MW00935904

Zoey

Lilith A. Bennett

↳ Keep your friends close

Lilith A. Bennett

KITSAP PUBLISHING

**KITSAP
PUBLISHING**

Zoey
First edition, published 2017

By Lilith Bennett
Copyright © 2017, Lilith Bennett

ISBN-13: 9 978-1-942661-70-2

Cover design based on iStock image license 108128956, 532875404

This is a work of fiction. Names, characters, businesses, places, events and incidents are either the products of the author's imagination or used in a fictitious manner. Any resemblance to actual persons, living or dead, or actual events is purely coincidental.

Published by Kitsap Publishing
www.KitsapPublishing.com

50-10 9 8 7 6 5 4 3 2 1

Prologue

Ezma is still asleep. I don't understand why she trusts me, given the circumstances. It's been months since we left Pryor Creek and we're still no closer to our goal. Just seems pointless...all of it. In the distance I can see the sun beginning to rise. She'll wake up soon. Just like every day since we left. I get to my feet and start walking back to the van. She'll be wanting to leave right after she wakes up. I've been awake since around midnight, keeping watch. I stop a few feet from the van and search my pockets. It takes me almost a full minute to remember why I can't find my cell phone. Ezma smashed it to pieces. She did the same with her own. She said they would find us if we hadn't.

I've been hearing her apologize more and more with each passing day. I can't tell if she really is sorry anymore. She's so difficult to read that I can't stand it. Each time I just nod my head and insist that she not worry about it. Maybe it's time to give up...go back home. The idea lingers in my mind for only a few seconds. We will go back someday. She said so herself. Just not today. It's too dangerous to go back with the way things are. We stirred up quite a mess. The horn honks and I'm thrust back into reality. I can see Ezma staring at me through the passenger window. Her expression is that of concern. I shake my head and clench my teeth as I walk toward the van. I climb into the front seat and close the door.

"Anything unusual?" she asks, starting the engine.

"Nothing."

"Good," she yawns, "Let's hope it stays that way." The van pulls forward and we begin heading down a well worn dirt road. The sun is flickering across the dash as we pass by countless trees. She keeps insisting on staying out in secluded areas every night. We only stayed in a motel a few nights. It's all about attracting as little attention as possible. We don't even make many stops along the road. Mostly just food and gas. Every other hour is filled with the endless sound of the van barreling down the road, talking to random strangers, following leads. A damaged section of the side door rattles in the silence. Every now and again, I glance over at Ezma, wondering what's going through her mind.

"Zoey?" Ezma says, breaking the silence.

"What?"

"You doing alright?" I let out a sigh and glance over at her. She keeps asking me if I'm okay. If the stress is getting to me. Each time my answer has been the same.

"Yeah..." I reply, "I'm fine."

"If you need to get some sleep, now's the time to do it," she says.

"I've only been up for a few hours," I insist, "I can keep going."

"You're no good to us if you start dozing off when it comes time for you to drive," she contends.

"How long are we going to keep this up?"

"As long as it takes," she answers. As long as it takes, huh? Am I supposed to expect this to last another month? A year? How long? I could ask her, but I know even she doesn't have that answer. With each passing day I regret my decision to tag along more and more. I turn my head and stare out the window. I know I said I wasn't, but I'm tired from keeping watch. My eyelids droop and soon even the glare of the morning sun can't keep me awake. Over the past three nights, I've been dreaming about what led up to this point. How I got here and why. I keep wishing I could go back and change things. I can wish all I want, but it isn't going to happen...

Chapter 1

Growing up, I always thought I'd lead a different life. One filled with all the things people often hope for. A good job, great friends, maybe a family of my own. A house on the waterfront, free time to see the world, to explore all it has to offer. Yeah...that was what I dreamed of. That may be because my life hadn't gotten off to the greatest start. By the time I arrived in Pryor Creek, I'd been through a lot. I was mad at the world. I had few friends, and moving several hundred miles to this new town wasn't the greatest way to stay in touch with them.

My parents fought day and night. There never seemed to be a break in the storm. It wasn't until I turned fifteen that they decided they couldn't stand each other any longer. It was nice to not have to hear the arguments anymore, but what I didn't like was the tug o' war that followed. Each of them wanted me to side with them. They never said that was the case, but they didn't need to. It was obvious to anyone, even a complete stranger watching from the nearest window. Not that people ever pressed their faces to the glass and watched them fight. Even so, it sure felt like the whole neighborhood was watching.

Dad would always storm off, get in the car, and tear out of the driveway. Twice he clipped our neighbor's garbage cans, and on at least one occasion, he tore chunks out of the lawn as he swerved out into the street. Mom was always drunk, leaving me to deal with my dad. Most days she was buzzed out of her head, not able to understand the most basic things. In one ear and out the other. It was like babysitting an overgrown child. How they stayed together for twenty years, I haven't a clue. Why they ever got married to begin with is an even greater mystery. They just seemed like the most mismatched couple anyone could imagine. Because of all this, I spent most of my time alone, locked away in my room. I would spend hours trying to do anything I could to escape reality. I read just about every book I could get my hands on and later started learning to write. It became my way of coping. After a few years, I'd accumulated several boxes full of spirals. All of which had been written in, cover to cover. I never bothered to get any of them out until today. We just finished moving into this new house about a week ago. My father won custody of me just before moving here. I imagine my mother's alcohol abuse played into that quite a bit. I suppose if I'm going to take a side, I should go with the one who wasn't too drunk to pay attention to me.

Flipping through one of my notebooks, I can see why I was so intent on putting these away. They're just...depressing. I never realized it at the time, but looking at them now with a clearer mind, it starts to sink in. Already I'm considering putting them away and leaving them in their boxes. I toss the spiral on the bed beside me and fall back onto my pillow. Staring up at the ceiling, my first thoughts are about school, and how much I don't want to go. I hate meeting new people. Always have. It's not that I don't find people I like, it's just that I always do something to push them away. The doorbell rings and I can hear my dad going downstairs to answer the door.

"Zoey!" he shouts from the doorway, "Someone's here to see you!" I have to take a moment to think about what he just said. I just got to this town. I haven't spoken to anyone. Who on earth would want to see me? Probably some overeager neighbor coming by to greet me before they spend the next however many years forgetting I exist. I groan and sit up, wondering if he's just pulling my leg. Wouldn't be the first time.

"What are you talking about?" I ask, opening my bedroom door.

"You have a visitor," he answers, "Come on downstairs. Shouldn't keep her waiting." I lumber down the stairs, taking more time than necessary and roll my eyes when I see that he's let her inside. She's standing just inside the door, glancing around the room. She looks to be about my age, maybe a year older. The first thing I notice is her smile. It's as though she's a little too happy to be in my house.

"Oh, hi!" she exclaims, her eyes falling on me, "My name's Ezmarelda." She gives a quick wave as I saunter toward her.

"I didn't ask, but okay." I'm hoping at this point that maybe I can do what I always do with these sorts of people. After a few minutes of making it obvious that I don't care who they are, they often leave and take to ignoring me. I'm not so desperate for a friend that I'm going to act like I care about the first person that wants to talk to me.

"So, what's your name?" she asks. She crosses her arms and tilts her head to one side. That grin is still plastered across her face. I can see she has braces.

"Zoey," I reply, "So...Ezmarelda?" She nods and continues to stare at me with her piercing green eyes. At this point I'm beginning to wonder if she wants something. Her expression seems genuine, but at the same time she seems a little too eager to talk to me.

"You can call me Ezma for short," she says, twirling some of her long black hair around a finger.

"Okay then. So...why are you here?"

"What do you mean?"

"Well, you must have come over here for something," I reply, "You looking to borrow something?"

"Of course not," she chuckles, "I just saw you the other day and thought I'd come see what you were up to. There's no one else my age around this neighborhood."

"So...what? You're looking for a friend or something?" I can't even describe how much I want her to go away. I think about shoving her out the door, but reconsider at the last second. I'm not sure why. Maybe, even though I just met her, I still enjoy the company.

"Perhaps," she replies, "Gets boring around here with no one to talk to, you know?"

"Don't you talk to anyone at school?" I ask. She shakes her head.

"Nope, I graduated a year ahead of my class. This year would've been my last."

"Must be nice," I say, "This is my last year. Can't wait to be done with it."

"I thought that too," she smiles, "But after several months of not going, it starts to get lonely. Well, for me anyway."

"Don't you have a job or something?" Why am I still carrying on this conversation? What on earth am I thinking? I want her to leave, not think she can come back.

"Yeah, but all the people I work with are kind of dull. Not that I expected to be friends with them, though. I mean, they are my co-workers. We're not there to socialize. Most of them are older than me too, so...yeah."

"Where do you work?"

"The library down the road," she answers, "You should come down there sometime. It's massive and has quite a selection." Seems she shares my interest in books. I'll admit I don't meet many people like that. I'd considered going down to the library after we first moved in, but now that I know she works there, I'm not so sure I want to.

"I'll have to check it out sometime."

"Are you busy at the moment?" she asks. I don't like where this is going. I'm tempted to make up an excuse, but what am I really doing?

"Um...no, not really." As soon as the words cross my lips I begin to regret them.

"Would you like to go down there with me? I don't work on weekends."

"Um...sure," I reply. The amount of effort it took to give that response was in itself exhausting. There are a few books I've been wanting to read. Maybe I'll be able to find them there.

"Great!" she says with an enormous grin, "Let's go."

"Dad!" I call, "I'm going to the library for while, I'll be back later."

"Alright then," he calls back, "Just be back by dinner." Ezma turns and walks out the door. I follow after her, closing the door behind me. She walks down the walkway and out the front gate where she turns and waits for me to catch up.

"How far is it?" I ask.

"Not too far," she answers, "I'd say a twenty minute walk from here." I suppose that's not too bad. I do get out and walk around from time to time, so it's not that I'm worried about. It's how long I'll have to tolerate her before I can ditch her among the bookshelves.

"So where did you move here from?" she asks. I close the gate behind me and catch up to her.

"Echo Point," I answer, "Crumby old town south of here." The two of us begin walking down the street, the sun high overhead and doing little to warm us.

"Never heard of it."

"No one has," I reply, "The people who either live there, or have lived there, seem to be the only ones who have."

"Pryor Creek's not really on the map either," Ezma says, "We don't get many visitors and even fewer people actually stay here. Can't really blame them. Most people have been leaving over the last few years."

"Why's that?"

"Well, our town got some bad publicity about five years ago," Ezma explains, "Some girl's parents were killed in the middle of the night. Some big mess about the parents abusing her or something. Couple people found out, went all vigilante on them with hatchets and knives."

"Sounds brutal," I reply. For the first time since she came to the door, she has my full attention.

"It happened in our neighborhood. I still remember the cop cars and ambulances and the like. Came roaring down the street in the dead of night. Whole neighborhood was outside watching."

"Wasn't my house, was it?" I ask.

"Oh no, it wasn't either of our houses," she assures me, "It was the red one at the west end of our street. 823 Sheridan Avenue. Boarded up, not hard to spot. So yeah...occasionally we get idiots up here looking to try and get inside the house for cheap thrills. Thanks to that, the city is often out here adding new boards to it."

"So, what? They think it's haunted or something?"

"Yeah, people spread rumors all over the place about it," she nods, "To be honest, I think it's a crock. Nothing haunted about it all. I broke in there one time when I was fifteen. It's creepy, but that's about it."

"If you think it's a crock, then why'd you go in?" I ask.

"I don't know, I was hanging out with an old friend of mine and we had nothing better to do. I like creepy stuff like that." I'm starting to like this girl. By the time we reach the library I've already decided not to ditch her. For the first time since I left Echo Point, I'm actually smiling.

Chapter 2

Upon entering the library, I realize that Ezma wasn't kidding. The place is huge. Getting lost among the many bookshelves seems like a very real possibility. Not that I would complain if that happened. As we walk past the checkout counter, a middle-aged woman waves at us and smiles.

"Afternoon, you two," she says. I wave back and smile. Ezma snorts as we head toward the fiction section.

"What's wrong?" I ask.

"Oh, nothing," she replies, "I work with her and she's just...I don't know. Hard to get along with, I guess."

"Really? She doesn't seem the type."

"Oh trust me, she is," Ezma mutters, "Anyway, let's not worry about that. What book did you say you were looking for?"

"Hang on, I'll check again," I say, taking out my cell phone, "I always forget what it's called." I pull up the note I typed and show it to Ezma. A smile spreads across her face and she leads me down several aisles.

"I know right where that one is," she says, "I just read it about a month ago."

"What'd you think of it?" I ask, "Any good?"

"Yeah, not half bad," she replies, "Definitely worth a read." She stops and begins searching the aisle.

"Ezma?" says a voice from near the end of the bookshelves, "You know you don't work today, right?" A man who looks to be in his twenties is standing at the end of the aisle staring at us, a stack of books in his arms. He looks at Ezma and squints behind his glasses.

"I'm helping my friend find a book, Michael," Ezma sneers, "What does it look like?"

"Relax, I was just kidding," Michael snorts, adjusting his hold on the books.

"Well your brand of humor annoys me," Ezma replies, "Why are you even talking to me, anyway?"

"Who's your friend? New in town or something?" Michael asks, ignoring her question.

"That's none of your concern," Ezma growls, "Now piss off, will you?"

"Jeez, I'm just trying to be friendly," Michael insists, "Why do you have to be so uptight all the time?"

"It's like you think I'm stupid," Ezma replies, handing me the book from the shelf, "I know what you've been up to lately."

"What, doing my job?" Michael snorts.

"Oh you mean your second job?" Ezma retorts, "Tell me, what are you hoping to accomplish?" As I look back and forth between Michael and Ezma, I start to feel a little uncomfortable. Ezma is scowling at Michael, her eyes burning with anger.

"Better watch yourself around that one," Michael warns me, "She's not right in the head. Probably why her parents were so eager to drive off that cliff." He laughs and adjusts the books in his arms. Ezma continues to glare at him for several seconds.

"Zoey...will you excuse us for a moment?"

"Um...sure," I murmur, "Where should I-?"

"Just wait at the counter," Ezma answers. I back away from the two of them and walk down the aisle. As I'm leaving, I catch some of the conversation.

"You know that's something you just don't say to me, Michael," Ezma growls, "You'd do best to watch your mouth around me."

"You finished yet?" he taunts, "Cuz I need to take these books to the back, and standing here isn't making them any lighter."

"Then start walking," Ezma growls. After that I was too far off to hear anything else. I thought about hiding behind a nearby bookshelf and listening to the rest, but something about the situation made me think twice. I glance down at the back of the book and continue walking. A girl looking to be about my age steps out of an aisle and bumps into me. I fumble the book and almost drop it.

"Oh my God, I'm sorry," I apologize, taking a step back.

"Oh no, it's no problem," she insists, holding up her cell phone, "I wasn't paying attention. Sorry about that." I apologize a second time and she walks off, pocketing her phone as she goes. She's about my height with black hair, green eyes, and a scarlet ribbon holding her hair in a high ponytail. I turn and watch her walk away, caught off guard by how much she looks like Ezma. Does she have a sister I don't know about? I shrug and continue on my way. I'll have to ask her later. Once I get back to the counter, I begin to think about what just occurred between Ezma and Michael. Part of me wants to ask the woman at the counter about it, but I decide against it. She scans the barcode on the back of the book and hands it back to me.

"Do you have your card?" she asks.

"I...uh...I just moved here so..."

"Would you like one?"

"I haven't changed my I.D. yet," I mumble, feeling embarrassed. I knew there was a reason my dad kept pushing me to go have it done.

"Oh, I see," the woman replies, "Hmm...how about Ezma? Perhaps she could check it out for you?"

"Would that be okay?"

"Of course," she nods, "Ezma and I may not always see eye to eye, but she has a clean record here. If it's checked out under her name, I'm certain she will see that it comes back."

"I'll have to ask her when she comes back. She's talking to some guy named Michael. Sounded like it was getting heated."

"Don't worry about it," the woman assures me, "Those two argue all the time." As the conversation continued, she told me that Ezma had a deep dislike of Michael. The two of them never got along since she began work there several months prior. I told her about what Michael had said about Ezma's parents. She told me that Ezma had been living on her own for years. It seemed unlikely that someone that young could keep and maintain a house of their own. Our conversation ends as Ezma emerges from the maze of bookshelves and makes her way to the counter. She still seems a little upset, but calmer nonetheless. She agrees to check the book out under her name, and the two of us leave soon after. Once outside, I ask her about Michael.

"What about him?" she asks, her smile fading from her lips.

"You looked pissed off when I left," I explain, "I was just a little concerned."

"I'm fine now," she assures me, "I suppose it goes without saying by this point, but I don't like him. He's rude to everyone, not just me. There are days where I consider quitting my job because of him."

"He did seem like a jerk."

"He is," she nods, "I'm sorry if I made you uncomfortable. That guy just...gets to me, you know?" I can relate, but I'm sure just about anyone else could too. I knew more than my share of people like that back home. Just something you learn to live with. Even moving to a new town doesn't mean you won't find more of them.

"I wanted to ask you something," I say, "I mean, if it's okay."

"Is it about what he said?" The two of us walk in silence for close to a minute. By the time she says something, I'm already wishing I hadn't brought it up.

"They didn't drive off that cliff on purpose," she explains, her eyes fixated on the sidewalk, "Someone tampered with the brakes and they swerved off the road. My aunt lives one town over. She's the only family member I have in this state. She's been helping me keep up on the bills since they died. She's a foster parent and she already has several kids, so me living there isn't an option."

"Why didn't you leave and go live with someone else?" I ask.

"My aunt's the only family I have that can tolerate me," she explains, "I didn't make it easy on my parents when I was younger. As for friends, well...I don't really have any around here."

"I see."

"What were you and Irene talking about?" Ezma inquires. She glances at me with an eyebrow raised.

"Nothing," I lie, "Just talked about books and how I should get a library card next time. Why do you ask?"

"I get this feeling that she talks about me behind my back," she explains, "She seems the type."

"Well she did talk about you," I admit, "but not in a bad way."

"What did she say?"

"She said that she was fine with you checking the book out for me," I say, "Said she felt you were responsible."

"That's a surprise," Ezma snorts.

"Why do you say that?"

"You know how I said I don't get along with her earlier?" she asks, "Well, she has this way of making me feel stupid while I'm working. I've heard her complain about Michael loads of times, so I just assumed she was doing the same to me."

"Sure didn't seem like it. What did you mean when you said Michael was up to something?"

"It's nothing," she says with a dismissive wave, "It's a long story and I don't feel like getting into it right now. Maybe some other time."

"Alright, no pressure," I say, "There was another thing. Do you have a sister who lives around here?" She shakes her head.

"No. I do I have a sister, though," she says, "No idea where she is, though. Left Pryor Creek a long time ago. Why do you ask?"

"Oh, nothing," I reply, "I just thought I saw someone who looked like you."

"I see," she chuckles, "Well, my sister doesn't look anything like me. Different hair color, eyes, etc. You probably just saw one of my doppelgangers. They say everyone has a few people in the world who look like them."

Several minutes pass and we find ourselves heading down our street. In that time, she's asked me if I can help her with something tomorrow morning. Since I have to be in class at eight, she suggests she come get me at five. She explains that it's going to take at least an hour and she doesn't want to cause me to miss class. I agree even though I'm not looking forward to getting up that early.

"I guess I'll see you tomorrow then," she smiles.

"Sounds good, see you then," I reply. She waves and trots across her front yard and into her house. As I step through my front door, my dad tells me that dinner will be ready in an hour. The smell of chicken is lingering in the air.

"You two have a good time?" he asks.

"Yeah," I answer, "I'd say so."

Chapter 3

I have to drag myself out of bed the following morning. I stayed up until almost midnight reading the book from the library. It's not the first time I've done something like this. I have to blink several times before my vision comes into focus. Since Ezma said she'd be by at five, I've gotten up a half an hour in advance. Or at least that was the plan. I hit my snooze button and wasted a few minutes. The night before, I told my dad about the incident at the library. For some reason I still can't get it out of my head. He said I shouldn't worry so much. That's his answer for most things. Maybe he's right. Still, some of what was said has left me with questions. I suppose it's none of my business. By the time I get dressed and saunter into the kitchen, I've got less than ten minutes before she's due to arrive. Scrounging around in the fridge, I end up settling for a few boiled eggs and a glass of milk. Hopefully that will hold me over until lunch. Right at five, I hear the doorbell ring several times in rapid succession. I roll my eyes and open the door to see her standing on my doorstep, broad grin and all.

"You know, once is fine," I murmur, "Maybe twice."

"Sorry," she giggles, "I'll remember that next time. I used to do that to an old friend of mine. Kind of like our special thing, you know?" The two of us walk over to her house and she steps inside, insisting that I stay outside.

"It's kind of a mess in here," she explains, slipping past the door, "I'll be right back, I just need to get a couple of boxes."

"Alright, I'll be here. You sure you don't want me to come in?"

"No, no, it's fine," she insists, closing the door. Minutes later, I can hear what sounds like something crashing down a staircase, followed by Ezma's muffled cursing. I'm almost tempted to walk in and see what's going on. I could care less if the house is a mess. Right now I feel useless standing out here not helping. I knock on the door and call to her.

"Ezma!" I shout, "You alright?"

"Yes, I'm fine!" she hollers back, "Be there in a second!" I glance through the nearby window to see that the curtains are closed. Instead I press my ear to the door and listen as I hear something being pushed across the floor. I back away as the doorknob turns and the door opens.

"That didn't quite go as planned," she laughs, "Good thing it's just useless junk in this thing." She gestures toward a large cardboard box behind her. It's pretty beaten up and has been sealed with duct tape.

"I just have one more," she says, "It's smaller than this one, so it shouldn't take as long." With that, she pushes the box out the door and onto the deck. She then goes back inside and closes the door behind her. I'm growing even more curious. While the door was open, what I could see of the house didn't look messy at all. If anything it seemed clean and tidy. I let out a sigh and stifle my urge to open the door and take a second look. Within minutes, she's back outside with a second box, also sealed with duct tape.

"Okay, now I need some help carrying it to my van," she says. I nod and lift one end of the box. We carry it to the back of the van and set it beside it before doing the same with the second. She takes her keys from her coat pocket and opens the rear hatch. The two of us lift the boxes into the back and she closes the van back up.

"Where are we taking these?" I ask.

"Oh we're just gonna dump them in the woods," she explains, "I don't want to drive all the way out to the dump and pay a fee on top of it; so I just take stuff out to the woods and throw it in a ravine. Most people around here do." The two of us climb into the van and Ezma turns the ignition. The engine roars to life and she starts the heater.

"How far are we going?" I ask, glancing at my phone.

"Just out to Hunter's Ridge," she answers. She puts the van in reverse and pulls out of the driveway, "It's just outside of town." She puts the van in gear and we begin heading down the street.

"Did you get a chance to read any of that book last night?" she asks, turning a corner.

"Yeah, I got about halfway through it," I answer.

"Wow, that fast? It takes me forever to get through books."

"Slow reader?"

"That's me," she replies, "I always wish I could get through them quicker. It's not that I don't enjoy them, it's just that there's so many I still want to read. Not going to be around forever, you know?"

"I know what you mean," I say, "My problem is that I read instead of sleep."

"You know what they say," she says with a grin, "You can sleep when you're dead."

"I don't know about that. I think I'd still be reading. Maybe find a good library to haunt."

"Now you're talking," she chuckles. Twenty minutes later, we pull off the main road and onto a well worn dirt path. She tells me that there used to be an amusement park nearby. One she went to with her parents when she was younger.

"It's about a mile from where we are now," she says, backing the van toward a large ravine, "It shut down the year after I went there. I think I was twelve at the time."

"Why'd they close it down?"

"Not really sure," she shrugs, "I heard it was something to do with money. Like they weren't earning enough to keep it open or something. Never looked into it. I just remember being really disappointed."

"That sucks," I say, unlocking my door, "Did you only go the one time?"

"Yep. Just once." The two of us walk to the back of the van and she opens the hatch. I glance down into the ravine and see that a large amount of garbage has accumulated at the bottom.

"Here, help me get these things out," Ezma grunts, pulling one of the boxes toward her. I take one side of the box and begin helping her pull it out. We push it to the edge of the ravine and she stands up.

"Would you like to do the honors?" she offers, prodding the box with her toe.

"Sure." I step behind the box and place my hands against it. Instantly I'm repelled by something slimy on the side. I look at my hand and see a clear, foul smelling fluid on my hand. I cringe and swipe up a few leaves.

"Sorry about that," Ezma apologizes, "This stuff's been sitting around for a while. That's why I wanted to get rid of it today. Any longer and I'm certain it would've started leaking...and smelling."

"Looks to me like it already has. What is it exactly?" I ask. I wipe my hand with the leaves and cast them aside.

"Old food and stuff," she mumbles, "It's kind of embarrassing. Up until a few weeks ago, my house was this huge mess, and well...I didn't do much to clean it up."

"That's pretty gross, no offense."

"Yeah, I know. I'm pretty disgusted with myself. You still want to push it?"

"I suppose." I lean down and this time avoid placing my hand in the same spot. I push it forward and watch as it tumbles down into the mountain of garbage below. We take the second one out of the van and this time she pushes it over the edge.

"I don't know why, but it's always fun to watch these tumble down to the bottom," she says, staring down into the ravine. She turns and closes the back of the van, then gets back behind the wheel. I climb in as well, and soon we're on our way back to town.

"Thanks for helping with that," she says, pulling away from the ravine, "I really appreciate it."

"No problem, glad to help out."

"Oh, that reminds me, I was gonna ask if you wanted to visit that old amusement park sometime. What do you say?" I look at her, confused.

"I thought you said it was abandoned?"

"It is," she smiles, "I go out there from time to time. It has this haunting feel to it that sort of helps me relax...if that makes any sense."

"No, I get it," I reply, "When were you planning on going out there?"

"How about tomorrow afternoon?" she suggests, "You busy then?" I shake my head.

"Sure. Let's do it." The rest of the day plays out better than I thought it would. Aside from the hours dragging by at school, I manage to get through it without any problems. There were a few times when I wished that Ezma was still in school. At least that way I might see her from time to time. No one speaks to me the entire day. Not unless they have to, anyway. Mostly just teachers and staff. After I get home, Ezma is nowhere to be found. I end up sitting in my room finishing my reading. Dinner time rolls around and still no sign of her. At that point

I stop expecting her to show up and sit down to eat. Dad seems frustrated with something and keeps grumbling at the table. When I ask what's bothering him, he says it has to do with my mother. It would seem that she's still trying to gain custody of me, despite the initial ruling. I tell him I hope she doesn't. He assures me that he won't let it happen. He then tells me that she talked about coming out to see me this week. I cringe at the very notion. The last time I saw her, she was spouting profanity and calling me a traitor.

"I don't want to see her. Not after the things she said to me."

"I don't blame you," he replies, spearing a piece of steak with his fork, "I told her it was up to you. If you ask me, she needs to get help with a few things before she starts trying to fix her relationship with you."

"I don't see that happening," I snort, "I don't think she could survive a day without a drink." The very thought of my mother going to rehab seems like a joke. The whole time I've known her, there wasn't a day that went by where she wasn't drowning herself in alcohol. The worst part of it was that she always blamed everyone else for her problems; and I heard it more than anyone else.

"I don't either," he continues, "I told her if she can't accept that she played a role in this, then she doesn't need to be in your life right now."

"Is she still blaming you for it?"

"For the drinking?" he asks. He chews and swallows a bite of steak.

"Yeah."

"She is," he murmurs, "Still all my fault. Still me that pushed her over the edge. I don't understand that woman sometimes. Whatever the case, it's your decision. If she comes here or not. You shouldn't let my opinion influence your decision."

"I might want to see her," I admit, staring down at my plate, "Just to tell her how I feel about her."

"Could do that over the phone. It'd be a lot easier."

"No, I'd rather say it to her in person." After dinner, I go up to my room and lie on my bed. I stare up at the ceiling and think about what I said at dinner. My mother was at times prone to violent outbursts. Maybe Dad was right. Maybe just telling her off over the phone would be enough. Even so, I'd rather not seem like a coward. She was a bully when I was a kid, and the least I can do is stand up to her. I spend at least an hour going over the pros and cons in my head before I end up falling asleep. When I wake up, it's because Ezma is shaking me awake.

Chapter 4

"What the hell?" I shout, sitting up on my bed, "What are you doing in here?"

"Time to get up," she laughs.

"Why are you laughing?" I hiss, "You think breaking into my house is a joke?"

"What are you talking about?" she snorts, "I didn't break in."

"Then how did you get in?"

"Your dad let me in," she explains, "It's seven-thirty." I stare at her in confusion and then glance at the clock. She's right. I'm late for school and I'm certain I've missed the bus. I swing my legs off the bed and walk out to the stairs.

"Dad!" I shout, "Did you let Ezma in?"

"Yeah, she showed up a few minutes ago," he hollers, "She said she was giving you a ride." I turn to face Ezma who stares back at me with her usual toothy grin. Minutes later, the two of us are out the door and heading to her van. I ended up swiping a few granola bars and a bottle of water from the pantry before we left, and as we head down the street, I'm trying my best to scarf them down.

"Sorry I startled you," she says, stopping at a red light. I try to tell her it's no big deal, but all that comes out of my mouth is a series of indistinguishable grunts. I let out a groan and continue chewing while Ezma giggles at my inability to speak.

"You don't have to say something right away," she chuckles, "I'm guessing you were trying to tell me not to worry about it? Something along those lines?" I nod as I unscrew the cap of the water bottle and down half of it in one go.

"Yeah, I said don't worry about it," I confirm, "I'm just not used to being woken up like that."

"I probably should've knocked first," she admits, "If that ever happens again, I'll make sure I do." We arrive at the school building a few minutes later, and I hop out onto the sidewalk.

"Later, Zoey," Ezma smiles.

"See ya." I close the door and wave before heading inside. Just as the day before, things drag on. Not that I expected my second day at a new school to be exciting. At last the clock strikes two and I'm on my way out of the building. Before I get even ten feet out the door, someone jumps on my back and almost brings me to the ground.

"What the hell?" I shout, shaking my attacker off. I turn to see Ezma giggling with her hand over her mouth.

"Surprise!" she laughs.

"Would've been better if you'd said that before you jumped on me," I grumble, making my way to the buses.

"But that would've taken all the fun out of it," she protests.

"How long have you been out here?" I ask, still a little annoyed.

"Since about one-thirty," she says, "I was bored so I thought I'd come meet you."

"I'm glad you did," I admit, "Sucks not knowing anyone up here."

"But you know me," she points out.

"Yeah, but you already graduated," I reply.

"What time to do you have lunch at?" she asks, "The teachers up here like me. I'm sure they wouldn't mind if I came to visit every now and then."

"Eleven-thirty."

"Perfect, that's when I take my lunch break," she smiles as we approach the bus, "Oh, I almost forgot I drove up here," she laughs, "Want a ride?"

"Sure, that'd be great," I say, "I'm not much for taking the bus."

"Yeah, me either," she replies, "As soon as I got my license, I quit taking it. I hate how crowded it gets. Usually I'd be scrunched between two people or something like that."

"That's exactly what I do pretty much every time," I groan, following her to the parking lot, "My stop is the last both ways. I know it's only my second day here, but I swear it was over capacity."

"It always is," Ezma replies, reaching the van, "They need more buses if ask me. They have too many people on that route for just one." The two of us climb in and we pull out of the lot.

"So, I just realized, how come you aren't at work?" I inquire.

"I got the day off," she explains, "The library's closed down for the moment."

"How come?"

"Not sure," she shrugs, "All I know is when I got there, they told me they were sending everyone home."

"Weird. I wonder what happened?" I reply, staring out the window.

"Beats me. You still up for going out to that abandoned park today?"

"Yeah, sure," I say with a shrug, "I don't see why not."

"I just need to stop by my place first," she says, "I want to pick something up before we go out there."

"Sounds good. I was gonna ask to stop at my place too. I need to get something to eat. Lunch just wasn't enough today for some reason." A few minutes later we stop outside our houses and I walk in to find something to eat. It's the week we usually go shopping, and as usual there isn't much around. I think about getting a few more granola bars from the pantry, but I've been eating those off and on over the past week and they just don't sound good. Even this morning I was forcing myself to eat them. The eggs are all gone and all that remains are a few protein shakes in the fridge. I suppose one of them is better than nothing.

I swipe one from the top shelf and close the door before going back outside. I glance at the van and see that Ezma doesn't seem to be in it. I lean against the side of the van and unscrew the lid on my drink. As I tilt my head back, I notice some movement in an upstairs window. That must be her. I finish about a third of the shake and already I'm thinking I might throw up. There's a reason I never drink these things, they taste terrible. Even so, I need something in my stomach. I wrinkle my nose and drink a little more while I wait. At last Ezma emerges from her house, carrying a metal box in one hand and a backpack over her shoulder. She closes the door and waves to me before trotting over to the van.

"That took a little longer than I expected," she grunts, pulling open the side door.

"What did you get?"

"You'll see," she says with a wink. She places the metal box behind my seat and hands the backpack to me. We climb in and she takes the bag from me.

"I ran into some drunk weirdos out there once," she says, opening the backpack, "So, because of that, I like to take one of these with me." She pulls a holstered pistol from the bag and hands it to me.

"It's not loaded is it?" I ask, examining it.

"All guns are loaded," she replies.

"No really, is it loaded or not?"

"It has no ammo in it, but it is loaded. Understand?"

"No, apparently not," I sigh.

"It's a basic rule I follow with any gun," she explains, "My dad used to say 'all guns are loaded, no safety works.' It's something that's stuck with me ever since. It means to always treat it as if it's loaded and never trust the safety."

"Makes sense to me," I say, continuing to look it over, "I've never fired a gun before."

"No problem," she smiles, "I'll show you once we're there. I'll have to take you with me the next time I go shooting. Good way to blow off some steam. You can hang on to that, by the way. I don't ever use it."

"So I can keep it?" She smiles and nods as she starts the van. Not exactly something I need lying around, but I guess there isn't any reason to complain. I've never had much interest in firearms, or shooting for that matter. I guess it couldn't hurt to try something new.

"Where did you get these?"

"They were my father's," she answers, "He was a collector. After my parents died, I was left to decide what to do with them. The guns weren't something my aunt wanted in her home. All those foster kids, something bad would happen sooner or later. So I ended up keeping them."

"I see."

"I've sold a few of them," Ezma continues, "but I kept a few for sentimental reasons."

"You mind if I ask something?" I inquire.

"What?"

"Well..." I begin, unsure if I should go through with asking, "Your parents. Did they ever figure out who tampered with the brakes?"

"I'm afraid not," she sighs, "My brother lucked out. He got into an argument with them just before the crash. They pulled into a gas station, they left the car idling while they followed him across the parking lot. He was shouting about wanting to kill himself, so they followed. Whoever did it must have tampered with the car while that was going on. He went on about how guilty he felt about it for years afterward."

"How come he doesn't live with you?" I ask.

"He did for a while," Ezma explains, "I got tired of him real quick, though. Don't get me wrong, he wasn't a bad guy. I mean...I sort of felt sorry for him. I kept telling him he didn't do anything wrong, but all he would do was get drunk and moan about how he should have been in the car with them."

"What happened to him?"

"He just...I don't know..." she groans, "He wandered off one day, didn't hear from him for months. I was worried sick the entire time. He comes back, says he's been through rehab, that he's getting his life together, and the next thing I know, that idiot says he's moving in with some girl he'd just met. He's a few years older, mind you. It was about two years ago, so I was sixteen at the time. He died not long after that."

"Must have been hard."

"It was," she says, "Just wish that jackass hadn't spent so much of our parents' life insurance money on booze and a ton of other useless crap. That money was what was allowing us to live here at the time; before our aunt took over helping. If he hadn't spent more than half it, then I probably wouldn't have had to bother inconveniencing our aunt in the first place."

"I was wondering about that. If she's got all those kids to look after, how is she able to help you pay bills?"

"She's pretty well off," Ezma replies, "Paying half my bills is like spending a few pennies to her. That's why she takes care of like eleven kids at a time. She has the space and plenty of money to do it." The conversation shifts to a more relaxed tone as we continue toward Hunter's Ridge. Instead of going off onto the dirt road like we did last time, we instead drive down an abandoned road filled with cracks and riddled with potholes. By the time we reach the end of it, I'm starting to get a mild headache. We stop at an iron gate on the edge of the woods and climb out.

"We'll have to walk from here," Ezma explains, "It's only a few hundred feet. Shouldn't take long." She opens the side door of the van and pulls out the metal container. She sets it down beside the van and opens the lid, revealing a pile of ammunition.

"Here, take your gun out of the holster," she instructs, nudging the container toward me. I do what she asks and she takes it from me.

"I have no idea what I'm supposed to do," I admit, feeling a little embarrassed.

"No worries," she smiles, "That's why I'm going to show you." She goes into detail about the basic operation of my weapon, telling me how to load it, as well us carry it safely.

"Do you know what a magazine is?" she asks.

"Not in this case." The only thing that comes to mind is something I'd find lying on my coffee table.

"It's this thing," she explains, pressing her thumb against the side of the grip. What I assume is the magazine falls out into her free hand and she shows it to me.

"Oh, okay."

"You load it like this," she continues, kneeling down beside the ammo container. She takes one of the cartridges out of the box and presses it into the top of the magazine, "Just do that until you have fifteen in there. Got it?" I nod and kneel down beside her. Aside from fumbling one of the cartridges, I do alright. Afterward she hands me two spare magazines and I load them both.

"Okay, next I'm going to show you how to use it," she says, "Oh, and if you've never fired a gun without ear plugs, it's not a pleasant experience. So if I tell you to plug your ears, do it; assuming we're not trying to defend ourselves, of course."

"What are the odds I'll have to use it?"

"You won't have to," she assures me, "This place isn't all that dangerous. It's just a precaution since there's a few creeps around from time to time." She then shows me how to hold it, how to chamber the first round, tells me to make sure I never point it at her or at myself. If she hadn't been smiling when she said that, I'm sure I would've taken it as an insult. Why would I ever point a loaded gun at myself? When she's at last satisfied that I know what I'm doing, she puts the box of ammo back in the van and locks the doors. We squeeze through the bars on the gate and begin walking down the cement path. I can see at once that the trees end a short distance away. Beyond that point is a massive open field. We stop for a moment as we approach. I take a few moments to glance around at the many dilapidated structures. Abandoned and decaying park rides lie before us.

"Well, what do you think?" Ezma asks with a toothy grin, "Pretty cool, huh?"

"Yeah...very." I continue glancing around as the two of us make our way toward a rusty ferris wheel.

"I still remember riding this back when the park was open," Ezma says, staring up at the top of the structure, "That was a fun day. I almost wish I could go back and live it again."

"Is that why you come here?" I ask, "To reminisce?"

"Yeah," she admits, "If I knew what I know now, maybe my life wouldn't have turned out the way it did. Try for a happier ending, I suppose."

"I know what you mean. I wish I could go back and fix my life too. Maybe my mother wouldn't be a worthless drunkard if I'd done something different."

"Is that why you live with your dad?" she asks. We turn and start walking toward a nearby merry-go-round.

"Yeah, the two of them always fought with each other. My dad was the one who paid attention to me. Mom just...I don't know...I hate her."

"Why do you say that?" Ezma asks.

"She's just...so...ugh," I groan, "She blames everyone else for her problems. She says it was my dad's fault she started drinking, she hates me because I sided with him during the custody battle, and she's just a terrible person."

"That must be hard," Ezma says, stepping up onto the ride, "I guess I can count myself lucky that I never had to deal with that."

"Honestly, I'd rather have two dead parents who loved me, than two that put me at the center of their problems," I declare.

"Be careful what you wish for," Ezma warns, "It's not fun losing your parents."

"No, I mean it," I insist, "I mean...I love my dad, he's always been there for me, and yeah, he isn't perfect; but at the end of the day, I hate how they still fight over me. I think after my mom lost the custody battle, it made her realize what a failure of a mother she is. The worst part is that she's still fighting tooth and nail to bring me back home with her."

"And you don't want to go back?"

"Not with her," I grumble, "I mean...I miss my friends, my old house... that whole town. It's where I grew up. If going back means I'd have to live with my mother, then forget it."

"How old are you?" Ezma asks, "I mean, I know you said you're a senior, but..."

"I'm seventeen," I answer, "Eighteen in two months. Why do you ask?"

"I was just thinking about what you were saying. I figured if you were eighteen, you could go back home and not have to put up with your mother. Sounds like you don't have long to wait."

"Living on my own would be nice," I reply, "but I know it wouldn't be that simple. I wouldn't know the first thing about getting an apartment or what it would take to keep it. That and I'm jobless with no savings or anything."

"I know we just met and all, but what if I came with you?" Ezma offers, "We could be roommates."

"What about your job here?"

"Eh, I'm sure they'd manage without me," she smiles, "I've been wanting to move out of this town for a long time now. Just haven't gotten ready to do it quite yet. That's part of why I started cleaning up my mess of a house. No one's going to buy it if it smells like something died in there."

"Wouldn't surprise me," I laugh. Somewhere nearby, I've been able to hear a crow for the past few minutes. It's been bothering me since around the time we began walking away from the ferris wheel.

"I hate crows," I mutter, "They're so annoying."

"I've been thinking that same thing," Ezma replies. We turn to see that the crow has left its perch in a tree and is now picking at garbage from an overturned garbage can. With little warning, Ezma draws her revolver and points it at the bird.

"Cover your ears, missy," she orders. I place my hands over my ears just in time to muffle the noise. I let go and glance over to where the crow was. It's now lying on the ground in a pool of blood, torn apart by the bullet.

"Um...okay then..." I mumble, "That's one way to do it."

"That's the only way if you ask me," Ezma replies, holstering her revolver, "Pesky little shits." At this point I'm not sure what to think. Yeah, I wanted that crow to stop making noise, but not because it took a bullet. Here she is capping birds when not even five minutes before this, she's suggesting we live together as roommates. The shock it seems shows on my face.

"Something wrong?" she asks, sounding concerned.

"Nothing, I um...hadn't thought to try that," I lie.

"They're considered pests around here," she explains, "Trust me, I'm not the only one killing them." As much as I want to believe that, I have a hard time doing so.

"I used to come down here and take pictures of all the rides a few months back," Ezma continues, breaking the silence, "I found some old ones of me that my parents took the day we came here...back when it was alive with people from all over. It's sort of eerie to compare them. Amazing how things have changed so much in only a few years."

"I'll have to see some of the older ones sometime," I say, trying my best to forget about the crow, "It'd be interesting to see how this place looked before it closed down."

"I'll have to dig them up this week. I'm not sure what I did with them. I found them to be upsetting at one point, so I stashed them somewhere in my house." Her gaze locks onto something behind me and her expression changes to one of irritation. I turn to see two men and a woman standing near the end of the walkway. The three of them are talking, but they're too far away to hear.

"Do you know them?" I ask.

"Yeah..." she answers, "That's Jason Rivers and his girlfriend, Rachel. I don't know who that other guy is. Probably one of his tweaker buddies."

"I take it you don't get along with them?"

"Let's go have a word with them, shall we?" Ezma says. She steps off the merry-go-round and begins walking over to them. I follow after her, nervous about what she's planning to do. As we approach, the three of them fix their gazes on us. Rachel steps in front of the others and crosses her arms.

"What's going on?" she asks, "Thought I heard a gunshot."

"Why are you following me?" Ezma demands.

"It's not following you if I was already on my way here," Rachel retorts, "We need to talk. Do you know about what happened to Michael?" I think back to the day at the library when Ezma was arguing with someone of the same name. Is she talking about him?

"What are you talking about?" Ezma demands, "The only thing I know is that he's a pain in the ass to work with."

"He said the wrong thing this time, didn't he?" Rachel says, cocking her head.

"I don't know anything about Michael," Ezma declares, "Why are you even bringing him up?"

"One of the library staff found him dead in a storage room," Rachel answers, "From what I hear, you were one of the last people to see him alive."

"So your immediate reaction is that I had something to do with it?" Ezma snorts, "Why would you come all the way out here just to tell me this? Do you get a kick out of pissing me off or something?"

"You and your friend here are being considered suspects," Rachel informs us. Is she serious?

"That doesn't answer my question," Ezma replies.

"I told you, I was already on my way here," Rachel says, "I didn't come all the way out here just for that. I know where you live, I could have just waited till you got home."

"I find that hard to believe," Ezma mutters.

"One is missing and another is dead," Rachel continues, "I thought we were done with this?"

"We're done when you and the others quit causing problems," Ezma snarls, "All I do is try to get by."

"This started back up again when your brother died," Rachel says, rolling her eyes.

"I never laid a finger on Brian," Ezma contends.

"I didn't say you did," Rachel says, "Guilty conscience?"

"You don't know anything about it, so quit acting like you do," Ezma growls, "He was my brother, not yours. If anyone should be concerned about what happened, it's me."

"Maybe so, but I still find it odd that you're a suspect in another murder two years later," Rachel continues.

"Yeah, like you're an angel in all of this," Ezma scoffs, "Quit following me around, alright? Next time you want to talk to me, you can come by my house like a normal person. I know there was something going on with Michael, and I may not know exactly what, but I'm sure I have the right idea. Come on, Zoey." She grabs me by the arm and leads me down the path. I glance over my shoulder to see that Rachel and the others are looking back at us as they move further into the park. Ezma lets go of my arm and remains silent until after we slip through the gate.

"I didn't kill my brother," she says, "Don't listen to them." She stops as she eyes her van. The side of it appears to have been keyed. She closes her eyes and takes a deep breath. At this point I'm certain she's about to fly into a rage. Instead she fishes a large folding knife from her pocket and walks over to a red convertible sitting nearby.

"Two can play at that game," she mutters, flicking the blade open. She stabs one of the tires, then moves to the next. She punctures that one, then does the same to the other two. She stands back, watching as the tires deflate.

"Hmm... needs something more," she says, putting the knife back in her pocket. She begins searching the ground near the car. After a few moments she picks up a large rock and approaches the front of the car. She lifts it over her head and hurls it through the windshield.

"Such a shame when rocks fall from the sky like that," she mutters, taking her keys out of her coat pocket, "It just needs one last thing." She selects one of the keys on the chain and proceeds to carve a vulgar word into the driver side door.

"There, perfect. Now let's get out of here before they come back. I don't think we'll want to be here when they do."

Chapter 5

"I can't believe those assholes keyed my van," Ezma grumbles as we reach the main road, "I've been putting up with that dumb girl for years now. Can't believe I ever used to be friends with the likes of her."

"You two were friends?" I ask, "Never would have thought."

"I know what I did was overkill," Ezma admits, "but after everything she's done over the years, I'd say she deserves it."

"Whatever you two have going on, I'd rather not get involved. That's between you and her. Just saying."

"No, no, I get it," Ezma assures me, "I shouldn't drag you into my business like that. We should've just left without saying anything to them."

"I sure hope the cops don't show up at my doorstep after what you did to their car," I grumble.

"Pff, they won't call the cops. She'd rather try to get even with me."

"That had better not involve me," I warn.

"I doubt it will," she replies, "She'll come after me for that. She knows I would do something like that. Anyway...if for some reason she does bother you, just let me know and I'll take care of it."

"I can handle myself," I reply, glancing out the side window.

"Not saying you can't, I'm just saying I can help you if you decide you need it."

"I'll keep that in mind." The rest of the ride home doesn't involve much conversation. All I can think about is how I don't want to be involved in a dispute between old friends. That was the last thing on my mind when I came here. Not even a month and I may just get pummeled at school for the way Ezma destroyed some girl's car. Some girl I don't even know. Wonderful. When we arrive back home, Ezma pulls the van into her driveway and we say our goodbyes. She apologizes a second time for what happened, and I tell her it's no big deal. Minutes later I find myself walking into my kitchen.

"Where have you been?" Dad asks. He sets his plate on the table and sits down.

"Out," I reply, prodding at my food.

"Just out?"

"Ezma and I went out to Hunter's Ridge," I explain.

"Where's that at?"

"It's just outside of town," I explain, "Wooded area. We went to look at an abandoned amusement park over there."

"How'd that go?" I think back to the crow and the three people Ezma spoke to. Then I think about the way Ezma trashed their car. At that moment I feel my heart skip a beat. The gun Ezma gave me is still loaded, and still on my belt. How did I forget to hide it? I can just imagine the lecture I'd get if he found it. I check to make sure my shirt is still covering it.

"Something wrong?" he asks, one eyebrow raised.

"No...nothing...I um...I'm a little distracted is all."

"I can tell," he replies, "What's on your mind?"

"Well...we ran into some people that Ezma doesn't like," I explain, "Nothing happened, she just talked to them for a few minutes."

"Why did she talk to them if she doesn't like them?"

"She said that one of them, this girl named Rachel, they used to be friends," I answer, "They were talking about a murder at the library. Apparently one of the workers was found dead."

"Heard about that this morning," he replies, "Someone at work today mentioned it. Everyone wouldn't shut up about it all day. Some guy named Michael Green."

"I saw him the other day when I was at the library with Ezma."

"You did, huh?"

"Yeah, Ezma was arguing with him about something," I explain, "I don't really know what since she insisted I leave them alone."

"You two didn't have something to do with the murder, did you?" he teases.

"Of course not," I scoff, "Ezma's a little weird, but I doubt she'd kill anyone." After dinner, I go up to my room and bury my nose in my book. I'm almost finished with it when eleven-o'-clock comes around. I tear myself away and flip on the T.V. I missed the news while I was eating dinner. Right now I'm hoping I'll learn something about what happened. While I'm waiting for the report, I start thinking about what Rachel said about Ezma's brother. I want to ask Ezma more about it, but somehow I doubt that would be a good idea. I turn up the volume as I hear Pryor Creek mentioned.

"A recent homicide has the residents of Pryor Creek, Michigan on edge tonight, after the body of a man in his mid-twenties was discovered in a storage room at the town library this morning. The discovery came at around eight in the morning, after an employee found the storage room door jammed." The camera switches to a reporter standing just outside the library.

"When Irene Donner first noticed a jammed storage room door, she thought little of it; but no one was expecting what would happen next. After requesting assistance from another employee, who forced the door open, the two made a gruesome discovery. According to authorities, the body is that of employee Michael Green. Investigators are looking to question two young women who are believed to have been two of the last people to see the victim alive. We would just like to emphasize that these two are not being considered suspects at this time, merely persons of interest. Due to the age of one of the girls, we cannot reveal her name, but we can say that the police are looking to speak with another library employee who reportedly had an argument with the victim shortly before the estimated time of death. The cause of death is suspected to have been strangulation, but as of now we are waiting for an autopsy to confirm this."

Rachel was telling the truth; or at least most of it. It was pretty clear to me that we aren't suspects. At least not right now. What they said about the argument taking place just before the time of death is a little disturbing. From what I saw, Michael was at least six-four, and had to be over two hundred pounds. He was a big guy. Ezma's not much taller than me and I'm five-six. Seems very unlikely that someone her size would be able to strangle someone like Michael. Just that realization removes a lot of the worry.

Chapter 6

The next morning, I'm yet again dragging myself out of bed. I'm almost surprised to see that Ezma hasn't snuck into my room. I know she only did it once, but I imagine she might try it again at some point. I head downstairs and eat a quick breakfast before going outside. The first thing I notice is Ezma loading another box into the back of her van. Whatever it is, it looks heavy. Just as she tries to adjust her grip on the box, it falls off and lands on her foot. She lets out a yelp and kicks the box in frustration, then curses under her breath.

"Need some help?" I call from the front gate. She turns and spots me, her usual grin appearing on her face.

"That would be great!" she responds. I trot out the gate and see that my bus is arriving at its usual spot near the intersection. I ignore the urge to run after it and keep walking toward Ezma.

"More garbage?" I ask.

"Yeah, I had a ton of magazines in one of the closets," she replies, "My brother used to collect a few different ones. I swear there were like three hundred of them up there. I have the next two days off, so I figured I should do some cleaning." We heave the box into the back of the van and she closes the hatch.

"Are there any more?"

"Yeah, I crammed about about half of them in this one," she explains, "I could barely get the damn thing out of the house. Thought I was going to give myself a hernia, then the thing falls on my foot."

"So I saw," I laugh.

"It's not funny," she chuckles, "It hurt."

"Sounded like it."

"Anyway, I noticed you missed your bus," she observes, "Want a ride again?"

"Up to you, I don't want to make it a habit."

"Don't lie to me," she teases, "You totally want it to be a habit." She walks around the side of the van and climbs into the driver's seat. I follow suit and climb into the passenger seat.

"Doing alright with the cleaning?" I ask, "I've had to clean out some things people left behind before. Not always easy."

"Yeah, it's not too bad so far," she answers, pulling out of the driveway, "Lot of memories coming back. Some good, some bad."

"I kind of feel like I'm intruding here, but...you mind if I ask what happened to him?"

"I don't mind," she replies, "It's kind of difficult to talk about, though."

"Oh, well I'm not trying to push you," I insist.

"No, no it's fine," she assures me, "I haven't ever really talked about it with anyone. The two of us were pretty close. Like I said before, we didn't get along all that well after our parents died. We once had the cops called over an argument one night."

"Should I ask?"

"If you'd like. It's not some big secret," she replies, brushing her hair away from her eyes, "I guess I could tell you the gist of it."

"If you want."

"He showed up at my house one night, pleading that I help him. He was hurt pretty bad, blood all over him. I'm sure his girlfriend was responsible for that. He said he had nowhere to go and I didn't want to just abandon him. I tried to call for an ambulance since it looked like he'd lost a lot of blood. He freaked out on me, broke the phone and ran out onto the lawn. So I locked him out and used my cell. When the police and paramedics arrived, we were both out on the front lawn, shouting loud enough to wake the dead.. Rachel lived across the street from me at the time, so she saw at least some of it."

"So what happened to the girlfriend?"

"Not a whole lot," she replies, "Got arrested and held for evaluation or something. Sounded like she took a hit to the head or something, I don't remember all the details. All I know is that for some reason, she got off with nothing."

"How does that even happen? She stabbed him, right?" I ask. Ezma nods.

"Brian sure as hell didn't get those wounds from me," she answers, "All I know is there was a lack of evidence or something."

"Sounds terrible. All of it."

"It really was," she sighs, "Brian made it sound like I attacked him which just made me even more upset. I would have never laid a finger on him. Never .He was probably too out of it to even know what he was doing. He was acting weird that whole time; God only knows why. Probably relapsed or something, I don't know. I told the cops that he'd shown up on my doorstep like that, all bloody and everything, but it didn't stop them from taking me to jail that night."

"How'd he end up dead?"

"They stabilized him at the hospital, fixed him up, but he only stayed a couple of days before he refused treatment. He overdosed on pain meds not long after that. I still don't know if it was intentional or not. Rumors started to spread that someone had killed him and made it look like a suicide. Guess who everyone thought that was?"

"You?"

"Yep," Ezma mutters, "Brian's girlfriend was still being held for evaluation when he died. Since I was the last to see him alive, everyone assumed I was involved. My brother was in a bad place, I'll say that much; but I wouldn't kill him. If you ask me, it was a cut and dry case. I guess the stress finally got to him."

"I don't know what to say," I mumble, "Sorry you had to go through that."

"Sorry I told you all of that," she apologizes, "I um...I don't know. Like I said, I never talk to anyone about it. My aunt barely ever has time to talk and I feel bad bothering her. Anyway...that's the story of how my brother died. I just wish people would leave it alone and stop bringing it up. Yeah, I'd love to say it was Sarah's fault, but I can't since she wasn't around to do it."

"Sounds frustrating."

"I'm sorry, I should shut up," Ezma murmurs.

"It's no big deal," I assure her, "I'm the one who brought it up. I don't mind listening."

"I appreciate that," she says, "But seriously, if I ever start to talk about something you don't want to listen to, just let me know."

"Will do," I reply. Minutes later we pull up in the school parking lot. At almost the same time, we spot Rachel standing across the street near the main entrance.

"Great, I bet she's here to rub the car thing in my face," I grumble.

"Just try to ignore her or something," Ezma mutters, "She gives up pretty quick sometimes. Let's just hope she isn't feeling persistent today."

"I don't usually run into her much," I say, "Thanks for the ride."

"No problem. See you after two." I shut the door and start toward the entrance as Ezma pulls out of the parking lot. I glance at Rachel who has stopped to talk to someone and is now looking right at me. I roll my eyes and start heading for the back entrance. I'd rather not give her the opportunity to bother me. As I round the corner and continue along the wall, I look over my shoulder to see that she's following me. I quicken my pace, but she ends up catching me anyway.

"What do you want?" I snarl, turning to face her.

"Whoa, relax," she says, "I just want to talk."

"If this is about your car, I had nothing to do with it."

"Okay, first, this isn't about my car," she groans, "Second, I do want to ask about that in a minute, so just hold onto that."

"Well, what is it?" I demand.

"I want to ask you why you're hanging out with Ezma," she replies.

"What does it matter?"

"It matters because I was once in the same position as you," Rachel explains, "Ezma is a terrible person to associate with. Keep it up and you'll see why."

"Is that supposed to scare me?" I snort.

"No, you're not getting it," Rachel continues, "I'm trying to help you. I was Ezma's friend for years, I know what she's like. Trust me, avoiding her is in your best interest."

"What's so bad about her?" I ask.

"I imagine she was the one who smashed up my car, right?"

"You keyed her van," I accuse, "Makes perfect sense for her to be angry."

"I didn't key her van," she declares.

"Then who did?"

"I don't know, probably Jason's idiot friend," she answers, "He stayed behind for a second, saying he had to...'do his business.' He probably did it then. At least I know who to blame now."

"I don't buy that you didn't follow us. What was really going on?"

"Following you, of course," she admits, "I wasn't planning on following you two out there. I'm no stalker. We just happened to see you two drive by us. I only went out there to make sure you were okay."

"To make sure I was okay?" I snort, "Why would you do that? You don't even know me."

"Haven't you been listening to me? I've seen what she does. I know her better than you do. I don't want you or anyone else she decides to make nice with, ending up hurt or worse. It's happened before and it will happen again."

"Or worse? Who did she kill?" I ask, "That's what you meant, right? Who was it?"

"Her brother for one," she answers, "She stabbed him when he came by her house one night."

"Ezma seems pretty certain that he showed up with his injuries," I reply, "We were just talking about it this morning."

"And you believe her? Of course she's gonna make it sound like it wasn't her fault. She probably even believes that's what happened. Come on, haven't you noticed anything weird about her behavior?"

"I haven't noticed anything odd," I lie.

"I don't believe you," Rachel continues, sounding irritated, "Look... just stay away from her. For your sake." She turns and walks back to the front of the building. I know she's right that Ezma's a little odd, but she never seemed threatening to me. I mean, she had a perfect opportunity to kill Rachel out in the woods. The nearest house was at least two miles from there. All she would've had to do was shoot her. After that, there were hundreds of wooded acres to bury her body. And what about Michael? I still believe it would be very unlikely, maybe even impossible for Ezma to have overpowered him. Rachel might act like she's trying to help me, but I can only guess what it is that's motivating her to do it.

Chapter 7

About thirty minutes before lunch, I'm sitting in my history class half asleep. I stopped paying attention within minutes of class starting. All I can think about is how the police want to talk to me, how Rachel seems like she wants to help me, and how upset Ezma would be if I stopped talking to her. So far she's my only friend here. And yeah, Rachel's right, Ezma is a little weird; but even so I still think Rachel is getting ahead of herself. How do I know she isn't hiding something? I didn't even know she existed until yesterday.

"Miss Parker," my teacher says, bringing me back to reality. I look up to see that he's standing in the doorway.

"What?"

"I need you to step outside for a moment," he says, opening the door. As I stand up, several heads turn in my direction. I walk to the front of the room and by the time I reach the door, I can hear people whispering. I continue out the door and into the hallway where my heart skips a beat. Two police officers are standing a few feet away. Great, now I'm gonna end up in jail.

"Morning Miss Parker," says the closest officer, extending his hand. I give it a firm shake and notice "J. Benson" on the front of his uniform. The other officer beside him shakes my hand as well. I can see "C. Harris" on hers.

"So...what's going on?" I ask, knowing full well what it might be.

"I need you to come with us," Benson says, motioning for me to follow him. As I follow them down the hallway, I'm beginning to wonder if Rachel is really looking out for me. She said she was in a similar situation at one time. I wonder if she meant this sort of thing? We head into the main office and toward a small room in the back where my school's principal is standing just outside. I've never met her before, but I've heard she's a little strict. She opens the door and the four of us step inside. Harris closes the door behind her and stands beside the door as the rest of us take seats at a table. The dull glow of the lights above me add to the tension.

"Hello, Miss Parker," says the principal, shaking hands with me, "I'm Mrs. Spencer. I don't believe we've met before." I shake my head.

"Alright," says Benson, clearing his throat, "Let's get on with this. First off, I want to say that you're a suspect at this time. Understand?" I nod.

"I'm here to ask about what went on the day you last saw Mr. Green," he continues, "According to Mrs. Donner, you and Miss Weston were speaking to him on Sunday."

"Well, Ezma was," I say, "I just sort of stood by and watched them for a second."

"What did you hear?" Benson asks.

"Michael sounded like he was being sort of a jerk to her," I reply, "He said something about her parents that she didn't like. Something about them intentionally driving off a cliff. I don't know why he brought it up."

"I think I may know the answer to that," Mrs. Spencer chimes in, "When I spoke to Rachel yesterday afternoon, she said that Michael would tease Ezma about her parents. It's because he heard some rumor that Ezma was somehow involved." Ezma? Involved in something like that? I hope it really was just a rumor. I wonder if Rachel heard the same thing? Is that why she seems so eager to help me? Regardless, rumors are just rumors. I'm only interested in facts. Even so, it still has me thinking...

"I see," Benson murmurs, continuing with his notes, "I imagine she was upset when he brought it up, am I right?"

"Sure looked that way," I answer.

"Do you know who started the argument?" he continues.

"Michael was the one who started it," I reply, "He was walking by and must have heard us talking. He asked her if she knew she wasn't working that day. He sounded like he was kidding, but not in a good way. Ezma said something, and then he made that remark about her parents driving off the cliff. After that, all I heard was him complaining that she was keeping him from doing his job."

"Anything else?"

"No, just something about how he should 'start walking' or something," I answer.

"So why did you leave after they started arguing?" he asks.

"Ezma asked me to," I say.

"Alright then," he says, tapping his pen on the table, "So Ezma was out of your sight after that?"

"Yeah. After that I ran into this girl who was nearby," I continue, "She stepped out in front of me and I almost knocked her over."

"And do you know this girl?"

"No," I say, shaking my head, "She looked a little familiar, but otherwise she was a complete stranger."

"Can you describe her to me?" he asks.

"Yeah, she was about my height, average build, long, straight black hair. She kept it in a ponytail with a red ribbon. Kind of pale with green eyes."

"Okay...I think that's all I need to know," he says getting up from the table, "We may want to speak with you again, Miss Parker," he adds as he and Harris exit the room, "So don't be surprised if we come find you again." He and Harris disappear through the office and I'm left sitting at the table with Mrs. Spencer. As I go to get up, she tells me to sit back down.

"I want to talk to you before you go back to class," she says.

"What about?"

"I wanted to ask you about your relationship with Ezma Weston," she explains, "I know you're new to this town and I imagine you know very little about her."

"Yeah, so?"

"She's not someone you should be hanging around with," she replies, "It is my understanding that you have a bit of a history yourself."

"At my last school?"

"Yes," she confirms, "I understand that you were involved in several fights, as well as at least two instances of vandalism among other things. Is that correct?"

"What does any of that have to do with Ezma?" I demand, "And how do you know about that?"

"Your old principal sent over your file," she explains, "All I'm saying is that it looks to me like you were attempting to stay out of trouble in the few months before you left. Ezma is a terrible influence and she has many of her own problems. I don't think you should be associating with her."

"I can decide for myself who I make friends with," I reply. I stand up and start toward the door. She grabs my arm as I try to leave and I shake her off.

"I am not telling you who to be friends with," she says, "I'm just trying to keep you out of trouble. Ezma is a very troubled young woman and I'd hate to see you end up like her."

"I can take care of myself," I grumble. I start toward the door again, expecting her to stop me, but she doesn't. I make my way back to class, only to get another series of stares as I return to my seat. I only just arrived in this town and already I seem to be caught up in something. Something that began long before I ever knew Pryor Creek existed. Somehow I get the feeling that I've only just scratched the surface. I wonder how deep this goes?

Chapter 8

When the bell rings for lunch, I walk out of the classroom and to my locker. I toss my books inside and close it. As I do so, I catch pieces of a conversation happening nearby.

"...heard she's been hanging out with that Ezma girl." I turn to see a group of people standing in a circle several feet away. Not one of them is paying attention to me.

"Rachel was talking to her this morning."

"Who? Zoey?"

"Is that her name?"

"I think so, I heard someone call her that the other day."

"What's she doing hanging out with Ezma? Doesn't she know about her?"

"She's new here, I bet she doesn't."

"I heard she's kind of like Ezma. Someone said they heard she moved here because she got kicked out of her old school."

"Did they say why?"

"Not really, but I heard they both smashed up Rachel Nolan's car yesterday." I grit my teeth and start walking in the other direction. As much as I'd like to thump the closest girl over the head and let them know I heard what they were saying, I really don't need anymore attention right now. I step outside and stand against a wall. I've got too much on my mind to feel hungry. I sit down against the wall and stare off down the street. My phone begins vibrating in my coat pocket and I take it out to look. It's my dad calling me.

"Hello?" I say, placing it to my ear.

"Hey Zoey, how are you?" Dad asks.

"Fine, I guess. Why are you calling me at school?"

"It's lunch for you right now, isn't it?"

"Well, yeah..."

"I just wanted to give you a heads-up about your mother," he explains, "Remember how I said she wanted to come talk to you?"

"She's not coming up here is she?" I inquire, pinching the bridge of my nose. The last thing I need is her making a scene at my school.

"Oh, no, no, no," he assures me, "She's supposed to be coming by the house at around five. I just wanted to know if you're okay with that."

"Sure," I say, getting to my feet, "I guess that's fine."

"Did you still want to see her?" I take a moment to think about that one. Last time I saw her, things didn't play out too well.

"Yeah...I do want to see her," I say, "I want her to know that it's not because I'm ready to forgive her. This is for me to tell her how I feel. Nothing else."

"I told her exactly that," Dad replies, "Anyway, since it seems you've decided, I'll expect you to be home by four-thirty. Okay?"

"Okay."

"Alright, have a good day, Zoey."

"Bye Dad," I mumble. I place the phone back in my coat pocket. Maybe this time I can make her understand why I've been avoiding her. She never seems to get it, no matter how many times I try to tell her. She always chalks it up to my dad brainwashing me. Just thinking of my last conversation with her is infuriating. I glance at the entrance, watching several students walking in my direction. I notice that Rachel is among them. She spots me and walks over.

"Hey," she says with a quick wave, "I heard the cops were here looking for you. Did you end up talking with them?"

"Yeah, why?"

"No reason, I was just curious," she says, "Have you given what I said any thought?"

"Not a whole lot," I lie. I don't want her to think she can change my mind that easily. I'm still not sure she isn't hiding something.

"I'm not the one you should be mad at," she says, "Really, I'm not."

"I'm not convinced."

"You don't have to like me, you don't have to like what I say," Rachel continues, "but you should at least consider what I'm telling you. I don't know if you've noticed, but people are starting to talk about you."

"I noticed."

"I'm not trying to taunt you with it, I just want to help."

"You can help by getting the hell away from me," I growl.

"Look...Zoey," she begins, "You've gotta trust me on this. I know Ezma and I know she's someone who should be avoided."

"I live right next to her," I argue, "If I did tell her to get lost, I'd still have to live on the same street as her."

"I had the same problem," Rachel explains, "It's a tough position to be in, I know. I can help you figure out what to do about that."

"I don't need your help," I groan, "Got that?"

"Were you even listening to me this morning?" she asks, "She's dangerous, Zoey. I was right where you are at one point...and I just wish someone back then had warned me about her."

"Look, all I know is that if anyone is acting weird, it's you," I argue, "Ezma smashed up your car and you don't even seem to be that upset. It would make more sense for you to be threatening me. What are you trying to gain from this?"

"I'm not trying to gain anything, and honestly I am pretty pissed about the car, but that's not what matters right now. What matters is that you're hanging around that psychopath!"

"How is she a psychopath?" I demand. I think back to when Ezma shot that crow. She didn't even seem to care. I've heard somewhere before that killing small animals is an indicator of a potential psychopath. Even so, that's all I've seen so far. And according to her, they're considered pests. My great-grandmother used to shoot anything that moved on her farm. Again, pests. That was a different era, I know...but still, isn't that pretty much the same thing?

"You remember when I mentioned her brother this morning?" Rachel asks, crossing her arms, "I brought that up because she knows I saw what happened. She knows damn well what took place and she just puts on that dopey grin and acts like it's all a game."

"I don't know why I'm asking this," I begin, "but what happened that night? As far as you're concerned, what took place?"

"What I saw was Ezma standing on the front lawn with a huge kitchen knife covered in blood. She was waving it around while she was yelling at Brian. Brian was shouting that he'd been stabbed and was hiding behind his car when the cops showed up."

"So you didn't even see her stab him?" I ask.

"No, but they had to hit her with beanbags to get her to drop the knife," Rachel explains, "They arrested her and carried her off to jail. She ended up with probation, but that was it. I still disagree with that. I think she should have been charged with attempted murder."

"You really think it was that bad?"

"Absolutely," Rachel declares.

"I'm still hung up on the fact that you didn't even see the whole thing," I reply.

"Fine, I'll grant you that," she says, "I did wake up in the middle of it, but you're forgetting that I know these people. You don't. I have reason suspect that Ezma was trying to kill Brian that night. I don't know why, but I'm sure that was the intended goal."

"What proof do you have of it?" I demand, "You're just telling me a story! I wasn't there, all I have is your word and Ezma's."

"Ezma is a goddamn liar," she warns, "She's manipulative, she knows just what to say and when to say it. Don't let her fool you. Whatever she told you is a crock."

"Prove it."

"Fine, if you want proof, I'll find it," Rachel says, "When I have something, I'll be sure to come find you." I glare at her for a few moments before she walks off.

Chapter 9

Once the bell rings at two-o'-clock, I try to leave as quickly as I can. I want to get out of here before Rachel comes back and starts bothering me again. As I make my way to the parking lot, I find Ezma sitting on the edge of the nearby sidewalk, smoking a cigarette. She looks up as I approach and snuffs it out.

"Something wrong?" she asks, standing up.

"Rachel's been hassling me," I answer.

"Oh?"

"She's acting like an idiot," I grumble, "She's trying to convince me to stay away from you."

"Eh, don't let her bother you," Ezma yawns, stretching her arms over her head, "She's just upset with me."

"If that's the case, then why doesn't she bother you instead?"

"She hates talking to me," Ezma answers, "Apparently I frustrate her." I glance over my shoulder. I can see Rachel talking to her boyfriend just outside the building.

"Come on," says Ezma, opening the van door, "Let's get out of here. I'm not in the mood to deal with her right now." I give a nod and climb into the passenger seat.

"What was she talking to you about?" Ezma asks, closing her door.

"She was bringing up your brother," I explain, "Said she followed us out to the park because she was worried about me."

"Sheesh, what a whopper..." Ezma replies, "And as for Brian, it's like I said. I wish people, including her, would leave it alone. It's over. I mean, Brian was my brother, not hers. It's not like talking it to death is going to bring him back."

"Yeah, exactly."

"She say anything else?" Ezma asks.

"She did," I say, "She said she saw you out in the yard that night, with your brother...that you had a knife in your hand."

"That's the same crap she told everyone else around here," Ezma grumbles, "I didn't stab Brian, his girlfriend did. Look, I didn't want to get into this, but what happened that night was a lot worse than I first made it sound," she explains, "You remember how I said he had an alcohol problem?"

"Yeah."

"He did get clean, but what happened after that, was he traded that addiction for another," Ezma continues, "He had blood all over himself because his stupid girlfriend attacked him with a knife and Sarah can deny it all she wants, but those wounds were not self-inflicted."

"Sarah?" I repeat.

"Yeah, Sarah Fenton, his girlfriend," Ezma answers, "He was so in love with her that he refused to call the cops. He said she was just dealing with her own problems and that he didn't want to see her in prison. Lucky for him, she didn't inflict anything too serious. I told him he was being stupid, that his obsession with that woman was going to be the end of him. I tried to call an ambulance since he refused to go to the hospital, but he took the phone and threw it against the wall."

"What happened after you two went outside?"

"We got into an argument and he said he didn't want to have to explain what happened to him. I told him he needed to and he tried to leave. I went after him, but unbeknownst to us, Sarah had followed him to my house. She jumped out and stabbed him. I managed to get her off, but not before she got me a couple times. The reason I had that knife in my hand was because I took it from her. She ran off as soon as I shouted that I was going to kill her. I imagine Rachel heard that too and thought I was talking to my brother." Why didn't Rachel mention that Sarah was there that night? Seems like an important detail to skip over.

"So what happened to Sarah?" I ask,

"She was caught later that night while my brother and I were being treated at the hospital," Ezma explains, "Like I said before, there was something about her getting hit in the head and being held for evaluation because of it. There was a mental evaluation that followed that and I didn't see her around town for a few days."

"What about Brian?" I ask.

"He decided after about two days in the hospital that he didn't want to be there anymore. Biggest mistake of his life," Ezma answers, "He was dead a couple days after that. Overdosed back at his place and that was the end of it. Brian had been suicidal for years, it wasn't exactly surprising."

"Sorry you had to deal with all that. Can't have been easy."

"It sure wasn't fun dealing with all that," Ezma replies, "It was hard, I can say that much. I'm just glad my aunt was around. She came and stayed with me for a while. That was before her husband died. Now she's so busy with her foster kids, I don't see her very often."

"I can see why you might get lonely."

"It's not so bad since you showed up," Ezma says, "I know it's barely been a week, but it's been nice to have you around."

"I could say the same," I reply, "I didn't expect to have any friends once I moved here. Doubt I'll make anymore since Rachel seems to have everyone talking about us."

"Why do you say that?"

"Well, I heard some things in the halls today. Sounds like someone, I don't know who, was telling people about Rachel's car."

"Can't say I'm all that surprised," Ezma sighs, "I figured one of them would say something."

"Everyone thinks I helped you trash it," I continue, "Funny how the truth always seems to get twisted. On top of that, the police came by and talked to me today. Not about the car, though. They asked me a few things about that Michael guy."

"The one at the library?" Ezma asks.

"That's the one," I confirm, "I imagine they might come looking for you too."

"Yeah, they already came by my place around noon," Ezma replies, "Damn pigs. Getting real tired of their crap. They said I'm a suspect."

"They said the same thing to me," I grumble, "Nice way to start off my life in this town."

"Don't worry about it too much," Ezma says, "It's not worth dwelling on. It'll blow over soon enough."

"I hope so."

"Neither of us had anything to do with what happened. They can't do anything without evidence."

"I hope my mother hasn't heard about this yet," I say, "It'll just give her a reason to act even more pompous than usual."

"I thought you lived with your dad?"

"I do," I nod.

"Do you still talk to her or something?"

"No, not really," I reply, "but she is supposed to be showing up at my house sometime around five today. Really not looking forward to that train wreck."

"Why is she coming up here?" Ezma inquires.

"She may have lost custody, but she still keeps trying to patch things up between us. Problem is, I don't want anything to do with her. Not until she quits drinking, not until she does some growing up."

"That bad, huh?"

"Oh, don't even get me started on her," I groan. The van lurches as we pull into Ezma's driveway, the seats creaking and items on the dashboard shifting. She kills the engine and the two of us climb out, closing the doors behind us.

"You mind if I stick around for a while?" I ask.

"Sure," she answers, "Just as long as you're alright with sitting on the porch."

"The house not ready for company yet?" Somehow I get the feeling that she's picky about how the house looks. Seemed fine the day I got a quick peek inside. I've known some people who had dishes piled all over their tables and laundry sitting all over the couch, among other things.

"Yeah, pretty much," she answers, "I need to rent one of those rug cleaners and use it in the living room this week. That and the upstairs bathroom is a mess, and it's the only one with a toilet that works. Downstairs one is just...I don't know, not in the greatest shape. I've had it overflow at least three times." She steps into the house and shuts the door. I sit down in one of the deck chairs and glance across the yard. From where I'm sitting, I can see one of my neighbors holding a rifle. He's aiming it at a few crows gathered around an overturned garbage bin. He fires, but I don't hear anything. Two crows fly off, leaving their deceased companion behind. I look further down the street and spot the girl from the library, the one with the ribbon in her hair. She's sitting on the front steps of the abandoned house Ezma told me about, talking to someone on her phone. The sound of Ezma coming back through the door breaks my gaze.

"Want one?" she asks, holding a bottle of water in front of me, "Sorry, it's all I have right now."

"That's alright." I take it and set it on the table next to me. Ezma seats herself in another nearby chair and looks across the street. The man I saw shoot the crow is now scooping it up with a shovel and taking it into the backyard.

"See?" Ezma says, "What did I tell you?"

"That people around here consider crows to be pests," I reply, "I didn't hear the shot, though. Thought he had a .22 for a moment."

"Folks in town usually use a pellet gun for that sort of thing," Ezma explains, taking a drink from her water bottle, "Kill the crow and keep the cops off your back at the same time. Well, unless you miss and take out someone's window or something. Most people just scare them off, but some feel that isn't good enough."

"How long have they been a problem around here?" I ask.

"Longer than I've been here," she answers, "Pryor Creek used to be a farming community back around the turn of the century, back when my great-grandparents were still young. By the late nineteen-fifties, much of it was getting pushed aside by urban development, and the Pryor Creek you see before you was born. It's still common for a lot of people around here, especially the families that have been here forever, to use at least some of their backyards to grow a portion of their food. The crows are just one thing that causes them problems."

"I see. Makes sense."

"Anyway, you were talking about your mom earlier?"

"Yeah, why?"

"I just wasn't sure if you were finished talking when we got out of the van," she says, "Thought I'd ask."

"Eh, there's not much else to say. Just that I'm sort of regretting my decision."

"What decision?"

"My dad asked me how I felt about her visiting me," I explain, "I said I wanted to tell her off and now...now I just don't care anymore."

"The anger died down, I assume?" Ezma asks.

"Yeah, it did," I nod, "I don't know if I feel like putting up with her right now. She's frustrating to be around."

"How come?"

"She's frustrating to be around." I explain.

"Is it too late to back out?" Ezma asks.

"Yep," I say with a nod, "I don't know what I was thinking. He called me a few minutes after I heard those people talking about me in the halls. I was still frustrated, angry. When Dad called me and mentioned my mother, I was itching to take my anger out on someone. Now that I've had some time to cool down, it doesn't matter anymore."

"Mind if I ask you something?" Ezma asks.

"What?"

"Well," she begins, "I don't know...I was gonna ask what happened. Like, what did she do to make you hate her?"

"It was all sorts of things," I say, "The main thing was that she was always drinking, and because of that she was violent. Actually when I say it like that it sounds like I'm giving her an excuse. That's what she always did. Made every excuse she could think of. Her favorite was that it was my dad's fault that she behaved the way she did."

"Sounds a lot like my brother," Ezma replies, "He wasn't violent when he drank, though. Regardless, he blamed me for a lot of his behavior. Anytime he was in a bad mood, it was because I was 'picking on him.' He was a complete downer when he was drunk. Always having pity parties and making every attempt to drag me down with him. I think he was just looking for someone to be depressed with."

"My mom did that too," I add, "Pity parties and whatnot. I guess you know how irritating it is, don't you?"

"Oh yeah," Ezma nods, "Very much so." She stops and glances down the road. I look in the same direction to see a blue car moving slowly down the street. We both watch as the car stops in front of the house. The driver climbs out, and I can see as she steps onto the lawn that she's holding a baseball bat.

"Get off my lawn, Melissa!" Ezma shouts.

"I heard you smashed my sister's car up!" Melissa snarls, pointing the bat at Ezma.

"What of it, deary?" Ezma taunts, "You gonna hit me with that bat?" She laughs and stands up. Melissa walks to the bottom of the stairs and stops with her bat over her shoulder.

"Depends on your answer," Melissa replies, "You gonna pay for it or what?"

"Wasn't really planning on it," Ezma says, "Why?"

"I see how it is," Melissa growls, "You just think you can get away with that sort of thing? Is that what's going on?" She storms up the stairs and pushes Ezma into her front door.

"I don't know what you think this is going to solve," Ezma snorts, "Rachel keyed my van. I just returned the favor."

"You did more than that!" Melissa snarls, "You caused several thousand dollars worth of damage!"

"And it wouldn't have happened had your bitch of a sister kept her keys in her pocket!" Ezma smirks, "Seems to me that you should be mad at your sister. Not me."

"You'll pay for the damages whether you like it or not!," Melissa hisses, "I bet that aunt of yours could cover the costs just fine, so don't tell me you can't afford it. I don't care where the money comes from just as long as you hand it over."

"Sounds like Rachel's gonna have to get used to taking the bus," Ezma sneers, "What a pity. The spoiled brat gets to go without a car for a week. Big deal."

"Keep it up. Keep being a smartass and see where that gets you," Melissa snarls.

"And what if I refuse?" Ezma asks.

"Then you pay for the car a different way," Melissa growls, slamming the bat down on a nearby railing.

"Hmm..." Ezma begins, "So...if I'm understanding this,I have three options,right?"

"I never gave you a third!" Melissa snaps, "Either you pay up or I crack your damn skull!"

"Or I can do this..." Ezma growls. She reaches into her coat and pulls out her revolver. She presses the muzzle against the bottom of Melissa's chin and cocks the hammer. Melissa's eyes widen in shock.

"You won't do it," Melissa whispers. Ezma cocks her head and smirks.

"And are you going to stop me?" Ezma taunts, "You'd be surprised to know how easy it is. I don't think you came here today because of the car. I think there was something else on your mind, wasn't there?" A tense silence ensues as the two of them glare at one another.

"For you, I'm sure it is," Melissa mumbles, "Even so, I doubt you're dumb enough to pull something like that in broad daylight."

"Legally I can shoot you," Ezma smirks, "You came onto my property, against my wishes, with what could be classified as a deadly weapon, and threatened to harm me with it. You're right, it would be messy, and I wouldn't want my hair to reek of your disgusting blood for the next few days, so how about I make you a deal? Leave now and I won't shoot you. Stick around and I will."

"You're bluffing," Melissa declares. Ezma takes the bat from Melissa's hand and throws it at my feet. I pick it up and place it over my shoulder. Movement across the street catches my eye. The girl with the red ribbon is now standing up, watching the scene unfold.

"Don't...test me..." Ezma hisses in Melissa's ear. She leans back and smiles at Melissa who by this time is beginning to sweat, "You know I'm not bluffing," Ezma continues, "Remember? I'm crazy. Isn't that what everyone says about me?"

"There's a reason people say it," Melissa growls, "You've changed, Ezma. We all see it."

"And there's a reason I'm contemplating blowing your head off," Ezma hisses, "I'm not the villain you and everyone else make me out to be. I'm the villain because you keep forcing me to be."

"No one's forcing you to do anything," Melissa snarls. Ezma shoves Melissa backward, sending her tumbling into the railing.

"Get off my property," Ezma growls, "Better hurry before I change my mind." She sits down in her chair and glares at Melissa who starts down the stairs.

"This is far from over, Ezma," Melissa warns, "You're on the losing side of this and you know it."

"I disagree..." Ezma growls. Melissa storms back to her car and slams the door. I lean the bat against the railing and brush a few stray hairs away from my eyes.

"I am so sick of this crap..." Ezma mutters as Melissa starts the engine, "This will be the year I move out of this town. I can't do this anymore." I sit back down in one of the chairs, watching Melissa's car speed down the road. She passes by the abandoned house before turning the corner. The girl with the ribbon has vanished.

Chapter 10

"Why haven't you left sooner?" I ask.

"Believe it or not, there was a time where I didn't want to leave," Ezma says, swinging the cylinder out of her revolver. I can see that all the chambers are empty. She begins loading it while I look on.

"So you were bluffing," I observe.

"Yeah," she nods, "I was cleaning it and forgot to load it again. After that whole thing, I can see I need to be more careful. Melissa is such a pain in my ass. It's not the first time she's paid me a visit like that."

"I take it you did something as bad as smashing up Rachel's car in the past?" I ask. Ezma shakes her head.

"No, it was part of something bigger than that," she explains, "Things have been tense between our families for a long time and Melissa always tries to threaten me when something goes wrong. Fine, maybe I shouldn't have smashed the car up, but that doesn't give her license to come and threaten me like that."

"What do you mean part of something bigger?" I inquire.

"It's nothing all that interesting," she sighs, "There's some bad blood between us and that's all there is to it. That car wreck didn't make things any better."

"How so?"

"Bunch of armchair detectives thinking they knew everything," Ezma explains, "The police investigated the crash as a homicide once they found that the car had been tampered with. Then of course people came to their own conclusions, didn't bother to wait for facts."

"What do you mean?"

"What I'm saying, is that people decided without any evidence that Brian and I had played a part in their deaths," Ezma explains, "My family wasn't exactly looked upon with favor if you know what I mean. Whole heap of reasons behind that, things I don't want to get into right now. I didn't know jack about cars at that age. How would I know anything about sabotaging the car? I wasn't even there that night and Brian was too busy arguing with our parents to do it. Everything settled down after a while, but once he started drinking, our relationship became strained." I watch as she places the final round into the revolver and locks it back into place.

"What did his drinking have to do with it?"

"Like I said before, he was depressing to be around," Ezma replies, "He pissed off a lot of people around here. Got kicked out of bars and liquor stores, that kind of thing."

"So, he died when you were sixteen, right? How much older was he?"

"He was twenty-two when he died," Ezma explains, "Six years my senior." I look over the fence to see my dad pulling into the driveway. It must be getting close to four.

"Your dad home?" Ezma asks.

"Yeah," I groan, "I guess that means my mom's gonna be showing up soon." I watch as my dad makes his way into the house, closing the door behind him. I wouldn't quite call it a slam, but he does do so with more force than necessary. I imagine he's not looking forward to having Mom around either. I've been so caught up in how I feel about it that I forgot how much this will effect him.

"Is he going to back you up?"

"I don't know yet," I reply, "Maybe, maybe not. Either way I don't care."

"You sound like you do," Ezma observes.

"I'm not so sure about that."

"I know this is a family thing, and that I probably shouldn't butt in, but...I wouldn't mind just standing off to the side. You know? Be there to help if you need it?"

"I wouldn't mind, but I imagine my dad might find fault with that," I reply, "Thanks for offering, though."

"Well, in any case, I'll be over here if you feel like talking once you're finished with her." I feel bad about turning down Ezma's offer, but my mother would find some way to pick a fight with her. And from what I've seen with Ezma, that could get very bad, very fast. I say goodbye to her a few minutes later and head into the house. My dad is sitting in the living room flipping through channels on the T.V. As soon as I close the front door behind me, I hear him call to me.

"Hey Zoey?" he says, "Can you come in here for a minute? I need to talk to you before your mom gets here." I let out a muffled groan and walk into the living room. As I plop down on the couch across from him, he mutes the television and turns to face me.

"I heard about what happened today," he says, "Apparently you had a discussion with the police."

"It's not like that," I protest, "I didn't do any-"

"I don't want to hear excuses," he interrupts, "I'm becoming concerned that you might be going backwards."

"I'm not like that anymore," I declare.

"I hope so," he replies, "When we moved out here, I thought it would do you some good. This is your chance to start over. If you fall back into bad habits, I'm not going to just pack up and move again. You need to take this seriously."

"I am," I groan.

"Getting calls from the sheriff's office makes me think otherwise."

"They told me I was just a person of interest," I lie.

"When they spoke to me, they said you're a suspect," he counters, "How the hell did that happen? It hasn't even been a month since we got here!"

"Why are we talking about this before Mom's visit?" I shout, standing up from the couch, "I'm already dreading that, and now here it is, not even ten minutes before she gets here! I don't need this right now, okay?" I storm off and head into my room. I don't understand why he always does that. Why he chooses the worst times to bring things like this up. I sit down at my desk and lean my elbows on it. The clock on my nightstand tells me only a few minutes remain. I wish I could just go back in time and fix this. Tell him that I don't want her here. It's nothing but added stress and it was unwise of me to agree to this. It's like arguing with a brick wall, I get nowhere with her regardless of what I say to her. A knock on the door sounds from downstairs minutes later. I can feel the pit of my stomach drop out. I know Dad's not going to bother to answer it. I saunter downstairs and look through the peephole to see my mother standing just on the other side. Her usual blood red coat and hat are unmistakable. I take a deep breath and open the door.

"Hello, Zoey," she smiles, "Aren't you going to invite me inside?"

"Dad doesn't want you in here," I lie. She raises an eyebrow.

"Is that so?" she snorts, "Lying isn't a good way to start this off." I let out a heavy sigh and open the door wider. I walk into the kitchen and seat myself at the table. My mother closes the front door behind her and follows me. She sits down across from me and removes her hat, placing it on the table beside her.

"So..." she says, "Where should we start?"

"How about you apologize for what happened?" I suggest.

"What exactly am I apologizing for?"

"Everything," I answer, "Every single thing you put me through."

"I've apologized countless times, Zoey. What else do you want me-?"

"I want you to be sincere about it this time!" I snap, standing up from my chair, my hands pressed against the top of the table. I glare at her for a few seconds before sitting back in my chair.

"See?" my mother snorts, "This is always the problem with you. You are never happy with anything I do for you. Anything I say to you."

"This whole thing isn't about me, Mother!" I snarl, "This is about you! This is about what you did! Not me!"

"It would be easier if you could give me specifics so we can work through them," she groans.

"Okay then, how about the dozens of times you left me sitting alone on the sidewalk for hours, because you forgot to pick me up from school...and soccer...and everything else I did! Oh and let's not forget the way you killed my gerbil!"

"I never killed any of your pets!" she contends, "Where are you getting this from?"

"You don't remember that, do you?" I growl, "I bet I know why that is. You were probably too drunk to remember doing it! Must be real convenient! I still remember that as if it happened yesterday! Not just that, everything. The way I'd wake up to the sound of you throwing dishes across the dining room because Dad hid your booze! I even remember how you got the both of us in a car wreck because you were too out of it to drive! What else do I have to remind you of?"

"That wreck was an accident!" she insists, "How dare you accuse me of such a thing!'"

"Truth hurts, doesn't it?" I retort.

"You're not telling the truth," she argues, "You're twisting it!"

"There were police reports, Mother!" I counter, "They tested you for alcohol the night of the crash. There was no arguing that you shouldn't have been behind the wheel! There is solid evidence that you did these things! You even spent time in jail for the whole gerbil fiasco! Are you so in denial that you can't bring yourself to accept the things you did?"

"I have no problem whatsoever, with accepting responsibility for my actions," she declares, "What I have a problem with, is my own daughter twisting the truth! The whole reason I came here today, was to clear the air with you, not start another argument!"

"You know what your problem is?" I snarl, "Your problem is that you don't take responsibility. You never have! It was always someone else's fault! The car crash was because someone else cut you off. I was left alone on the street for hours after school because it was Dad's fault for not reminding you, or just getting me himself, when you knew how much pressure he was under at work. And you know why that was the case? He was always having to take care of not just me, but you too! We both tried to help you and you just blew us off. If you would just admit that you screwed up, I wouldn't be so upset with you!"

"We failed as a family," she argues, "Do you even remember the way your father took out part of the neighbor's fence with the car when he stormed off? It wasn't just once either! He was even arrested for vandalism and reckless endangerment! What bothers me most about you, Zoey, is the way that you constantly defend your father! You focus all your negativity on me and ignore all the problems your father has caused!"

"He had to deal with you on a regular basis!" I shout. I turn to see my father walking into the kitchen. I imagine he's been listening this entire time. He sits adjacent to the two of us and crosses his arms. My mother and I look at one another, then back at him.

"What?" he says, "Don't stop just because I'm here."

"This is between me and Zoey," Mom hisses.

"I understand that," Dad replies, "I'm just here to make sure you two don't have a repeat of the last time you saw one another." I heave a sigh and stare down at the table in front of me.

"This is exactly what I mean," Mom mutters.

"Quit playing the victim," I groan.

"No, really," she continues, "Every single time, you two gang up on me. It starts to get tiring after a while, you know?"

"I'll be eighteen in a few months," I say, "This whole 'siding with Dad' thing isn't going to matter after that."

"This isn't about custody," she insists, "This will go on long after that if we don't resolve the situation."

"Oh, it's a Christmas miracle!" I exclaim, "That's the first time I've ever heard you talk sense."

"Knock it off, Zoey. Can we please try to discuss this without arguing?"

"I'm sorry," I snort, "Did you forget that you were the one who started the argument?"

"It doesn't matter who started it," she groans, "I just want it to stop."

"Then apologize," I demand. I glare at her for what seems like minutes before she at last says something.

"Zoey," she says, "I'm sorry. Okay? I'm...sorry."

"For what?"

"For not being the mother you deserved," she continues, "I can apologize as many times as you like, but it won't erase what happened."

"It's not about that," I reply, "It's about accepting responsibility."

"Please don't start acting superior," she growls, "Like I said before, we failed as a family. We all did something to contribute."

"How am I acting superior?" I demand, "I know that things got a lot harder after I turned thirteen. I know I contributed, and I know it didn't help the situation."

"Do you really?"

"I've done some growing up," I insist, "I know I'm still young, but I'm old enough to realize when my actions aren't helping a situation."

"Then why has it come to my attention that you're being investigated for murder?" Mom demands. I can't stand to be around her anymore. As much as I want to stand up and leave the room, something keeps me in my chair.

"That doesn't have anything to do with the discussion," Dad chimes in.

"Why did you tell her about that?" I demand.

"Don't blame your father for this, it's you we're talking about and I want an answer," Mom scolds, "It was bad enough when you were in trouble for fights and vandalism, but I never once thought I'd hear this about you."

"Says the gerbil killer," I mutter.

"Don't turn this around on me, young lady!" she snarls, "You need to explain yourself! So start talking!"

"I was in the wrong place at the wrong time," I explain, "It was bad timing, nothing else. It could have been anyone!"

"Well I certainly hope so," she replies.

"Helen, we aren't here to discuss that," Dad chimes in, "I only let you show up today because the two of you have past issues that you have yet to resolve. So maybe instead of going on about the murder investigation, the two of you should do what you came to do."

"I didn't ask for your opinion, Walter!" Mom snarls.

"It's not an opinion," he argues, "It's fact. If you're not going to do what we agreed, then I see no reason for you to stay. To be honest, I'd like to know what you've been doing since the last time we saw one another."

"What do you mean?" Mom asks.

"I want to know how you've helped yourself since then," he answers.

"We all know I went to rehab," she grumbles, "We don't need to discuss it."

"It's not just about that," Dad continues, "Last I heard, you were still searching for work. I want to know if you've gotten your act together."

"I have, Walter," Mom says, "I'm out of that rundown apartment and I'm working a new job. I would say I'm doing much better now."

"What about relapses?" he inquires.

"I haven't had any."

"In how long?" I ask.

"Never," Mom insists.

"I find that hard to believe," I mutter.

"So if I go out to your car right now, I won't find any alcohol?" Dad asks.

"No, of course not," Mom replies.

"You don't sound too sure of yourself," he says.

"There's nothing out there, Walter," Mom declares.

"Last chance, Helen," Dad warns, standing up as he speaks.

"So, what?" Mom snorts, "You're gonna rifle through my car or something?" She gets to her feet and places her hat back on her head. Dad shakes his head in frustration and starts walking out of the kitchen.

"If there's nothing incriminating in there, I don't see why it's an issue," he says, heading for the front door. Mom follows after him and I stand up and do the same.

"That's not how it works, Walter!" Mom snarls, "That's an invasion of my privacy! I came here to speak with my daughter, not bullshit with my arrogant ex-husband!"

"Where are your keys?" he asks.

"I'm not giving you my keys."

"You've been drinking, haven't you?" he continues, "Give me the keys. I'm not letting you drive home. Not tonight."

"I haven't been drinking!" Mom insists.

"Don't lie to me, Helen!" Dad shouts, "I can smell alcohol on your breath!"

"So I had a drink!" she admits, "It's been a rough week for me! What's the big deal?"

"The big deal is that you're a recovering alcoholic," Dad answers. He opens the door and walks toward Mom's car.

"I'm not giving you the keys," she growls, following him outside. I knew it, I could sense it a mile away. Dad's never been innocent in any of this. He always says he's looking out for Mom's best interests, but the reality is that all he's doing right now is harassing her. It's his way of getting back at her for a failed marriage and everything he went through. It's childish and I can't believe he's decided that this is somehow more important. It wouldn't surprise me one bit if he wanted to have one more opportunity to make her miserable. As much as I despise my mother, I can't defend Dad's behavior.

"Will you just leave her alone?" I snarl at him, "I don't care if she had a drink! I wanted her here to talk to her!" Both of them stop in their tracks, exchange glances, then look at me.

"Zoey, this is about whether or not your mother is going to put other people in danger if she drives home," Dad explains, "We can get back to your conversation as soon as she gives me her keys. That's all I want from her. If she doesn't want me to search the car, then fine, whatever."

"You and I both know you'll search my car at some point, you goddamn liar!" Mom snarls, giving him a rough shove, "I don't know how many times I've apologized to you, Walter, but you will never understand what it's like to kick an addiction you've had since your midteens! We are not married anymore! It's time for you to stay out of my goddamn business!"

"It's my business if I let you leave and you end up killing someone!" Dad thunders, "You think this is some kind of joke? Just give me the keys and we'll go back inside!"

"Don't you stand there and bullshit me!" Mom hisses, "You love creating a spectacle and your goal has always been to humiliate me! If by some miracle I did agree to stay here tonight, you'd probably sneak out and check the car while I'm sleeping!"

"Will you two cut it out?" I shout, "Dad, you hijacked this whole damn thing! This wasn't supposed to be about you!"

"Exactly!" Mom snarls, "I came here for Zoey, not you! What I do in my personal life is none of your business!"

"It's my business as a father!" Dad growls, "You've said it many times before, you want to be back in Zoey's life, and it's not going to happen until I know you're clean!"

"This was only supposed to be a brief visit, I'm not asking her to come back to Echo Point with me!" Mom rages, "You're the one causing the problem here! I know I screwed up and it haunts me every day of my life, Walter! I thought this would be a step toward normalcy, but here we are, indulging your selfish need to piss me off instead!"

"Give me the keys..." Dad sighs, rolling his eyes, "I'm not backing away from this, Helen, I'm not going to have it hanging over my head while you drive home; all the while wondering if you've caused a wreck or not."

"You're not getting my keys, Walter!" Mom hollers. This is getting ridiculous. It's like nothing I say matters. Fine, if they want to fight, they can do it on their time.

"You know what? To hell with both of you!" I shout, "Have fun doing what you're doing!" I turn and start back toward the front door. People have started coming out of their houses, most of whom are standing on their front lawns or porches. Ezma is one of them. I catch her eye for a moment as I place my hand on the doorknob. Before I can step into the house, my mother stops me.

"Zoey, please don't run off," she pleads.

"Why the hell not?" I demand, turning to face her, "I don't want to do this in front of a bunch of strangers! Besides, it doesn't matter what I think! It's all about you two!"

"That isn't true, I came all the way up here to see you!" she protests.

"Yeah and started making excuses right off the bat and now you're more interested in arguing with Dad!"

"Zoey, I'm sorry, I really am," she apologizes.

"I don't want to hear it!" I snarl.

"Zoey, don't talk to her like that," Dad warns.

"Oh now you're done making a spectacle?" I snort, "Screw this, I'm leaving." Mom stops me again and I turn and shove her away from me. She slaps me across the face and I clench my fists.

"What the hell?" I rage, "What'd you do that for?"

"First off, young lady, you're going to be a legal adult in a few months," Mom growls, "You need to quit putting your hands on people. Did you learn nothing from what happened at your last school?"

"Did you learn nothing from all the times you were too shit-faced to know left from right?" I retort.

"Don't change the subject!" Mom snarls, "You're no saint and neither am I. I get it, Zoey, I know what it was like to have a lousy mother. I'm sorry I put you through all of that, I really am, but I try more than you know. I don't want to go back. I know you don't either, but I had a rough time growing up, and there is a lot that I'm not ready to deal with. I have been struggling with this for years and you can't expect me to just fix everything in two!"

"More excuses," I growl. She slaps me a second time and grabs me by the arm.

"Don't you sass me, young lady!" she hisses. At that instant, I can't take it anymore. I ball my free hand into a fist and strike her in the cheek. She stumbles backward and I drag her to the ground. Dad shouts and runs toward us. I manage to land two more blows before he drags me off of her. I spot her keys on the ground and pick them up before either of them notice.

"What the hell is wrong with you?" Mom screams.

"I could ask you the same thing!" I shout back.

"Both of you knock it off!" Dad thunders. Mom and I glare at one another and for a moment I consider trying to hit her again. She spots her keys in my hand and narrows her eyes.

"Why do you have my keys?" she demands.

"Because you dropped them," I retort.

"Give them to me!" she orders, trying to move toward me. Dad holds her back.

"Let go of me!" she rages. She tries to throw Dad off, but he maintains his hold.

"Not until you calm down," he replies.

"I want my damn keys," she continues, "Give them to me, Zoey!" Dad looks at me and shakes his head. I place them in my pocket and cross my arms.

"I'm keeping them for now," I declare.

"I want to go home," she says, "And I can't do that without my keys."

"You're staying here," Dad declares. The two of them go right back to fighting and shouting, once again leaving me on the sidelines of a fight I helped start. Having her come here was a terrible idea. I should have never agreed to it. Sirens in the distance bring me back to the present and I look down the street to see flashing lights approaching.

Chapter 11

Two hours later, I find myself sitting on the sidewalk in front of my house. Ezma is sitting beside me. Both my parents were taken in for questioning a short time ago. Seems someone called the cops after the argument became a fist fight. I happened to recognize one of the officers who showed up. It was Harris, the woman who was accompanying Benson when he questioned me at the school.

"I'm sorry that didn't go well," Ezma says, lighting up a cigarette.

"I am too," I mutter.

"Did they say how long they'll be gone?" Ezma asks.

"No, not really," I mumble, "Just that it could be a few hours."

"So...if you don't mind me asking...what happened?"

"I don't mind," I assure her, "My dad cut-in during our conversation. I don't think it would've gotten so out of hand if he hadn't done that."

"Why was he asking for her keys?" she inquires.

"She was drinking before she showed up," I reply, "He didn't want her driving off. Although, part of me wishes she had. Too bad I can't make sure she slams into a brick wall instead of another car."

"Is that just some left over anger, or do you really hate her that much?"

"I hate her that much," I grumble, "She's already caused a couple of wrecks in the past. She never got much either time. Spent six months in jail the first time it happened, then the second time, she got a year plus probation. After that, she always made someone else go get her alcohol instead."

"I don't know what to say," Ezma says. She takes a drag on her cigarette and exhales a large puff of smoke in front of her. The breeze carries it away and she tucks her hair behind her ears.

"It's a frustrating position to be in," I sigh, "On one hand, she's my mother and I want her to get better. On the other, I think she'd be better off dead."

"Why do you say that?"

"She's too far gone," I say, "Even if she can overcome her addiction, it won't change what it's done to her. She's just this...hateful, angry, condescending person. She says she's not ready to face her demons yet. I have to face the things that happened to me, so why can't she? It's the same thing with my dad. We've tried to explain to her that we could help her, but she just doesn't want to be helped. She's already dead as far as I'm concerned."

Ezma and I remain on the sidewalk for another hour before we part ways. I head inside and go straight to my room. My mind is racing after all that's taken place today. I think about what Rachel said the other day about Ezma, and how Ezma handled the incident with Melissa. My mind moves from that to the incident with Ezma and Brian. All at once, my mind is swimming with questions. I let out a sigh and sit up on the bed. Maybe I can dig something up if I take a look around. I stand up and seat myself at my desk. I turn the computer on and wait for it to start up. I lean back in the chair and stare up at the ceiling for a moment. I begin to wonder if what happened tonight will effect how I'm perceived around here. I've already been talked about in the halls at school. Now this whole mess I'm sure will just add fuel to the fire.

I turn my attention to the monitor and start working. After about twenty minutes, I manage to dig up a few articles from various newspapers. Some from nearby towns, and one of which was published in the Pryor Creek Tribune. They all say essentially the same thing. There was an argument on Ezma's front lawn, Ezma was taken to the hospital and later to jail that night. She was let go on bail, her brother refused treatment after a short period of time in the hospital and left. He was found dead two days after that, Ezma was named a suspect. There isn't any definitive answer that I can find. All three articles vary slightly in what occurred.

There are two things that always remain the same. Sarah Fenton is always mentioned, and each article states that Ezma was shot with "less-lethal rounds" after she refused to drop a large kitchen knife. For the time being, it seems both Rachel and Ezma are telling at least some of the truth. I brush my hair from my face and start searching for police reports, but nothing comes up. Seems I would have to request the information from the local station in person. I continue searching, but no new information emerges. With that I decide to look more into the murders Ezma mentioned on our way to the library.

Everything I find at first gives vague details about what occurred. No names, only the date. February 20th, 2010. Over five years ago. I find a photo of each of the victims. According to what it says beneath the photos, their names are David and Miriam Beckett. They had a daughter named Myra, but no photo of her is shown, likely due to the fact that she was fifteen at the time of the murders. From what I can tell, she's about two years older than Ezma. The descriptions of the crime scene and the murders themselves are nothing short of disturbing. Several crime scene photos are posted at the bottom of the article. One shows the inside of a bedroom, the walls are splattered with blood, as are the sheets on the bed. The article states that the victims were hacked to death with a hatchet and machete.

I keep reading through the article and manage to find something new. The killers and their accomplices are named. Jeb and Gloria Weston, and Fredric and Avery Nolan. As I suspected, the first two are Ezma's parents. Why didn't she tell me about this? I suppose there are a myriad of reasons, but none of it matters. I keep looking through the article to see that Ezma's mother is named as the mastermind behind the murders. The article goes on to say that she enlisted help from the Nolans in committing the murders. Ezma's mother allegedly witnessed a distressed Myra Beckett attempting to escape her house one night. After that, I find that Myra is Ezma's half-sister. Same father, different mothers. The article states that this was part of the reason the Westons went after the Becketts.

Twenty minutes later I've found another article that claims that the Nolans held a grudge against David Beckett after he sent a man named Nelson to prison. He was later found innocent of robbery, but not before he was executed. It sounds like the Nolans were out for revenge, and the Westons appeared to have used that to their advantage. Further on, I discover that Jeb Weston brought forth evidence against the Nolans, a well-off family that once owned a series of department stores around the state, for fraud and tax evasion. The Nolans were tried in a separate case and lost their empire as a result. This all shows that

Rachel has more reason to hate Ezma than she lets on. I knew she was hiding something. I hear a knock on the front door and I go to answer. It's gotten dark outside and I have to turn the porch light on to see that it's Ezma.

"What are you doing here?" I ask, poking my head outside.

"I noticed your folks still weren't back," she says, "Thought I'd see how you were doing."

"Not too bad," I reply, "You wanna come in for a while?"

"Sure." Ezma steps inside and I close the door.

"So, what have you been up to?" she asks.

"Not a whole not," I answer, "Just digging around on the internet."

"What were you looking for?"

"I was looking into those murders you told me about," I say, "The ones that happened on this street."

"Find anything interesting?"

"Actually yeah, there was one thing," I reply, "You want to come up to my room or...?"

"Yeah, that's fine," she smiles, following me up the stairs, "So, what was it you found?"

"Well it says Rachel's family was involved...and yours..." She plops down on the end of my bed and I sit down in my chair.

"Yeah...it's um...it's one of those shameful family secrets everyone wants to forget about," she explains, staring down at the floor, then up at me. She shrugs and I glance at the monitor.

"Sorry, should I have not brought it up?"

"No, no, no, it's fine, it really is," she insists, "I just um...I didn't know what you'd think of me if I said my family was involved in that mess."

"So, the Becketts' daughter was your half-sister?" She nods.

"Yeah, she is," she confirms, "Never knew it until the trial. There's a whole story behind that too. A lot of it came to light after my parents bit the big one. They were a couple of strange people. Both of them came from some pretty dark backgrounds. To me they were just my parents. No different from anyone else's, you know? Looking back on it, it's kind of eerie that I lived in the same house with them."

"What makes you say that?" I ask.

"Well, my dad was a drug dealer when he was younger," she explains, "Started in his teens, got a lot of people hooked, started making some good money off of it. Then one day he gets shot, just about dies in the hospital. You'd think that would be the moment he decides to get his life together, but no...he found the guy who shot him and beat the piss out of him with a bat. Served five years in prison for that. Once he got out he met my mother and seemed to straighten up his act after that."

"What about your mom?"

"She was abused as a kid, grew up in some crappy foster home since her dad was dead and her mother unfit to raise her," she explains, "She was deaf in one ear as a result of the abuse. She finally got sick of it and stabbed her foster mother to death during an argument when she was sixteen. Messed up the father pretty good too, but she got pummeled pretty good in the process. My aunt says she wasn't the same after that. She still thinks my mother suffered brain damage from the beating, and maybe she did if she lost some of her hearing, but I don't know if that's the case or not." The door downstairs swings open and I can hear my parents arguing. I roll my eyes and let out an exasperated sigh.

"I'm sorry about them," I murmur, "God they're embarrassing..."

"I should probably leave. I'll come by in the morning. If that's alright with you."

"Sure," I reply, "Here...I'll go down to the door with you. I can just imagine my mother's reaction otherwise."

"Thanks." We make our way downstairs, and as I could tell by the arguing, neither of my parents have moved far from the door.

"Forget it, Walter! I'm not staying here with you!" Mom snarls, "I'll stay at a motel."

"Your license is suspended, you're staying here," Dad replies, "It's just for a little while, okay? Lizzy will be here to pick you up whenever she has time."

"Great, now I get to spend time with my two awful sisters," Mom grumbles, "Just what I wanted to do on the drive back. There's a reason I never visit them. I don't even know when she will have time since Becky has to come with her to get my car, which means I'm either stuck here with the likes of you or at some crappy motel until then! This could have been avoided, Walter. All you had to do was mind your own damn business for once in your life." As we reach the bottom of the stairs, her eyes fall on Ezma.

"Who is that?" she asks me, gesturing toward Ezma.

"She's my friend, Mom," I groan, "She's leaving."

"Wait, is she the friend your father told me about?" she demands, "The one who's also in trouble?" Ezma glares at my mother as she walks past her. She goes to open the door, but my mother grabs her by the arm and spins her around. "Would you leave her the hell alone?" I snarl as Ezma wrenches her arm free. Dad steps up beside Ezma and places a hand on her shoulder. He scowls at my mother, who rolls her eyes and backs off.

"I'm sorry about that, Ezma," Dad apologizes, "She won't be here long."

"Don't you sit there and defend her!" Mom growls, "The two of them can't have been friends long! This is just like before! Zoey starts hanging out with people she shouldn't and the next thing we know she's in handcuffs!"

"Nice to meet you too," Ezma mutters. She turns to leave and again my mother stops her.

"What did you say to me, you little brat?"

"Helen!" Dad barks, pulling her away from the door, "Stop harassing her!"

"This is why she gets into trouble!" Mom rages, "It's all because you aren't strict enough with her! You never were!"

"I can make my own decisions, Mother!" I shout, "You don't even know her, so piss off!" I shoo Ezma out the door in a huff and slam it shut behind us, "Swear to God if she pulls that crap again..."

"Don't worry about it," Ezma assures me, "It's fine."

"She'll be gone soon," I say, "Too bad I can't make her stay gone."

"You sure you'll be alright?" she asks.

"I'll be fine," I answer, "I've had years of practice. Anyway...I'll see you tomorrow morning." She smiles and nods before walking through the gate. I'm so embarrassed right now, I don't know what to say. It isn't the first time my mother has done something like this.

Chapter 12

The next morning I make my way downstairs earlier than usual. My parents were up arguing until almost midnight. I managed to get to sleep through all of it a short time after ten, but kept waking up every twenty minutes or so until after midnight. When I awoke at close to five, I decided to get up. Once I enter the kitchen, I find my dad sitting at the table. A steaming cup of coffee sits beside the newspaper spread out before him. He looks up as I walk in.

"You're up early," he observes. I open the fridge and start looking inside.

"Couldn't sleep," I reply. I take a few boiled eggs and a piece of left over steak from the fridge. I suppose this will suffice.

"Me neither," he says, "I swear...your mother is a handful sometimes."

"More like all the time," I yawn, sitting down at the table.

"Is Ezma alright?" he asks. I start peeling one of the eggs and clear my throat.

"Sounded like it," I answer, "She didn't seem all that upset."

"That's surprising," he says, turning a page in the newspaper.

"Not really," I say with a shrug. I finish peeling the egg, then take a bite of it and set the other half on my plate, "She's usually pretty calm."

"Usually?"

"Well, she gets frustrated with a couple of people," I admit, "One of them is this girl I go to school with."

"I think you mentioned her before. Rachel, right?"

"Yeah, that's the one," I nod, popping the rest of the egg in my mouth. I hold up my index finger and continue chewing.

"No rush," Dad assures me. I swallow the rest of the egg and start peeling another.

"Rachel and Ezma used to be friends," I continue, "Few years back. Other than that, all I know is that she's a senior, same as me. She has this annoying habit of badmouthing Ezma to me."

"She badmouths her?"

"Yeah," I groan, "I can't even begin to describe how irritating it is. I've told her I don't want to hear it, but she keeps coming back. She's under the impression that she's helping me."

"I see," he sighs, taking a drink of his coffee.

"So...where did Mom go?"

"I finally gave in and drove her to the Cedar Springs Motel across town," he explains, "Couldn't stand to listen to her another second. That and I figured the shouting was keeping you awake. I'm sorry about that. I should have just taken her there after we got back. I just assumed she would get in more trouble. It was bad enough at the police station."

"What did she do?"

"Oh, nothing," he snorts, "Just picked a fight with anyone who touched her. I'm amazed she didn't struggle when they handcuffed her in the yard."

"Did they charge her with anything?" I ask.

"She didn't assault anyone," he says, "She just shouted a bunch. Never heard so much cursing in my life; but they did suspend her license. She's not supposed to be drinking. When they tested her she was still plenty over the legal limit. Court order from the sound of it. Not allowed to purchase or posses."

"So she got a slap on the wrist, huh?"

"Pretty much," Dad nods, "Part of the agreement for allowing her to drive and to receive outpatient treatment was for her to follow that order. I don't know what she was thinking."

"She's not coming back here, is she?"

"Only to get her car out of here," he answers, "Your Aunt Lizzy is pretty upset about having to come up here to do that." I finish the rest of my food in silence and trot back up to my room. Before I can get to the top of the stairs, the doorbell rings. I groan and go to answer it. As I predicted, Ezma is waiting on the other side.

"You're a little early," I say, glancing at the clock.

"Sorry," she apologizes, "I've been up since three with not a lot to do. I can come back later if you want."

"No, no it's fine. Come on in."

"I didn't interrupt anything, did I?" she asks.

"No, really, it's fine," I insist, "Make yourself at home. I'm just getting ready." She steps inside and I close the door behind her.

"Hi, Mr. Parker!" Ezma says as my father wanders out of the kitchen. The newspaper is folded and tucked beneath his arm.

"Oh...hi, Ezma," he replies, seeming surprised, "Couple of early birds today. Sorry about last night. Helen just...she gets a little out of control sometimes."

"No worries," Ezma assures him, "I'll try to stay out of her way next time."

"Oh, there won't be a next time," he declares, "She's not allowed to come here anymore after that outburst. She won't cause you anymore problems."

"Well, I appreciate the apology, nonetheless," Ezma replies, "Best of luck sorting everything out, I suppose."

"I'll need all the luck I can get," he murmurs, "Zoey, I think I'm going to stay home the next couple of days. I'll be up in my room if you need anything."

"Why are you staying home?" I ask.

"I don't think I can focus with your mother in town," he answers, "No telling what trouble she might get into. Holly...I mean Dr. Clarence is supposed to be stopping by around noon and I need to be away from work in order to help her with Helen. She seemed frustrated."

"Mom or Dr. Clarence?"

"I was talking about Dr. Clarence, but I guess the both of them are," he explains, "Anyway, I'll leave you two alone." He saunters up the stairs and out of sight.

"Hey, so...part of why I couldn't sleep was because of what happened last night," Ezma admits, following me into the living room.

"My mom or that discussion we had about the Becketts?" I inquire, sitting down on the couch.

"Don't you need to get ready?" Ezma asks, sitting across from me.

"I will in a minute," I answer, "So which was it?"

"The discussion," she replies, "I guess I'm just feeling insecure about it or something. You know? Like I said last night, shameful family secret."

"Should I just drop it or...?"

"Well, no I don't expect you to just forget about it," Ezma says, crossing her legs, "If I were you I'd have questions. Perfectly fine if you'd like to ask a few." I glance at the clock, then back at Ezma. I've got plenty of time to get ready, but I still feel like I'm in a bit of a fog. I suppose I can chalk that up to poor sleep. Maybe it would be best to put the topic aside for now.

"How about we talk after school?" I suggest, "My head still feels a little fuzzy."

"Works for me," she smiles, "I'm feeling sort of the same, like I can barely stay awake."

"You could hear them next door, couldn't you?" She averts her gaze and clears her throat, before looking back at me.

"Unbelievable..." I mutter, "I'm sorry about that." I get up from the couch and stretch my arms over my head.

"It's fine, don't worry about it," she yawns, "I'm sure I'll sleep better tonight. Oh, I was going to ask...do you still have that gun I gave you?"

"Yeah, why?"

"You want to take it out to Hunter's Ridge and get acquainted with it?" she asks, standing up with her arms crossed. I look at her with an eyebrow raised. What's that supposed to mean?

"I meant shoot some targets with it," she continues, reading my expression, "You know...containers of all kinds, old furniture, anything else we can scrounge up. That sort of thing."

"What made you decide to ask me that?"

"You seemed stressed out last night," she explains, "Thought it might be a good way to blow off some steam."

"Sure. When's a good time?"

"Maybe Saturday." Later on, once I get to the school building, I'm counting the minutes until two. Our plans to go to Hunter's Ridge this weekend, gives something to look forward to as the day drags on. I'm almost surprised to see that Rachel is nowhere to be found. For some reason I notice a strange heaviness in the air as I move through the halls. People are glaring at me as I make my way to class. Just as I'm beginning to become unsettled, someone places their hand on my shoulder and turns me around. I recognize him almost at once. It's Jason, Rachel's boyfriend.

"We need to talk," he says, "Come on." He leads me past a group of other students and out into one of the courtyards. He stops once we're out of earshot and turns to face me.

"What's going on?" I ask.

"I really don't want to be apart of this, but I'm doing this as a favor to Rachel," he explains. He drops his backpack on a nearby bench and removes a manila envelope. He hands it to me and slings his bag back over his shoulder.

"What is this?" I ask.

"It's the police report from the night Ezma had that fight with her brother," he answers, "Rachel was supposed to bring it to you today, but something came up."

"Where is she?"

"Didn't you hear what happened?" he asks.

"No, what?"

"Her sister, Melissa was killed late last night," he says, "No leads, no witnesses, nothing. She's down at the station talking with the police." I can't believe what he's saying. Just yesterday, Melissa was alive and well. What could have happened to her in such a brief span of time? My thoughts immediately go back to what happened to Michael.

"What happened to her?" I inquire, suspecting I already know the answer.

"She was hanging in a tree behind her house," he replies, "They said someone drugged her before they strung her up. Look...I need to go. You didn't get that report from me, okay?" He tries to leave, but I stop him.

"Hey, just one more thing," I say, "Maybe this is something I should ask Rachel, but...what do you know about her family?"

"Her family?" he repeats, "What do you mean?"

"The Beckett murders from a few years back. I read somewhere that the Nolans were involved."

"Look, I can't tell you much about that," he says, shaking his head, "It's uh...it's one of those things you don't talk about, you know? Rachel's never said much to me about it."

"So what can you tell me?"

"Like I said, only a little," he answers, "All I know is that the Becketts screwed one of the Nolans over. That pissed them off and they wanted revenge. I mean, who wouldn't? Guy lost his life for something he didn't even do."

"Why would the Becketts want him dead, though?" I ask, "Just to prove they could?"

"It was more complicated than that," he continues, "I heard that guy the Becketts railroaded...he had evidence against the Becketts, but I don't know what it was. I just heard the Becketts had that guy locked up so he couldn't make his case. Had him stabbed to death in his cell by two inmates."

"Wait, they ordered a hit on this guy? I read that he was executed by the state."

"That's what they say, anyway," he replies, "I don't know the specifics. All I know is that officially, they said the guy went to the electric chair. I don't know if any of this is true, so don't go around quoting me on any of it. Rachel doesn't like to talk about what her family did. It might be difficult to get anything out of her. I quit trying a long time ago." He turns to leave and walks back inside the building. I stare down at the envelope, uncertain of what to think. I stuff it in my backpack and walk back into the building.

Once two-o'-clock approaches, I decide to leave the police report in my bag until I get home. I won't tell Ezma that Jason handed it to me. Even so, I wonder why he seemed so nervous when I spoke to him? Maybe Melissa's death rattled him more than most. I make my way out to the parking lot and find myself being followed by three senior girls. I know one of them from class. I speed up the pace, but it does no good. The three of them hurry after me and I break into a run. I have a feeling they're pissed off about what happened.

Earlier that day, there had been an assembly in Melissa's memory. Judging from what I saw, she was well-liked by most of the community. It's my guess that the people following me must think I have something to do with her death. One of the girls catches up to me, the blonde girl I recognize from one of my classes. She latches onto my arm and attempts to drag me to the pavement. I punch her in the cheek and shove her off of me as the other two arrive. Before I can get even ten paces, the same girl manages to catch me off guard. She hits me in the nose and sends me reeling. I can tell at once that she broke my nose. Blood drips from my nostrils and stains my shirt. I squint through the pain to see her fist coming at me for a second time. This time she lands a blow on my cheek and splits my lip. The other two girls are standing nearby, watching the scene unfold.

By this time, the fight has attracted a crowd. Everyone is egging this girl on, laughing while I try to defend myself. I grab the girl by the throat and squeeze as hard as I can. By this time, I'm so furious that I almost can't feel my broken nose. Her arms flail about as she tries to pry my hands off. Before I know what's happening, someone strikes the girl in the side of the head, sending her to the ground where she chokes and gasps for air. Without thinking, I kick the girl in the ribs, much to the dislike of the crowd. I don't care, though. She attacked me first. I realize then that it was Rachel who struck the girl.

"Attacking Zoey isn't going to bring my sister back!" she shouts, "You think this is how you honor her memory?" The blonde girl glares at me as she's helped to her feet.

"You're a punk, Parker!" she snarls, "You're lucky Rachel saved you."

"I saved you, dumbass!" Rachel hisses, "In case you didn't notice, she was strangling you!"

"What the hell are you even mad about?" the girl rages, "She probably helped kill her!"

"You don't know what happened!" Rachel thunders, "I don't blame Zoey for it and neither should any of you!" She points at several people in the crowd and spits on the girl's feet before storming off with me in tow.

"You alright?" she asks, "Looks like Lisa got you good. Here, take this; you're bleeding everywhere." She removes a small package of tissues from her bag and hands it to me. I take some out and put the rest in my pocket.

"I didn't need your help," I grumble, holding the tissues to my still bleeding nose.

"You're being investigated for murder," she hisses, "You think that's a good way to prove you're innocent? Strangle some dumb girl in front of a bunch of witnesses?"

"It was self-defense," I counter, "It's not like I was going to choke her to death. Besides, there were like fifty people standing around."

"You don't get it," Rachel replies, "Sure, there were a lot of people there, but I'm guessing you noticed that none of them helped you. No reason to believe they would have helped Lisa either."

"Whatever," I mutter, "Any idea why she attacked me?"

"She was a close friend of my sister," Rachel explains, "Since everyone thinks Ezma is responsible, they also think you are."

"So because I hangout with Ezma, that's enough reason to break my nose?" I growl.

"I didn't say it made sense," Rachel argues, "I'm just telling you how it is around here. I hate to say it, but I told you so." As we approach the parking lot, I see Ezma sitting on the sidewalk near her van. She spots us and jumps to her feet.

"What the hell happened?" she demands, throwing down her cigarette, "Why is she bleeding?"

"She got in a fight," Rachel answers.

"And I imagine that was your fault?" Ezma growls.

"Relax, Ezma, it's fine," I say.

"Like hell it is!" she shouts, "Who attacked you?"

"Ezma, seriously, it's nothing to get worked up over," I insist.

"Who was it?" she demands.

"Lisa Trent," Rachel chimes in.

"I am not talking to you!" Ezma sneers, "Get lost, will you?"

"This involves me as much as it involves you!" Rachel snarls, "Lisa attacked her because of what happened to my sister!"

"So now Zoey is suddenly a murderer to everyone?" Ezma snorts, "I doubt she had anything to do with it."

"They think that because the two of you are always together," Rachel explains, "They think she's your accomplice."

"I had nothing to do with what happened to Melissa!" Ezma hisses, "Frankly, I'm glad that stupid bitch is dead! Did you hear what she did yesterday afternoon?"

"What, the thing with the bat?" Rachel asks, "Yeah, I know all about it, Ezma! I didn't tell her to do that and not that you care, but I tore into her for it when she got back! All that aside, you do still owe me for that car since I wasn't the one who keyed yours!"

"Liar!" Ezma snarls, shoving Rachel backward.

"I heard someone say that Jason's friend did it," I cut in, "I know you don't believe her, but I don't think she did it."

"I don't care about the car right now," Rachel declares, "I'll worry about it some other time. As for you, Zoey, I'd be careful if I were you. Lisa's not the only one upset about this."

"Is that some kind of advice or a threat?" I ask.

"Figure it out." She turns and walks across the lot, disappearing behind a row of cars.

"I should probably get my nose checked out," I groan, climbing into the van, "That's gonna be fun..." Ezma climbs into the van and closes the door. She gives a heavy exhale and starts the engine.

"Are you asking me to take you to a clinic or something?" Ezma asks as we leave the lot.

"Might as well. Dad will drag me to one the second he sees it." I remove the tissues from my nose and wait to see if it continues bleeding. When it doesn't, I ball the tissues up and clench them in my hand.

"What was that girl's name again?"

"Lisa," I answer.

"Right, I just don't remember the last name," Ezma explains.

"I think Rachel said Trent." The entire way to the clinic, Ezma grumbles about what happened. I'd be lying if I said I wasn't still furious. A broken nose is not something I wanted to deal with. It isn't until much later, after I've had some time to cool off, that I remember the police report. Still tucked away in my bag. At the clinic, I'm asked how my nose was broken. As soon as I admit to having been in a fight, the nurse asks if I took it up with the school's administration. I lie and tell her that I did, but now I'm anticipating having to deal with that. I don't care enough to report it, and each time I've been in a fight before this, I've never bothered to do so. Just isn't the way I do things, I suppose. When the doctor comes in to have a look, he straightens my nose back out, something that feels almost as painful as having it broken a second time.

Sounds like I have a fracture and that it will heal the rest of the way on its own. He tells me to ice it every once in a while and refrain from blowing my nose. Ezma insists on paying for the visit, despite my attempts to convince her otherwise. After leaving, we head to Ezma's house at her suggestion. I don't want to show Dad my broken nose at the moment. Once at Ezma's house, she leads me around to the back patio and I sit down in one of the chairs. The backyard looks like it was recently mowed. The smell of recently cut grass is absent and a mower sits beside a large metallic shed. I'm guessing it was used a couple days ago. The shed has a large tree near it with a piece of rope wrapped around a thick branch. It looks like someone cut it. Near the tree and leaning against the shed is a well worn tire.

I think back to what I heard about Melissa's death...that she was strung up in a tree. I glance over my shoulder and check to see if Ezma's watching. She said she was going to make some tea, but I don't have a clue how long she'll be gone. I sneak up to a window and glance through it. She's nowhere to be found. I suppose this is my chance. I'll have to make it quick. I trot over to the tree and look up at the rope. I was right. I can see for certain that it's been cut now. A small branch is broken off near the end of the larger one that once held the rope. It looks fresh. I hurry back to the patio and sit down. A few minutes later, Ezma comes back out onto the patio. She sets two cups of tea on the table and sits down across from me.

"How's the house looking?" I ask, "Making progress?"

"Yeah, for the most part," she answers, leaning back in her chair, "It's slow going, but there's not a whole lot left to do."

"So, hard part's over, that sort of thing?"

"I would say so...and...just what the hell happened to my tree?" she exclaims, standing up from her seat.

"What happened to it?" I ask, trying to play innocent.

"There used to be a tire swing and...what the hell?" she continues, walking over to the tree. I get up and follow her, wanting an excuse to look things over a second time. She pulls on her hair and swears under her breath, stopping a few feet from the tree.

"Why would someone cut this thing down? Why? Seriously, what kind of jackass does this kind of thing?" she rants, "My dad put that up there when I was seven! I swear to God when I figure out who did this I'm going to string them up by their neck!" Jason said Melissa was strung up in a tree. Is this where the killer obtained the rope? Why would they take it from here? Who else would know about it without snooping around? I glance at Ezma for a second and feel the pit of my stomach drop out. Is she just putting on a performance for me? Is she really upset? She yanks on her hair a second time and walks over to the shed, grumbling and muttering curses.

"Do you...do you think...?" I begin. I can't bring myself to say the rest. I have a feeling she'll think I'm accusing her. She undoes the lock on the shed and scowls at me for a moment, before opening the doors.

"Do I think what?" she asks. She steps inside for a moment and comes back out with a machete. The branch is just within her reach. She swings the machete at the broken branch, leaving a gash at the end of it.

"That...someone took it to use..." I continue, trying to force the words out of my mouth. She hits the branch a second time and lets her arm drop to her side, the machete gripped in her hand. She glances over her shoulder at me, then turns around to face me.

"Seriously?" she snorts, "You think someone took the rope to kill Melissa?"

"I didn't say that," I argue, "I was just-"

"Alluding to that," she interrupts, rolling her eyes, "Great. What a nice way to honor what few good memories I have at this crap shack." She turns and swings the machete one final time, cutting the branch loose. It falls to the ground and I step back a few paces. Ezma returns the machete to the shed and locks it without another word. Just as I'm thinking I should say something, her phone begins to ring. She fishes it out of her pocket and heaves a sigh.

"Hello? Oh...hey, Aunt Tillie," Ezma says, "Fine. Something happened and I'm kind of pissed off about it. No, nothing like that..." I wave to get her attention and point to the patio. She nods and gives me a thumbs up. With that, I return to the patio and pick up my cup of tea. Ezma sits down on a splitting block with her back toward me and continues her conversation. I take a sip of my tea and set it back down on the table. My bag catches my eye and I remember the police report. Maybe if I'm quick I can take a peek without her noticing. I take the report out of my bag and slide it out of the envelope. I glance back over at Ezma one more time to make certain that she isn't watching me.

I look back at the report and start reading it. The date reads, November 18, 2013. The report states that there were three people involved in the incident. Ezma, Brian, and Sarah Fenton. The report goes on to say that a call to 911 was made at 11:27 that night. Ezma had reported that her brother was bleeding from several "knife wounds" and had requested an ambulance. Two police units and an ambulance were dispatched to the house where Ezma and Brian were standing in the front yard.

Ms. Weston was shouting while waving a large kitchen knife in a threatening manner. She appeared to be speaking to her brother who remained behind his vehicle. When ordered to drop the knife, Ms. Weston pointed up the street and began shouting that someone by the name of "Sarah" was fleeing the scene. Another officer spotted Ms. Fenton [Sarah], and accompanied by another officer, proceeded to give chase. Mr. Weston was rushed into a waiting ambulance while another officer and I, again ordered Ms. Weston to drop the knife. She ignored our orders and was subsequently shot with a non-lethal round from Officer Davidson's shotgun. Ms. Weston dropped the knife and bolted for the front door. Davidson fired a second round that struck Ms. Weston in the ribs, causing her to stumble and fall to the ground. Before either of us could move in to detain Ms. Weston, she leaped to her feet and barricaded herself inside her residence.

Officer Davidson and I ordered her to open the door, but she refused. Concerned that Ms. Weston may have intended to arm herself, we were left with no other option than to force the door. Ms. Weston was discovered in her living room, unarmed and bleeding from several slash wounds. Ms. Weston claimed that she had struck her head on the edge of the deck after she was shot the second time, and because of this could not stand. Davidson and I detained her without further incident and escorted her from the premises. A second ambulance was requested and arrived soon after. Ms. Weston was then taken to the hospital for both physical and mental evaluation.

The other two officers returned approximately twenty-five minutes after Ms. Weston had left in the ambulance. With them was a woman whom was later identified as Sarah Danielle Fenton. Ms. Fenton was found to be unarmed and appeared to have suffered at least one stab wound to the arm. She was immediately taken in for questioning while other residents were interviewed. Several witnesses claimed they saw Ms. Fenton struggling with Ms. Weston, both of whom appeared to be fighting for control of the knife. It is believed that Ms. Weston may have had the knife because she had taken it from Ms. Fenton.

I look up from the report and see Ezma still sitting with her back to me. I stuff the report back in the envelope and set it atop my bag. A minute later, Ezma stands up and pockets her phone, before walking back toward the patio, shaking her head. I'm still wondering why Rachel would bother to have Jason give me the report. It didn't seem to say anything that would further her arguments about Ezma. Yeah, Rachel had been right about one of the officers shooting Ezma, but what did that prove? Rachel is clearly biased. She probably sees the events of that night in a different way.

"It's like she knows when I'm upset or something," Ezma grumbles, seating herself at the table, "Sorry that took so long. Talked my ear off."

"No worries." I glance back over at the tree and then at the cup in my hands.

"Something wrong?" Ezma asks.

"It's nothing," I lie, "Just thinking about what happened."

"Trent?"

"That and what happened to Melissa," I say, "It's just...well...first there was that Michael guy, and now Melissa is dead too. I just don't know what to think of it."

"I think it's fantastic," Ezma replies, "Two people I despise, dead in the same week." I know I've had moments where I would have loved to hear that someone I hated had died, but Ezma's attitude regarding these murders is starting to bother me.

"Sorry about the tire swing," I say, "Sounds like it had some sentimental value to it." She turns her head and stares off across the yard.

"It did, but..." she begins. Her voice trails off and she remains silent, continuing to stare at the tree.

"But what?"

"It has me confused," she answers, taking a drink of her tea. She wrinkles her nose and sets the cup down.

"Too cold?" I ask. She nods.

"Yeah, I need to warm it up," she says, "Maybe in a little while. I don't feel like getting up at the moment. Anyway...like I was saying, I can't make sense of it. Why take the rope from my house? Assuming it was used for that. I mean...maybe it was, maybe it wasn't. I didn't notice it until today."

"When was the last time you saw the swing intact?" I inquire, finishing my tea. I set the empty cup down and Ezma taps her fingers on the table.

"The last time I was out here was three days ago. I don't come out to the patio very often. Not in the past couple of weeks, anyway. Ever since I started cleaning the house up, I've been focusing on the interior. Last time I was out here was to mow the lawn. Took forever with how tall I'd let the grass get. Still, I guess the point here is that I remember the swing being intact at that time."

"So whoever took the rope must have done it between now and then," I surmise, "Did you hear anything, see anything?" She shakes her head.

"No, nothing," she replies, "That's what I don't get. Usually I'm pretty observant. I'd like to think I'd notice someone coming into my yard; although...they could have done it while I was at work."

"Or while you were asleep," I add.

"That's probably it right there," she says, glancing at the tree again, "God that gives me the creeps. Weirdos coming into my yard in the middle of the night."

"Well, however the rope was stolen, it still seems kind of messed up, what happened to Melissa," I say, leaning back in my chair.

"Are you kidding me?" Ezma snorts, "She deserved it. Hell, you saw what she did the other day. Girl was out of her mind, coming onto my property like that. On top of that, she lived to torment her sister. Not that I care all that much about it anymore."

"Why do you hate the Nolans so much?" I inquire, "I mean, from what I can gather, it was Rachel and Melissa's parents who were the real problem. At least, that's how it sounded last night. They tried to put it all on your family in the end."

"You must have heard that somewhere else, because I don't recall telling you that part." She looks at me and catches my eye for a moment. Something about her expression is making me a little uncomfortable. Before I can stop her, she reaches for my bag and swipes up the manila envelope. She opens it and glances over the report.

"The hell did you get this from?" she demands, "Wait...no, don't tell me. It was Rachel, wasn't it?"

"No, she wasn't at school today," I answer, shaking my head, "She was off at the police station, talking to the cops about Melissa. Look, Jason gave it to me, alright? I didn't ask for it, Rachel insisted upon it." Ezma scowls at me, then looks over the report again. She rolls her eyes and sets it on the table, heaving a sigh as she does so.

"Fine...I believe you," she murmurs, handing the report back to me,

"I'm sorry I got upset. It's been difficult to make friends ever since Rachel and I quit talking. Don't let her run you off. She doesn't know what she's talking about."

"Sure seems that way," I reply, "She's already wearing on my nerves as it is."

"You said this morning that you wanted to finish our discussion from last night," Ezma begins, leaning her elbows on the table, "Since we're already on the topic, now seems like a good time. This is what I can tell you. The Nolans are crooks, Zoey. They're terrible people and they got my family in a lot of trouble in the past. It wasn't just about the murders. That was on us, the Westons. That was our idea and I'll get to that in a minute. Rachel sided with her family, I sided with mine. That's why we aren't friends anymore. As you can probably tell by your busted nose, and that Trent girl's reaction to Melissa's death, the Nolans were and still are in fairly high standing around here."

"So, what then? That fight's just the start of things?" She nods.

"It's not a good sign, I can say that much," Ezma replies, "You might want to be a little more careful now, but I wouldn't expect the whole town to come marching out in the streets with torches and pitchforks. Anyway...the Westons, like I said, were the ones responsible for the murders. Everyone looked down on my parents. I mean, think about what I told you about them last night. They were the kind of people everyone feels they have some kind of moral obligation to hate. Even after the Becketts were killed, people just viewed my parents as criminals who did one good thing in the world. When my father testified against the Nolans in court, things only got worse for us."

"I read something about that," I reply, "The Nolans owned a bunch of stores around the state."

"That they did," Ezma nods, "When Rachel's parents went down for their own crimes, the stores started closing down and people around the state, including those here in town, lost their jobs. So of course they blamed my father for that. They were ticked off that he'd brought evidence against them, thought it would have been better if he'd just taken the fall for the murders, and let the Nolans worm their way out with dirty money and a bullshit plea deal."

"So basically the whole town is divided?" I ask, "I mean...they didn't want the Becketts around, but they were okay with the Nolans breaking the law?"

"David Beckett's law-breaking was causing direct harm to people," Ezma explains, "Stop and frisk operations, trumped up drug charges, police brutality, bribes...even hits. People looked at the Nolans as job creators, didn't care if they were doing anything illegal. I hate to admit it, but I can understand that. It seems like a victimless crime to folks, especially to the poor and lower middle-class people around here."

"Wait, go back for a second," I say, remembering something Jason told me, "You said the Becketts carried out hits, right?"

"Yeah, there's some story, a rumor about what happened to Nelson Nolan. The guy Beckett screwed over."

"Jason was telling me about that today," I recall, "He said he was stabbed to death in his cell by two other inmates. Said it was covered up and that David Beckett ordered it."

"And that's why people were happy to see him go," she sighs, tilting her head back for a moment, "Good riddance. Worthless piece of shit. I still can't believe what he did to Myra."

"Your half-sister, right?"

"That's her," Ezma confirms, "She was the result of an affair my father had with David Beckett's wife, Miriam; If you can believe that. I imagine that's why the Becketts hated her so much, you know?

I heard something about David viewing her as a reminder of his wife's infidelity. He was an egotistical guy, couldn't cope with the fact that his wife had cheated on him. He was controlling from what I understand. Miriam on the other hand, my father mentioned that she wouldn't speak to him anymore. I'm certain David used to abuse Miriam, and it wouldn't surprise me one bit if one of two things happened. Either Miriam felt she couldn't help Myra and stayed out of the way, or she also saw her as a reminder. One that refused to allow her to forget her mistake."

"So the question is, did Miriam stand by out of hate or fear?"

"My money is on hate," Ezma continues, "Cousin of mine who was there at the house a few times before the Becketts died, I heard she mentioned that Miriam sometimes took part in the abuse. I suppose that way she could sort of 'redeem' herself or something."

"That's all kinds of screwed up if she did."

"Tell me about it," Ezma says, leaning back in her chair, "My parents tried to get Myra back, or at least my dad did. He tried to gain custody of her, but David, sick bastard he was, he probably threatened the judge or paid them off or something. Ruled in David's favor and so began our little feud."

"Feud?" I repeat.

"It was with the Becketts at first; then the Nolans once the Becketts weren't around anymore. Giving each other grief any way we could, innocent things David couldn't arrest us for, things he couldn't prove we did," Ezma explains, "It was childish to say the least. Letting air out of Beckett's tires, playing music too loud until he came storming over to shout at us. I wish it had stayed that way...harmless and petty, but no...Mom had to go and involve the Nolans. If we hadn't done that, then maybe Rachel and I would still be friends, maybe this whole thing wouldn't have blown out of proportion...and maybe people wouldn't be turning up dead."

"You think the deaths lately are linked to that?" I ask.

"Probably," she shrugs, "I don't know what else it could be. During the whole custody battle, I was too young to know what was going on. I was about four or five, maybe a little younger. I would see Myra from time to time across the street, but I didn't know we were related until I was thirteen. That was the year the Becketts were killed. Back in 2010."

"What set your mom off?"

"The final straw was this one night when she saw Myra trying to escape the house," Ezma answers, "She was emaciated, bruised, bloody. They beat her so much, I heard she went blind in her left eye. They locked her in her room like a jail cell, kept her in there for days at a time. Starved her, threatened her, and worst of all...they sold her like a cheap toy."

"Wait...they prostituted her?" I gasp, "Christ, how old was she?"

"I don't remember all of what I heard, but I think it started when she was about eight or something."

"Jesus..."

"Yeah..." Ezma murmurs, "I don't understand it. Who does that to a kid? What has to happen to make someone walk down that road? Whatever the case, I'm just glad the Becketts got what they deserved."

Chapter 13

That night I'm back in my room, staring at the computer screen. I've been online looking up everything I can about the murders on my street. So far everything seems to match up with Ezma's story. David Beckett was indeed the police chief at the time, there were allegations of abuse made by the Westons and the Nolans, but since the Becketts were dead, there was no one to bring up on charges for it. Myra was taken into foster care, and still I can't find anything on her. Nothing that I can find, anyway. The only lead I have is that she was taken off to Ohio somewhere. Headlights flash across the front of the house and I feel a surge of anger. I'm willing to bet that's my mother.

I stand up from the desk and peer through the blinds. The car hasn't pulled up in my driveway, rather it's parked alongside Ezma's van. It's difficult to see, but I can tell it's Rachel. Ezma is standing on the front porch, her arms crossed and her expression impossible to make out. I crack the window as quietly as I can and glance outside. I can hear them talking, but I'm only hearing bits and pieces of the conversation. Rachel seems calm, but Ezma sounds irritated. I close the window back up and walk out to the stairs. I quickly trot down them and place my hand on the front door. No...I should go out the back. If I open the front, they'll notice me. I turn and head to the back of the house, going through the kitchen and around to the back door.

It's difficult to see beyond the glow of the porch light, but I manage to find the back gate. Remembering how it creaks, I try to unlatch it quietly. From here I can make out every word, but it's still faint. I unlatch the gate and push it open. I feel a sense of relief when I manage to squeeze past without it squeaking. I crouch and let the gate sit back against the latch. For a moment I consider leaving it, but I can feel a slight breeze. I don't want it swinging back and forth. I latch it closed and crouch back down before making my way along the length of the fence.

"...not my problem if that's how you cope with things," Ezma growls at Rachel, "We all went through some rough times. It wasn't just you, you know."

"My issue is that we went into this as friends and came out as enemies," Rachel responds, "I didn't want it to happen, I really didn't."

"You abandoned me in my darkest hour," Ezma snarls, "You left me behind, just so you could show some kind of twisted loyalty to your family. Just...why did I even let you come here tonight? Nothing you say, nothing I say, is going to make a difference in all of this. I want to know why you've been participating in this smear campaign against me. Why are you harassing Zoey? This has nothing to do with her!"

"I'm not running a smear campaign and I'm not harassing her!"

"Why did you have Jason hand off that police report? Hell, why didn't you do it yourself if you wanted to make me look bad?"

"I was helping make arrangements for my sister's funeral, thank you very much," Rachel growls, "I'm not trying to make you look bad, you do that all by yourself. You're delusional. That's why I'm not friends with you anymore. You're unstable!"

"This again," Ezma grumbles, "There's nothing wrong with me. You act like I'm some kind of psychopath."

"Because you are!"

"No more than you," Ezma snorts, "You can try and pin this on me all you want, you can try and convince people that I'm behind the murders, but I know it's you, Rachel. I know who you are. I know you hated your sister and I wasn't the only one whose nerves that Michael guy grated on! The first week we met, I still remember you arguing with your sister, then after it was over you muttered something about wanting to kill her. I lost track of how many times you said it."

"You know damn well I wasn't ever serious! After having to deal with Brian, I'm sure you know what it's like to have a sibling who chips away at your sanity!"

"She pushed you down a staircase and then laughed about it," Ezma continues, "You want to talk about psychopaths, start with your sister!"

"Don't you dare talk about her like that!" Rachel hisses.

"Everything you do, all your little quirks, your behaviors, it all makes sense to me after seeing what you grew up around," Ezma replies, "You're a terrible person, you know that? You're the product of shitty parenting!"

"And your parents were any better?" Rachel snaps, "Your mother plotted the murders! She helped carry them out!"

"So did yours!" Ezma growls, "Also where the hell were you the night my parents' brake lines were cut? You've given me almost a dozen different answers. I bet you were part of that, weren't you? Pissed off because my family caught yours in a web of unrelated illicit activity! You're nothing but a spoiled little shit, angry that you lost all that money to a poor family."

"Your aunt seems pretty well off," Rachel snorts.

"That dumb woman just happened to marry into a lot of money," Ezma explains, "Quit distracting from the issue. Where were you that night, huh? Tell me!"

"I don't need to tell you where I was."

"Oh but I think you do," Ezma growls, "The day after that was the day we became enemies...all because you wouldn't give me a straight answer. Funny how I overheard your cousin Sarah Fenton saying she was talking to you at that gas station around the time my parents were there. I wonder why that is?"

"That is a boldface lie!" Rachel accuses, angrily pointing at Ezma as she speaks, "I was never at the gas station that night and I know Sarah didn't tell you that!"

"Oh yeah? Why don't you go ask her?" Ezma retorts. A tense silence ensues. Almost a minute passes before someone speaks again.

"Addison's been missing for three weeks now," Rachel says, "Last time anyone saw her, she was walking into your house. You wouldn't happen to know what happened to her...would you?"

"Piss off, Rachel..."

"No really, I'd like an answer," Rachel insists, throwing her hands up in frustration, "Let's hear it, Ezma!"

"After you refused to tell me whether or not you were at the gas station?" Ezma snorts, "Fat chance."

"I wasn't at the gas station!" Rachel declares, "I don't know who told you that, but I wasn't there that night!"

"I don't believe you," Ezma says.

"I know you don't and I don't care."

"Fine, whatever," Ezma grumbles, "As for Addison, I'll say it again, I don't know anything about your dead friend."

"No one said anything about her being dead," Rachel points out, "What makes you think she is?"

"The last time anyone saw her was along highway nineteen, not at my house," Ezma replies, "Don't bullshit me, Rachel. Yeah, she stopped at my house, so what? She mouthed off at me and we got into an argument."

"And you killed her, didn't you?"

"First, no I didn't, and second, if I had at that time, then I guess Jacob Fawver saw a ghost along highway nineteen at five in the afternoon!"

"I bet you followed her out there," Rachel accuses, "Her car was abandoned along the road. Engine still running, radio still on, and no sign of her anywhere."

"I told you, I didn't do anything to her!" Ezma insists, "Why would I? Seriously, give me a reason! Come on, tell me! I bet you've cooked something up already, haven't you?"

"I bet you were pissed off about what happened to Eric, weren't you? That's why you did it."

"Of course I was pissed off about that!" Ezma exclaims, "I knew they used to fight all the time and I tried a million times to convince them both to split up. Instead of acting like adults, she tried to kill him! That whole bullshit lie she told about Eric abusing her was a crock of shit if I ever heard one! Yeah, they both yelled at each other, but he would never have laid a finger on her! I know my own cousin, I know he didn't deserve having his skull cracked with a skillet! He doesn't even remember me or anyone else anymore. Five months now...five months he's been acting weird because of what that stupid bitch did to him, and it's not going away! What she did is permanent and she doesn't give a rat's ass!"

"Is that what you two were fighting about?"

"Damn right it was!" Ezma confirms, "She straight up admitted to me that she lied about what happened. I accused her of lying, she started arguing with me, and the next thing I know she lets it slip. Whatever happened to Addison, it was too good for her."

"You just don't care who you hurt, do you?" Rachel growls, "She was a family friend, Ezma. Is a family friend. If I find out you had anything to do with her disappearance, there will be consequences."

"You're full of shit, Rachel. You won't do anything to me. I mangled your car and you still have yet to pay me back for it. Your dead sister had more guts than you'll ever have."

"Who said I was going to do anything to you?" Rachel sneers. She turns and climbs back into her car. The headlights switch on and Ezma hops off the porch and follows her into the street as the car pulls out of the driveway.

"Coward!" Ezma roars, kicking the side of Rachel's car as she goes, "You stay away from Zoey, you got that? You so much as touch her and I will kill you, Rachel Nolan! You hear me? It'll be the last thing you ever do!"

"Psychopath!" Rachel shouts through her open window. She hits the accelerator and then makes an obscene gesture at Ezma before she tears down the street, leaving the smell of burnt rubber lingering in the air. Ezma curses under her breath and storms back into her house, slamming the door behind her.

Chapter 14

When Saturday morning arrives days later, I find myself sleeping in until almost noon. I climb out of bed and fifteen minutes later, Ezma is knocking at my door. By this point I've barely had the time to put my shoes on. I sigh and let the second one drop to the bedroom floor before proceeding to the top of the stairs; one foot in a shoe, the other with only a sock. Near the bottom of the stairs, I slip on my socked foot and fall with a thud. I let out a yelp and my dad walks into the room holding a phone in one hand.

"You alright?" he asks, sounding a little amused, "Did that myself the other day."

"I'm fine," I reply, getting to my feet, "Butt's a little sore, but whatever." Ezma knocks again and I open the door to see her standing outside with a baseball cap and a dark coat.

"Come on in, I'm just finishing up," I say, beckoning for her to follow me.

"Morning, Ezma," Dad says, dialing as he speaks. He puts the phone to his ear and listens.

"Morning, Mr. Parker," Ezma replies.

"You alright, Dad?" I ask, "You look worried." He shakes his head and removes the phone from his ear.

"I've been trying to get a hold of your mother since eight this morning," he explains, "I'm just a little concerned."

"Why? Who cares what she does?" I snort.

"Zoey," Dad groans, "Don't talk like that, she's your mother."

"The mother who got in a fist fight with me the other day," I mutter, starting up the stairs, "One that she started."

"I'm not looking to argue with you, Zoey," he replies, Ezma following after me, "Also, I thought I'd mention that your mother's therapist is coming by around five today. So don't be surprised if you come back around that time."

"What's she coming over here for?" I ask from the top of the stairs.

"She's looking to speak with me about the fight and your apparently relapsing mother," he explains.

"She's not looking to talk to me too, is she?" I ask.

"No, not unless you want to," Dad replies, "I'm sure she'd appreciate it if you did, but it's up to you."

"I think I'll pass," I sigh. Dr. Clarence is someone I've only met a few times, and what stands out to me more than anything about her, is her hopeless optimism, like she doesn't understand that she's wasting her time trying to help my mother. I guess I can at least give her points for tenacity and patience. Ezma follows me to my room and I push the door open.

"I hate to always be the one asking you for your help with things, but I have a couple of things I need to get out of my house before we leave. Too big and too awkward to carry alone."

"It's no problem," I say, tying my shoe as I speak, "I guess now I get a chance to see how much cleaning's been done in that house of yours."

"Just as long as you avoid the downstairs bathroom," she replies, sitting on the end of my bed, "Toilet's busted and the sink needs cleaning."

"I doubt I'll need to use a bathroom while I'm there, but sure thing." I stand up and pull a messenger bag out from under my desk. Inside is the pistol Ezma gave me and a few other things. I sling it over my shoulder and Ezma stands up.

"So why do you need whatever these are out today?" I ask, walking down the stairs.

"Well they're ugly as sin and have some bad memories attached to them," Ezma explains, "It's just an old table and a file cabinet. Rollers on the bottom of it broke off like a year ago and one of the drawers is busted, won't open. Of course it's the biggest one because that's the kind of luck I have."

"I take it that drawer is still full?" I ask, leading her out the front door. She closes it behind us and follows after me.

"Yep, that it is. I'd try breaking it open or something, but I'm not concerned about what's in it. Just some old papers, nothing important. Figured it'll provide some ballast while we're putting a few holes in it."

"Oh, so that's the reason you want them out today," I chuckle, "Now I get it. How come you don't donate them instead? Well, the table at least. Sounds like the file cabinet is a lost cause."

"Well the table is all rickety and one of the legs is shorter than the other. Used to have to keep a book under it. Got busted a long time ago when Brian was all pissed off about something. Kicked it and voila... busted table leg." We walk up onto Ezma's porch and she opens the door. Inside is an old oak coffee table, a very worn leather couch, an old TV, and a tattered arm chair. Sitting beside the fireplace is a pump shotgun and a box of old newspapers. The carpet looks to have been cleaned recently and the scent of bleach is wafting from the kitchen.

"Sorry about the smell," she says, propping the door open, "I have the windows in the kitchen open, but I guess it's not helping much."

"It's fine," I smile, "Where's the table and whatnot?"

"Upstairs. Come on." I set my bag in the arm chair and follow her upstairs. The stairs are carpeted and seem to be stained in a few places. Once at the top, she opens a nearby door and leads me inside. Inside is a large bedroom with an old bed, stripped of sheets, exposing the well worn mattress. The shelves have a series of small clay statues along them, along with a few dozen books, an old radio, and a flashlight. An old desk sits against the far wall beneath the only window, and beside it are two guitars, one acoustic and one electric. Both are leaned up against the side of the desk. An old file cabinet is in the closet and an old wooden table sits in front of it, looking somewhat out of place.

"Whose room is this?" I ask.

"Brian's," she answers, "Haven't been in here much since he died. Decided that I needed to start cleaning it out. It's not like he's coming back."

"Seems kind of harsh," I say, walking over to the guitars, "I don't know if I'd be able to do something like this. I don't have any siblings, so it's hard to put myself in your shoes, but...yeah...I'm sorry he's not around anymore."

"It's not your fault," she sighs, "Thanks, though. It's still hard, but it's getting easier. He may have been a thorn in my ass, but he was still my brother."

"Was he a musician?"

"Yeah, he loved music," Ezma replies, "He used to write songs, lyrics and everything. You can pick one of those guitars up if you like. You look like you're itching to."

"They're both pretty nice," I observe, picking up the acoustic one, "You could probably get a good chunk of money off these if you're planning to get rid of them."

"I take it you play guitar?" she says as I strum the instrument a few times.

"Yeah, I started when I was about...seven, I think? I can't remember for sure. Somewhere around then. My dad's been playing all his life. He's the one who taught me."

"You can take them both if you'd like," Ezma offers. I stop playing and suddenly feel a little embarrassed. Yeah, I'd love to have another guitar again, but it seems weird to take her brother's old ones.

"Oh, well...you don't have to-"

"I want to," she smiles, "Really, it's fine. I'd rather I give them to someone I know."

"How much do you want for them?" I ask, still feeling a little bad.

"How about you help me take the table and cabinet downstairs and we'll call it even?"

"Sure...I suppose," I murmur, "Just kind of feel bad taking them like this." I set the guitar on the bed and she props the door open with a book from the shelf.

"It's not like you're stealing them," she chuckles, "It's fine, really." I help her move the table to the door, where we begin the process of trying to get it through the doorway. We try a few angles, but nothing works.

"How did he even get this thing in here?" I ask.

"Honestly, I have no idea," Ezma shrugs, "It still baffles me. Especially considering that he got it in here all by his lonesome."

"You're kidding," I chuckle, "Thing weighs a ton." After a few more minutes, we manage to get it through the doorway and down the stairs. With some effort, we get it in the back of the van, then return for the file cabinet. We carry it downstairs and Ezma and I place it in the van with the table.

"You can go get the guitars real quick if you'd like," she grunts, pushing on the bottom of the file cabinet.

"Well I don't want to hold us up or anything," I reply.

"No worries," she assures me, "I have to go close the windows and everything anyway." I trot back up onto the porch and into the house. Inside I find that a stray cat has wandered inside.

"Hey! Get!" I say, shooing the cat. It runs away from me and into the downstairs bathroom. I follow after it and it hides in the tub right as I step inside.

"Shoo! Get out of there!" The cat leaps out of the tub and bolts out of the bathroom, disappearing into the kitchen seconds later.

"What the hell...?" I whisper, pulling back the curtain. In the base of the tub is a splotch of bloody water. What's even more alarming is that a hacksaw is lying beside the toilet. I hear Ezma walking back inside and hide behind the door. Once I hear her walk into the kitchen, I bolt up the stairs just as she spots the cat and starts shooing it out the back door.

"Gus, I don't have any food for you! Get out of here!" she moans. I quickly grab one of the guitars and begin heading back down the stairs.

"What's going on?" I ask, trying to sound innocent.

"Oh nothing," she groans, "The neighborhood stray got in. Looking for food again, I guess." Once down the stairs, I see her standing in the kitchen, closing the back door.

"Well, at least he didn't knock over a picture frame or something... again," she sighs, walking toward me, "Anyway, I guess now you just gotta get the guitars out of here and we're all set." She smiles and I nod."

"Oh, yeah...right," I smile, "I'll go put this one away and come get the other. I'd rather not try to carry both at the same time." Ezma walks back into the kitchen and I hurry back to my house, uncertain of what I just saw in the bathroom. I think back to those boxes Ezma had me help her toss out. There was a foul smelling liquid that got on my hand when we were out at Hunter's Ridge. Those weren't...no...no that's ridiculous, right? I set the guitar in my room and retrieve the other from Ezma's house.

Now that I think of it...that bleach smell seems a little weird. What was she cleaning up? Something about this doesn't seem right. If she was cleaning something up in the kitchen, then why not just rinse out the tub and hide the hacksaw too? It's not like it would be that hard. Certainly easier than asking me to say out of the downstairs bathroom and hoping I listen. It has to be some kind of coincidence. Once back at Ezma's, she closes and locks the front door, then climbs into the van. I do the same and crack the window as we pull out of the driveway. A breeze catches some of my hair and I take a deep breath. Should I admit to what I saw? Say I was in that bathroom and hope she can give me a decent answer, or keep it to myself and overthink it? I guess I don't have much choice. I'll keep a lid on it for now.

* * *

When we arrive at our destination, Ezma finds a small open area with a large wall of earth along one side. Near the mound about fifty feet away, is a small shack and an old rusted truck. One by one, we carry the table and a few other items over to the base of the mound and set them up. The table we flip onto its side and the cabinet we place beside it. After that we set up a few chairs and a couple of boxes with a series of cans, jars, and bottles set atop them. Once everything's set up, Ezma tosses me a pair of ear plugs and starts loading her revolver.

"Want to take the first shot?" she offers.

"Sure, why not?" I raise my pistol and take aim at one of the jars, roughly twenty yards from where we're standing.

"Just imagine it's Trent's head," Ezma says with a mischievous grin.

"If only it was," I reply. I squeeze the trigger and watch as a small cloud of dust rises up along the earth mound. I fire twice more and one round grazes a can while the second sheers a glass bottle in two.

"There we go," I chuckle.

"My turn," Ezma smiles, blasting two jars and a can without missing.

"Way to make me look bad," I tease.

"Eh, I'm out here a lot," she says with a shrug, "Just takes practice." Five more rounds and I've struck two of the cans.

"So, I heard you shouting the other night," I say, "Thought I heard Rachel's name."

"Yeah, sorry about that," she apologizes, pausing to fire her last three rounds, "Rachel came by to talk about something and it got out of hand."

"Why was she at your house at eleven at night?"

"Because I'm an idiot, that's why," she sighs, "She called me up, said she wanted to talk in person, and I said yes. She's making accusations about her friend again. Some backstabbing psycho bitch named Addison. Did I ever tell you about her?"

"No, you haven't." I shoot another bottle off one of the boxes.

"She's quite the piece of work," Ezma mutters, shooting another can, "She went missing out near here about three weeks ago and Rachel's got it in her head that I had something to do with it. It's like I said to her last night. Jacob isn't some two bit liar. If he says he saw her out along the road over here, then I believe him."

"I don't think you've ever mentioned Jacob before," I say.

"He's just some guy I know," she replies, "Not really a friend, but more like a friend of a friend, that kind of thing. He's known my cousin Eric for a long time now, several years older than me. Not someone I'd hangout with, am I making sense?"

"Yeah, I understand," I nod, "Kind of like a family friend or something?" She nods.

"Pretty much," she says, "He only really talks to me and Eric, though. Family friend to me seems more like someone everyone in a family knows and talks to, but I guess the meaning is somewhat subjective."

"So how does all that tie in with Addison?" I ask.

"Rachel thinks the last time anyone saw Addison was when she showed up at my place and started a fight with me," she explains, "If that were true, then why did they find her car out here several hours after that? And why does Jacob seem so convinced he saw her? I don't know...I can't say I'm sorry that Addison is missing. Thanks to her, my cousin has brain damage, and because the cops in this town suck at what they do, she didn't get any time for it."

"What? How?"

"She lied and said he was abusing her, that he attacked her first," Ezma replies, "Cops claim she had injuries consistent with her story, but I think the Nolans were behind that."

"Why do you think the Nolans were involved?"

"When aren't they involved in shady shit like that?" she snorts, "Like I told you yesterday, there were cops, judges, people in that line of work who were happy to see the Becketts dead. They helped my family by destroying evidence, no reason they wouldn't also do the Nolans a favor. Especially since few people sided with the decision to fine them into oblivion."

"Sounds like one complicated mess," I say, shifting my weight and glancing up at a bird flying from a nearby tree.

"It really is! It's maddening! I feel like I have to look over my shoulder wherever I go. My family made a lot of enemies around here and it's not like they're easy to spot. I know I said I was glad Michael and Melissa are dead, but that doesn't address the feelings of paranoia, you know? It's not like we know who's doing it. It could be someone who just hates the Nolans for whatever reason, or someone looking to get me too." She shoots the table again and puts two more rounds through the file cabinet and the final through a can.

"Sounds like the deaths have you more worried than you let on," I observe.

"I can take care of myself, but there's no telling who else might end up dead. That's what bothers me. If someone hadn't cut the brake lines on my parents' car, then maybe none of this would be happening right now. Someone was bitter about the outcome of the trial, that's all there is to it. Now I get to deal with something I didn't even start. Brian's gone, my parents are gone, my cousin's not himself anymore. It has to stop. I just hope I'm still around to see it."

"Getting a little dark there, Ezma," I say, trying to lighten the mood.

"Sorry, sorry..." she apologizes, shaking her head, "I'm just venting."

"I understand. Hell, I could go on a tirade about my own life."

"You know, I feel bad about wanting to ask this, but...who the hell hits their kid like that?"

"My mother, apparently," I mutter, shooting one of the boxes.

"I can't imagine living with someone like that."

"And I can't imagine living with a perpetually wasted brother."

"That's a good thing," she says, "Like I've said before, he was my brother, I loved him, but he didn't have any right to put me through that. It was painful to watch...which is kind of why I'm glad this table is out here." She finishes reloading her revolver and fires all six rounds through it in rapid succession.

"That's not meant to be for your brother, is it?" I ask.

"Nah, just the memories...addiction...everything that ruined him," she sighs, "By the way, you can fire at that shack too. Nothing but junk in there."

"Sure, I suppose," I shrug, turning to face it, "Should I go for a window?"

"That's what I would do," she replies, "Twenty points if you shatter it, only five for a hole." I raise my pistol and fire at one of the remaining front windows. The glass shatters and I let out a chuckle.

"Alright, how about I go for the peep hole?" I suggest.

"I'll pay you fifty bucks if you hit it," she laughs, "No really, I will."

"Why, because you think I'm an awful shot?"

"No, it's just so tiny from here." I raise my weapon and fire the last remaining rounds in the magazine; not a single one of them ever hits the peep hole.

"You gonna try?" I ask.

"Nah, I'm just gonna hit that window a couple of times," she says, raising her revolver. She fires twice, both rounds taking chunks out of each pane they strike. I reload my pistol and try for the peep hole a few more times, but I still can't hit it. The closest I come is about two inches.

"I'll pay you eighty if you back up twenty paces and hit it," Ezma says with a wink.

"I'll be an old woman by the time I hit it," I laugh, "I'd rather just go for another window." I blast out another broken pane and lower my weapon. Ezma shoots off the doorknob and throws her free hand up in celebration.

"First shot!" she exclaims.

"I don't see anymore windows on this side," I reply, "None that are intact, anyway."

"Yeah, looks like it," she says, firing at the file cabinet, "Hey, I've been meaning to ask you. What happened to Lisa Trent?"

"That girl who broke my nose? Nothing really. School administration didn't do anything since it was just off campus. I could have pressed charges, but passed on it."

"How come?"

"Just didn't seem worth it," I shrug, "I strangled her half to death last time. Figured that was enough. Plus everyone hates me anyway. No need to give them any reason to try something else."

"I'm sorry that happened," Ezma apologizes, "I still feel like that was partially my fault."

"Hey, you aren't the one you slugged me. Don't worry about it."

"Yeah, but she only attacked you because you know me."

"She attacked me because she's trash," I snort, "I can decide for myself who I make friends with. No one's business but mine. If Trent has a problem with that, then that's on her." I can't decide if I mean that or not. The more I talk to Ezma, the more I'm around her, the more uneasy I feel. Even right now, I have a strange feeling in the pit of my stomach; one I can't quite explain. At this point I think I'm either in denial about Ezma, or I'm just afraid to quit talking to her. Maybe even both. "Do you hear that?" she asks, taking her earplugs out. I do the same and listen in the silence.

"Hear what?" She shushes me and we both stand in silence. Somewhere nearby I can hear the sound of a phone ringing. The feeling in my stomach worsens.

"Is that yours?" I ask. Please tell me it is.

"Not mine," she replies, shaking her head, "Mine's in my pocket." She takes it out of her coat and shows it to me.

"Well, that's not mine either. You don't think someone followed us out here, do you?" I ask.

"Keep that thing ready just in case," she instructs, pointing at my pistol. I nod and we begin walking toward the source of the noise.

"I think it's coming from the shack," I say, pausing to listen. Ezma goes ahead of me and pushes open the shack door. The ringing stops, leaving a tense silence behind.

"Great, it stopped," Ezma grumbles, peering around the darkened shack, "You got a light or anything?"

"No, nothing."

"Oh wait, never mind, I got it." She takes her lighter out of her pocket and flips it open. After a few clicks, a flame appears. We begin searching the shack, checking everywhere we can. There are only a few rooms to search. One contains a broken down couch and a toppled bookshelf. Another has only a table and chairs. The aging floorboards creak and groan underfoot as we come to the last room. Ezma pushes the door open and steps inside.

"Dammit, there's something on the floor," she grumbles, "Just stepped in it. Can you see what it is? I hope it's not gas or something."

"I think we would have smelled it by now," I reply, stooping down to look at the floor. My heart skips a beat.

"Oh my God..." I whisper.

"What? What is it?"

"That's blood..."

"You're joking, right?" I look past Ezma and feel the pit of my stomach fall out. Behind her is someone sitting in a chair against the wall; slumped over and not moving. The phone begins ringing again and I realize it's on the body. Ezma turns toward the noise and gasps.

"Oh no..." I gasp. Sitting in the chair, tied up and gagged, is my mother...

Chapter 15

The phone continues ringing for several seconds before going silent again. Ezma and I stand in shock, staring at the body. The copious amounts of fresh blood on the floor suggests that she was alive until we started shooting at the shack.

"No, no, no, no, no!" I panic, "Why? Why is she here? How the hell did she get here?"

"Calm down," Ezma says, holstering her revolver.

"I killed my mother, Ezma! I fricken shot her! There's blood all over the place and...oh my God...I can't do this."

"Come on, let's get out of here." She brushes past me and leads me out of the room.

"How the hell are you so calm about this?" I demand, "I mean...what are we supposed to do? We can't get the cops involved, not with everything else that's been happening."

"We're not involving the cops, so don't worry about it," she replies. We step back out into the daylight and she closes the lighter.

"Then what are we going to do?" I demand. She pauses for a moment and pockets her lighter. She takes a deep breath, and turns to face me.

"We're going to be here when they come back," Ezma says, narrowing her eyes, "Whoever left her here didn't finish her off themselves. They'll be back to get her. Now come on. We need to clean things up, make it look like we were never here." She leads me over to the targets we set up and over the course of about twenty minutes we begin picking everything up. First the cans and bottles, tossing them in the boxes they sat upon. Next we carry them to the van and come back for the filing cabinet and table. Once everything is loaded up, we get in the van and drive to the ravine where Ezma parks the van and we begin unloading everything. We push the table down into the ravine, then the file cabinet. Next go the boxes.

"So what do we do once they come back?" I ask, taking one of the boxes out of the back.

"Nothing good, I can say that much," Ezma answers. She tosses one of the boxes down into the ravine and I do the same with my own.

"What are you gonna do? Torture them or something?"

"Maybe," she shrugs, walking back to the front of the van. She and I get in and she parks it behind some bushes. We sit in silence for a few minutes while Ezma does something with her phone. My heart is still racing from what I just saw. Ezma looks up from her phone with a look of concern.

"You doing alright?" she asks, "You look like you're about ready to have a panic attack."

"Can you really blame me?" I snap.

"Relax, will you? I'm just trying to help," Ezma replies.

"How do you expect me to relax after what I just saw?" I demand, "I don't think I've ever seen so much blood in my life, let alone a dead body! And it doesn't help that it was my mother!"

"Weren't you telling me just the other day that you didn't care if she died?" Ezma recalls.

"Are you fucking serious?" I rage, "You're gonna throw that in my face now of all times?"

"I'm not throwing it in your face, I'm just confused!" Ezma insists. I reach forward and grab her by the front of her jacket. I'm so mad I might just hit her.

"Did you have something do with this?" I snarl, "Tell me! Tell me right fucking now!"

"I didn't do anything!" she shouts, "Let go of me! Jesus Christ! Get a hold of yourself!" She throws me off, but I grab her a second time.

"Don't fuck with me, Ezma!" I shout, "I will fucking kill you! You hear me? I'll tear you apart!" She pushes me off and throws open her door. She climbs out and I follow after her, slamming my door behind me. We both stand at the front of the vehicle and Ezma backs away a few paces with her hands raised in front of her.

"You need to calm down!" Ezma orders, "Right now! Okay?"

"I saw the blood, Ezma! The blood in the bathroom, the saw! What the hell did you put in those fucking boxes, huh?" She looks at me as though she thinks I'm crazy and shakes her head.

"What in the hell are you talking about?" she demands, "Boxes? The ones we threw in the ravine?"

"What else would I be talking about?" I demand, taking a step forward. She hesitates, appearing to be about to step back again, but instead holds her ground.

"Okay, question..." she begins, taking a deep breath, "Why the hell were you in my bathroom? I told you not to go in there!"

"Yeah and now I see why, you fucking psychopath!" Her demeanor instantly changes to pure rage. She looks down at the ground and slams her fist down on the hood of the van.

"First off, never call me that again!" she hisses, looking up at me, "Second, those boxes were full of garbage, just like I told you. What the hell even brought this on? We were talking about your dead mother!"

"Oh, I dunno, Ezma," I snort, "I just think it's really odd that we were talking about my mother one day and the next she's shot to shit in a shack! It was your suggestion to shoot at it in the first place! To even come out here!"

"So that makes you think I did this?"

"What about the saw, the blood?" I demand. She claps a palm to her face and holds out her hand. Her thumb is bandaged and a small amount of blood has seeped through.

"I cut my finger on the stupid thing," she explains, "I was out using the saw for something and I slipped up."

"Then why was it in your bathroom?" I ask, "Seems a little odd, doesn't it?"

"I forgot to set it down until I got to the bathroom. And I assume because you saw that and blood in the tub, you immediately assumed I was cutting up bodies in there, right?"

"Well...yeah!" I reply. She lets out a frustrated groan and takes hold of her pant leg. She pulls it up to her knee and I see that she has three fresh cuts, all parallel to one another, just below her knee.

"I cut myself in the shower this morning," she groans, "Okay? There was still blood in there because it kept bleeding after I shut off the water and I was in such a hurry I forgot to rinse it. It's like I said before, I only told you to stay out of that bathroom because the toilet is busted. Okay? Do we have all this squared away now? The saw was part of a project I had going in the backyard, the blood is mine. Alright?" Wait minute...project in the backyard? That injury on her thumb seems fresh; maybe within the last day or so. Unless she really cut it. Even then it seems like she'd have stitches in it. Somehow I doubt that since it hasn't seemed to slow her down at all. It's the same hand she uses to reload her revolver. Didn't look like there was any problem moving it while she did that. She told me she was last out in the backyard three days ago. If the wound's as fresh as I think it is, then she's lying to me. Unfortunately I can't be sure enough to call her on it.

"Alright...I'm sorry," I apologize, running my fingers through my hair, "Let's um...let's figure out what to do." Without another word, the two of us climb back into the van and Ezma rolls the windows down before lighting a cigarette. I try to push all my suspicions about Ezma aside and focus on the task at hand. Right now we have a dead body we're partially responsible for. We need to decide what happens from here. After about twenty minutes of sitting in an awkward silence, I look over at Ezma.

"What now?" I ask, "Throw her in the ravine or something?" She shakes her head while taking a drag on her cigarette and blows the smoke out the window.

"Like I said wait for them to come back," Ezma says, flicking ashes out the window.

"What makes you think they will?" I ask.

"A corpse doesn't bleed all over the place like that," she explains, resting her elbow on the door, "Blood goes all over the place like that when there's a beating heart to pump it. She was alive until we...well... the point is whoever kidnapped her left her here alive, and that says they'll be back for her."

"And how long are we gonna have to wait for them to show up?" I inquire.

"Hell if I know," she shrugs, "Only thing we can do is wait and see. Hopefully it's soon."

"Hopefully..." I turn my head and look out the window, watching the bushes and trees rustling in the breeze.

"You mind checking the back for something?" she asks.

"Sure, what is it?"

"I need you to find one of the extension cables I keep in the back. Should be somewhere around the very back seats." I nod and climb back out of the van. Extension cable, huh? Now I'm starting to lean back in the direction of believing Rachel. Okay, maybe it wouldn't be weird if she was a carpenter or something. It would make sense to have things like that sitting around. Once at the back, I hear the click of the hatch unlocking and pull it open. After about a minute of searching, I'm not seeing any extension cables.

"Are you sure they're back here?" I ask. She turns around in her seat to face me.

"Yeah, it should be right around there," she replies, pointing to one side of the vehicle, "It might be in that cardboard box under there." I check under the very back seat and find a small cardboard box I already checked. Inside is a folded up tarp and some tools. Buried beneath all of it are two extension cables. I take one out and put the box back before closing the hatch and returning to my seat.

"Why do you keep these in here?" I inquire.

"I have my reasons," Ezma replies, turning back around in her seat. I shake my head set the cable on the floor in front of me.

"And what sort of reasons are those?" I continue.

"Oh my God, Zoey..." she groans, "Sometimes I need an extension cable, alright? Quit overthinking it."

"I don't like where this is going," I sigh. I turn back toward Ezma and watch as she unlocks the revolver's cylinder and glimpses the cartridges inside. She locks it back into place and puts it back in her holster. She catches my eye and looks down at the steering wheel.

"If you really didn't have a hand in this..." I begin, taking a deep breath, "Then is it possible that this is related to the recent murders?" She places both hands on the steering wheel and tilts her head back for a moment.

"It's possible," she says, "I don't want to jump to conclusions, but we should at least keep it in mind." She looks up suddenly and glances out the side window, moving so she can see past me.

"What is it?" I ask. Right as the words cross my lips, I hear the faint sound of a car engine in the distance.

"Someone's coming," Ezma says, "Come on, keep quiet and follow my lead." I nod and we both climb out of the van and close the doors as quietly as possible. My heart is racing and my palms sweating. We duck down near the edge of the bushes and wait as the sound of the engine comes closer.

A small white car, dented and scratched, pulls into the clearing and turns the corner into the area that contains the shack.

"Come on, let's get after them," Ezma says, "We need to hurry. Bring that cable with you and be ready for anything." We stand up and dart out from behind the bushes. I can't really make sense of what I'm feeling. It's sort of a mixture between anger and unease. I want to know who's responsible for what happened to my mother, but at the same time, neither of us know what we're walking into. We sprint across the grass and duck back down once we come near the clump of trees the car turned past. Ezma leads me along them and she stops me by sticking out her arm in front of me. A man and two women are standing around the car. One of them, a woman of average height with long, braided, platinum blonde hair and gray eyes, seems to be giving the other two orders.

"I know her..." Ezma whispers, "That woman ordering the others around."

"Who is she?"

"That's Sarah Fenton," Ezma answers. The other two disappear into the shack and Ezma beckons for me to follow. Sarah has her back turned toward us. She lights a cigarette and blows a puff of smoke into the air. Ezma sneaks up behind her and in one swift motion, loops her arm around Sarah's throat, pressing the gun up against her temple.

"Scream and you die..." Ezma hisses, covering Sarah's mouth. She tries to free herself and Ezma cocks her weapon. Sarah mutters something incoherent and Ezma motions for me to hand her the extension cord. Ezma forces Sarah onto her knees behind the vehicle. I hold my pistol to her head as Ezma quickly ties Sarah's hands behind her back.

"I see you have a new friend, Ezma," Sarah mutters, "What kind of lies did you feed this one?"

"Open your mouth again and I start breaking your fingers," Ezma growls. She pushes Sarah over onto her stomach and instructs me to watch her. Ezma peeks out from behind the car and I do the same on the other side. The other two are walking out of the shack. Ezma stands up and points her weapon at them.

"Jack...Stella..." Ezma says, "Long time no see. You shoot out any windows lately?" Both hold up their hands in surrender.

"Just yours," Jack responds, "Are you the one who shot her up?"

"Not on purpose, I didn't," Ezma replies, "You mind explaining what the hell that woman was doing here?"

"Don't answer that!" Sarah shouts. I grab the back of her head and smash her face into the dirt.

"Not another word," I growl.

"Put the gun down and we'll talk," Stella pleads.

"Oh, now you wanna talk?" Ezma snorts, "You sure didn't feel like talking that night a bullet came sailing through my living room window!"

"Get fucked, Weston!" Jack sneers.

"Excuse me?" Ezma chuckles, "What did you just say to me?"

"You heard me," Jack sneers, "Too bad I missed that night." Ezma brushes some of her hair behind her ear and gives a sinister scowl.

"You'll regret it even more soon enough. This wouldn't have anything to do with the recent murders, would it?" Ezma demands, "Kidnapping this woman?"

"What, did you hit your head or something?" Jack snorts, "Those were two of ours, you idiot!"

"I don't care if Michael and Melissa were part of the Nolan clan or not," Ezma snarls, "Everyone knows you've been losing money ever since the trial. I just thought maybe you were squabbling over inheritance or something. Don't you two have a couple of grandparents in the hospital right now?"

"So what if we do?" Stella growls, "That's none of your business!"

"Maybe that isn't, but what is my business is when you three fuckoffs start screwing with outsiders!" Ezma rages, "What the hell is wrong with you?"

"We could ask you that same question!" Stella says, "Maybe we were pissed off at your idiot father, but we didn't have anything against you until the night you attacked Brian and Sarah!"

"Your jackass cousin is the one who started that whole thing!" Ezma snarls, turning and pointing at Sarah as she speaks.

"Oh, is that what you told this one?" Sarah chimes in, "That's a crock and you know it!"

"Do you wanna get shot?" Ezma snarls, brandishing her weapon at Sarah. Ezma kicks her in the ribs and spins back around to face the others. Jack, who has taken a few steps forward, backs off at once.

"What? You trying to be a hero?" Ezma growls, advancing toward him, "Here, let me fix that." Without warning, she shoots Jack in the stomach. He falls to the ground in agony, cursing and clutching his wound. Ezma just stands there with a dull look in her eyes.

"Christ! What the hell? You crazy bitch!" Stella shouts. Ezma cocks the hammer again and points the revolver at Stella's head. Stella's eyes widen.

"You know, I don't much care for cowards who shoot at me through my living room window!" Ezma snarls, "I didn't realize it was possible, but now I feel even less sorry for killing Addison! Especially after what she did to my cousin!" She shoots Stella in the thigh, sending her to the ground in a heap. She clutches her leg as blood begins seeping from the wound.

"You know...I always felt like the world would be better off without certain people..." Ezma says, pacing back and forth, "Some people are worthless wastes of flesh, whose sole purpose in life is to cause problems for everyone else! So why should anyone care if they die?" She shoots Jack in the throat and stands there motionless and unfazed as he chokes on his own blood. Seconds later, he stops moving.

"You're fucking crazy!" Stella panics.

"Oh how you all love to say that about me!" Ezma snarls, "I get in a knife fight with Sarah one time, and suddenly I'm some unstable whackjob to everyone in town!"

"And were we wrong?" Sarah demands.

"I was defending myself!" Ezma shouts, "I was keeping your sorry ass away from my brother, Fenton! I am sick and tired of this pointless fucking feud! I just wanted to live my life in peace, but instead I lost my parents, my brother, and my fucking sanity!" She shoots Stella between the eyes and storms back over to Sarah.

"Zoey, help me get her up," Ezma orders, glaring down at Sarah, "We're going to have a nice chat with her..." I help Ezma stand her up and lead her back toward the van.

"I don't know what you're hoping to accomplish with this," Sarah mutters, "Now you've got two bodies to deal with."

"Three if you count the Parker lady," Ezma growls. She stops Sarah in her tracks and spins her around. Ezma slugs her in the jaw and I struggle to keep Sarah from falling over. Once she regains her footing, I see that blood is trickling from her split lip. She spits some of it on the ground and glares at Ezma.

"That gal behind you, the one keeping your ass off the ground," Ezma snarls, "That's the girl whose mother you kidnapped. Her mother is dead because of you. I imagine she's pretty pissed about that, don't you think?"

"And your point?" Sarah snorts. Ezma holsters her weapon and grabs Sarah by the front of her shirt.

"The point is that she gets to decide what happens to you." She spins Sarah around and gives her a rough shove forward. Before I can grab her arms again, Sarah takes off at a full sprint.

"Grab her!" Ezma barks, racing after her. I lunge for her arms and trip on the uneven terrain. I fall to the ground and Ezma keeps running after her. I scramble to my feet in time to see Ezma tackle Sarah. The two of them hit the dirt with a thud. Ezma pins Sarah on her back, then slugs her in the cheek and again in the jaw.

"That's it...I'm not having that happen again," Ezma growls, "Zoey, hold her down for a second. I'll be right back." I do as she asks and she trots off to the van with her keys in hand.

"Look, I'm sorry about your mother," Sarah apologizes, "I didn't know who she was, I didn't want her to get hurt."

"Save it..."

"I really didn't," she insists, "This can still go another way. Help me get out of here and I'll return the favor."

"Return it how?" I demand, "Why should I believe you?"

"I know it looks bad right now, I get that, but I'm not the bad guy here, alright?" she replies, "Ezma is playing you for a fool. Come on, there's no denying who and what she is at this point."

"And what exactly do you want me to do?" I demand, "You kidnapped my mother. I don't care why you did it, it doesn't change what happened...and for the record, I don't care about what Ezma is doing at the moment."

"Somehow, I don't think that's the case. I think you do care," Sarah replies.

"This conversation is over," I growl.

"Just listen to me!" she hisses, "Quit being so hard-headed! What do you really have to lose here? Ezma just killed two people right in front of you and only God knows what she's planning for me. Is it really going to hurt to help me? All I did was kidnap someone in a panic. It was a stupid decision, but I didn't mean for anything like this to happen."

I take a moment to think about what she's saying. As much as I really hate to admit it, she's right. What is there to lose? Is it worth letting Sarah go? Will I regret it?

"How do you expect me to get you out of here?" I demand, "Assuming I did want to help you."

"Did you forget already? Ezma said she would leave my fate up to you. You have all the control here. Ezma may be a crook, but she's still plenty smart. Tell her you want to let me go, that we're calling a truce or something."

"And if I do let you go, what can you tell me?" I inquire.

"Did Ezma happen to mention what happened to her parents?" she asks.

"So what if she did?"

"You've probably heard it several times already, but Ezma really is delusional," Sarah insists, "I'm not trying to use it as an insult, I'm just stating fact. She always tells people that someone else cut the brake lines, that she wasn't there when it happened, but she was! I saw her from the window in the gas station! She was futzing with the brakes while her parents were arguing with her brother."

"How do I know you're telling the truth?"

"You don't, but you've got to trust me on this." I look up to see that Ezma is coming back with a lug wrench.

"You know what I think the truth is?" I growl, "I think you're lying to worm your way out of this. Desperate people will say anything, right?"

"Did she tell you anything interesting?" Ezma asks, approaching us.

"Nothing worth repeating," I reply, "Just saying whatever she can to try and change our minds."

"Is that right?" Ezma snorts, stooping down in front of Sarah, "Shame, I guess I'll have to break your legs after all."

"Hey, whoa, wait a minute!" Sarah panics, "Just chill out, okay? Let's talk this out."

"Talk it out?" Ezma repeats, still glaring at Sarah, "Alright fine. How's this? Who's been ordering you around? Hmm? And don't give me some bullshit answer about that, you know damn well what I'm talking about."

"No one's ordering me to do anything," Sarah declares, "Why would you even think that?"

"What, you think I'm fucking stupid?" Ezma snarls, "What had you and Zoey's mother in the same place to begin with?"

"We were meeting someone at the Cedar Springs Motel," Sarah explains, "She just happened to be there for whatever reasons. That's all I'm telling you."

"I'm sorry, do you not understand how this works?" Ezma hisses, slamming the lug wrench down in the dirt, narrowly missing Sarah's head, "Start talking or I start breaking bones!"

"We were meeting with someone who said they knew where Addison was," Sarah answers through gritted teeth, "I figured it was some bullshit lead, you know? Someone just messing with us. He said she was alive somewhere, and since the police are of no help for reasons you and I are both well aware of, we took him up on his offer. We were waiting for him to show up, but he never did. By the time we kidnapped Parker, it was almost an hour past the agreed meet-up time. Now I know for sure that it was useless information, seeing as you just confessed to having killed her! You killed a battered woman, you know that? She was the victim!"

"I am so sick of you defending her!" Ezma bellows, slamming the lug wrench down a second time, "She is nothing but a manipulative sociopath! She was using him for money the entire time they were together, and she laughed about it whenever she had the chance! She admitted it to me, Sarah! She started the fight! Eric was defending himself and she tried to kill him for the life insurance money! She screwed up and her plan didn't work! Eric's still alive and she gets nothing! She mocked me and said I would never be able to prove it, because who would ever believe that she was the aggressor? Addison deserved what she got!"

"You're so fucking delusional you can't even get your facts straight!" Sarah snarls, "Eric was beating on her and you know it!"

"She! Cracked! His! Skull! He has a brain injury! She condemned him to that for the rest of his life, all to cover her own ass! I would not have gotten involved if she'd listened to me! I told her to back off! I told her to just leave! And she decided that attempted murder was the better solution!" She gets to her feet and paces back and forth in front of Sarah.

"Yeah, keep believing that!" Sarah growls, "I'll probably never know the real reason you killed Addison, but don't act like you're some kind of noble vigilante! You barely even knew her!"

"Why did you kidnap her mother?" Ezma demands, crouching back down in front of Sarah, "Huh? Let's talk about that."

"I'm not telling you squat!" Sarah sneers. Ezma takes a deep breath and exhales. She looks at Sarah, then stands up again and begins tapping the palm of her free hand with the end of the lug wrench.

"Give me one of her arms..." Ezma says, still staring at Sarah, whose eyes widen. Sarah begins struggling with all her might and kicking her feet.

"Hey, whoa! There's no need for that!" she panics.

"Consider it payback for what you did to my brother," Ezma hisses as I pin one of Sarah's arms out to the side. She struggles to get loose and Ezma stoops down beside her again, this time grabbing Sarah's wrist and pinning it to the dirt.

"I didn't do anything to your brother!" Sarah shouts, "I never touched him that night! You're the one who had the knife! Not me!"

"Don't fucking lie to me!" Ezma roars, smashing the lug wrench down on Sarah's arm. A sickening crack reaches my ears just before Sarah lets out a pained yelp. She grits her teeth and curses several times.

"You feel better now?" Sarah snarls, "Did that bring your brother back?"

"Keep talking to me like that and I start breaking fingers," Ezma growls, "Why did you kidnap her mother? Tell me!"

"Piss off, Weston!" Sarah hisses.

"Oh, so you do want some busted fingers?" Ezma taunts, "Fine then!" She smashes the lug wrench down on Sarah's thumb and index finger, snapping them both.

"I swear to God when I get loose, I'll skin you alive!" Sarah bellows.

"That's two," Ezma growls, "Here's a couple more!" She smashes Sarah's remaining three fingers in one violent swing. Sarah howls and writhes in agony, still struggling to get loose.

"I can do this all day!" Ezma warns, "Start talking!"

"Zoey, come on!" Sarah shouts, "Quit letting her do this! I'm sorry, alright? Just let me up already!" I roll my eyes and let out a sigh.

"Alright, fine," I grumble, "Let's get her up. I think she's had enough for now." Ezma looks at me, then places the end of the lug wrench beneath Sarah's chin. She lifts Sarah's head up and the two glare at one another for several seconds.

"You're lucky she's calling the shots here..." Ezma mutters, "Consider this a temporary truce."

"I need more than just your word," Sarah insists. Ezma draws her revolver and unlatches the cylinder. She removes the four spent cartridges and the two remaining live ones, placing them all in her coat pocket.

"Zoey, hand me yours too," Ezma says, holding out her hand. I hand it to her and she removes the magazine, then the round in the chamber. She pockets the magazine and loose cartridge, then hands the weapon back to me.

"Lose the lug wrench too," Sarah says. Ezma rolls her eyes and tosses it to the side.

"So...you want to get off of me, Zoey?" Sarah asks. Ezma nods to me and I stand up. Wincing in pain, Sarah stumbles to her feet and clutches her wounded arm.

"Your turn," Ezma says, "Spill it."

"We never planned to kidnap her," Sarah explains, "It just came out of the blue. Jack was being loud and obnoxious while the three of us were at the Cedar Springs Motel. He was pissed off about Addison's disappearance and kept going on about how he wanted to kill you for it. He knew just as well as the rest of us that our informant was a fraud. Stella and I started arguing with him and he stormed out of the room to go to his car. He said he was going to get his gun, then go to your house that night."

"So, what? You followed him?" Ezma asks. Sarah nods.

"We did and he just got even more upset," she replies, "He took the gun out of the car, started waving it around, and the next thing I know, that woman comes out of her room and starts shouting for us to shut up. She saw the gun and muttered something about calling the cops. So Stella and I chased her back into her room and gagged her."

"What were you planning to do with her after that?" Ezma asks, "I assume you took her out here to keep anyone from finding her."

"We weren't planning to kill her," Sarah insists, "Jack wanted to, but I told him to back off. I said we should leave her alone for now. Decide what to do later."

"You sicken me," Ezma mutters, "All of you."

"Look who's talking," Sarah snorts, "You're no more innocent than the rest of us. Now if you'll kindly piss off, I'd like to speak with Zoey in private for a moment."

"You really think I'm going to just leave you two alone?" Ezma snorts, "Whatever you want to discuss with her, you can do it in front of me."

"I think I told you to piss off!" Sarah growls.

"And I think you want to get hit again..." Ezma snarls, clenching her fists, "Get on with it. I don't have all day for this." Sarah lets out a groan and tilts her head back for a moment. She looks down at the ground and shakes her head before looking at me with intense frustration.

"That was for kidnapping her," I say, "The arm, fingers...that's why."

"Whatever helps you sleep," Sarah mutters, "Gas station on Ricky Road. Midnight tomorrow night. Keep this psycho away from me, you got that?" She glares at Ezma, then looks back at me.

"You come alone," I say, "If I see anyone else, or I think you're trying to trick me, I'm leaving."

"Deal," she agrees. We shake hands and step back from one another. She turns to Ezma.

"You got anything else to ask me before I leave?" she inquires. Ezma crosses her arms and cocks her head.

"Who killed Melissa and Michael?" Ezma asks, "I'm convinced you know something about it and I want to hear it."

"I assumed it was you," Sarah answers, "I can't think of anyone else who'd want them dead. I don't know anything about it. All I know is the same thing everyone else has heard, the causes of death and whatnot."

"I didn't touch them," Ezma declares, shaking her head, "I really didn't."

"I don't believe you," Sarah growls, shifting her weight, "You already confessed to killing Addison, you killed Jack and Stella, I've got no reason to believe you."

"I swear to God I never touched them!" Ezma insists, "I'm not kidding around! I really didn't!"

"Then who did?" Sarah demands. A tense silence follows as she and Ezma lock eyes.

"Blame me all you want, but it doesn't make it true," Ezma says, "Do I look like I could have strangled Michael to death? I'm five-nine and a hundred-fifty pounds, he was twice my size. How could I have strung Melissa up in a tree like that?"

"They were drugged, Ezma," Sarah replies, "Just that alone means it could have been you. It's easy to kill someone if they can't fight back."

"I suppose I can give you that," Ezma sighs, tilting her head back, "Still doesn't change that I didn't do it, though. My guess is it's someone outside our two families. Someone who has an issue with your family at the very least."

"Say that turns out to be the case," Sarah says, "What then? How would we even know who it was? How would we find them?"

"Your guess is as good as mine. All I know is to me it sounds to me like we have a rogue killer running loose."

"Even though I agree it could be possible, I'm not going to assume you're innocent; not after what took place here today. If there is a third party at work, I'll believe it when I see it," Sarah murmurs, brushing past Ezma, "I'm getting my car. Zoey, remember what I said. Tomorrow at midnight; the gas station."

"I'll be there." Sarah walks off and leaves Ezma and I standing in silence.

"You sure you know what you're doing?" Ezma asks.

"I can handle myself," I reply, "I'll be fine. I'm hoping maybe she can tell me something useful. Maybe something she wouldn't say in front of you."

"Sure hope so," Ezma sighs.

Chapter 16

Looking down at my phone, I can see that it's almost midnight. I'm standing across the street from the gas station, sitting with my back against a wooden fence, just out of the reach of the nearest streetlight. Over the past twenty minutes or so, I've seen five cars come through the station. None of them are Sarah's. At this point I'm starting to wonder if I should leave. I don't see her anywhere. It takes several more minutes before her car pulls into the lot. She steps out of the car and glances around as I make my way toward her. Her left arm is in a cast and her fingers splinted. I'm almost surprised she managed to drive herself with her arm like that.

"There you are," she says, right as I come up to the curb, "Over here. I don't want the staff bothering us. They don't like people loitering out here, especially this time of night." She leads me along the side of the building and away from the windows.

"Alright, that should be fine," she says, turning to face me.

"So what is it you wanted to talk to me about?" I ask.

"First off," she begins, pointing at her broken arm, "this hurts more than you can imagine. I'm still pretty pissed off about that, so don't go thinking I've forgiven you for your role in this."

"I didn't expect you would."

"Getting to the point of why I asked you here," she continues, "I was here at this station the night Ezma's parents were killed. Like I told you on Saturday, I saw Ezma tampering with the car."

"Why don't you start from the beginning?" I suggest, "Tell me the whole thing. What did you see and hear?"

"It was about eight months after the Becketts bit the big one," she begins, "I'd turned twenty-one a few months prior and managed to land a crumby job here at the station. It was about an hour after sunset and there were a few folks coming through the place, nothing unusual about that. One of my co-workers was out at the pumps. This couple was out there making a huge fuss about it not working and being late getting somewhere because of it, something like that."

"And who were they? The Westons?"

"No, just some obnoxious people I remember from that night," she explains, "I'm just giving you all the details. It looked like they had a kid, but I can't remember for sure. It was difficult to tell from here, you know? I'm in there trying to pay attention to customers and occasionally glancing outside in the process; I missed a few details, I'm sure. Anyway, that's not the point. Around that time, a car pulled into the lot, swerved off the street, then parked across from that couple. Brian got out and his dad followed him across the lot. They were both shouting up a storm, trading insults, the works. So not long after that, Mrs. Weston got out of the car and joined them. They all kept on arguing for about five minutes or so, until my manager went out and told them to leave."

"And what about Ezma?"

"I noticed movement near the Westons' car while my manager was talking to them," she explains, "The car was parked near that streetlight over there. So when she stood up, I could see it was Ezma. I didn't realize what she'd done until I heard the news about the accident."

"What happened after that?" I ask.

"Manager flipped out on me for eavesdropping and told me to go stock shelves. Last thing I saw was Ezma walking along the side of the car. I heard the Westons leave soon after that, but that's all I saw. Left both their kids behind and the rest is history."

"You're certain you saw her?"

"One-hundred percent," Sarah nods.

"What about Brian?" I ask.

"What about him?"

"What happened that night in Ezma's front yard?" I inquire, "I want to hear your side of the story."

"I don't know what you've heard, but I assume Ezma made me out to be the 'psycho girlfriend,' didn't she?"

"I would say so."

"Brian wasn't bloodied up when he came to that house that night," Sarah declares, "Brian didn't throw the phone, he had nothing to do with why it broke. I know that's what Ezma says, but Brian had a different version of events. That whole incident that night was the result of some kind of heated argument, one that Brian never got a chance to talk to me about. That to me is suspicious in its own right. That he just happened to die before I could get back to him? I think he saw something he wasn't supposed to. That's why I think Ezma was trying to shut him up. Keep him quiet so some dirty secret of hers never got out. What that was is anyone's guess."

"That seems a little far-fetched, don't you think?"

"Hey, I thought the same thing at first," she says, "Ezma cared about her brother, but...I don't know. Rachel noticed it too. Ezma wasn't herself after her parents died. The changes were subtle, but they're there. You just have to know what you're looking for."

"Can you give me an example?" She takes a moment to think about it, glancing off across the parking lot, then over my shoulder.

"I don't know if I can put it into words," she says at last, "It's one of those things, you know? You have to know the person for a long time. I'll try, but I don't know how much help this will be. You know how people have these idiosyncrasies about them? Just certain things they do, little habits of theirs?"

"Yeah, I know what you mean," I nod.

"I don't know how much of this was due to grief or what, but Ezma wasn't so...wasn't so dark, you know?"

"You lost me," I sigh, crossing my arms.

"Rachel told me she saw her shoot a crow in front of you at the old amusement park," Sarah says, "Did that happen or is Rachel giving me shit?"

"Oh it happened, alright," I nod, "I thought they were pests around here?"

"They are, they spread trash all over the place, they get at the food in gardens, all sorts of stuff," Sarah explains, "But that's not the point. The old Ezma, the one Rachel knew before the Westons died...she never would have done that. Not in a million years. Ezma used to volunteer at the animal shelter when she was younger. She loved animals and she hated it when people would kill crows, rats, anything anyone considered a pest. That's what I mean."

"So her personality changed?"

"Exactly," she nods, "Like I said, it was subtle. Come on, I bet you've noticed other strange things, am I right?" I think back to the hacksaw in the bathroom and the smell of bleach in the house the first time I came in. Even the missing length of rope on the tree in her backyard. I probably shouldn't mention that last one to Sarah. I'm sure I'll just set her off.

"A few things," I admit, "Her house reeked of bleach the first time I went in there. That was right after we'd taken these boxes off to Hunter's Ridge. She keeps insisting that it was just garbage, but I'm not convinced. When we took the first few, there was this foul smelling fluid leaking out of one of them. Smelled like something was rotting in it. I just assumed it was food, but...later on she told me to stay out of the downstairs bathroom. Someone's cat got inside and I chased it out of the house...not before I saw blood in the tub and a hacksaw by the toilet."

"And what kind of pathetic excuse did she give you for that?"

"She said she'd cut herself in the shower, showed me a few cuts around her knee, then said she'd been using the hacksaw for something in the backyard. Apparently she forgot to set the saw down when she cut herself and that's why it ended up in the bathroom. Look, I've had a feeling that something was wrong with Ezma from near the start. Just before I met you, she told me to get one of the extension cords out of the van, and I know she put them in there for the exact purpose we used one of them for."

"To tie me up?" Sarah asks.

"Exactly," I confirm, "And before we get too much further into that, you never told me the rest of what happened the night Brian ended up in the hospital."

"After Ezma broke the phone, she pulled a knife on him and chased him out of the house," Sarah continues, "From what I heard, Ezma was the one who called 911 first. I imagine that was to divert suspicion. Brian had left his cell at our apartment and that was part of why I went to check up on him. I didn't trust Ezma and I wanted to make sure Brian wasn't starting a fight with her again."

"How do you know what went on in the house if you weren't there?"

I ask.

"It wasn't a full conversation or anything, but Brian gave me a quick version of events when I got there," she explains, "He was shouting about how she'd broken the phone, that she was trying to kill him, and then there was this crazy bit about how he was convinced she wasn't actually his sister. He kept saying she was a fake, an impostor. He was all cut up and bleeding, Ezma came at me with the knife and stabbed me in the arm, what was I supposed to think? I tried to take the knife from her and ended up hurt even worse. I ran off and she started shouting that she was going to kill me."

"Apparently Rachel mistook that for Ezma shouting at Brian," I say, "That's what she told me, anyway."

"I doubt she was the only one to make that mistake," Sarah says, "I was off behind another house trying to stem the bleeding. I barely remember that part, to be honest. Cops rounded me up a little later. I ran mostly just because I wanted to get away from Ezma before she killed me. That and since my family had some involvement in the Beckett murders, I never know when I might run into a cop who takes issue with that. Part of the reason that part of the night is so fuzzy to me is because when the cops arrested me, they tackled me and I hit my face on the pavement. Knocked me out cold, so I was kept for observation. For that and because I'd lost a fair amount of blood. It was just one huge mess."

"Did they charge you or anything?" I ask. She shakes her head.

"Not with anything to do with the incident," she replies, "They tried to get me for resisting arrest, but it happened right near a traffic camera at an intersection. The camera caught the whole thing. I was so out of it that all I did was look around like I was drunk off my ass or something. I guess I was just in shock." Sarah's story seems to match up with what was written in the police report. It said that she fled the scene, but there was no mention of her being tackled or injured because of it. If I remember right, it made it sound like they brought her back without injury; aside from the stab wound to her arm that Ezma allegedly inflicted. The question now is, did they omit that from the report for some reason, or is Sarah making that part up? The report also went on to say that witnesses claim to have seen Sarah and Ezma fighting for control of the knife. Seems like she's being mostly truthful, but that missing part from the report, about how she'd been knocked out cold during her arrest, makes me wonder if I can trust what she's said so far about Ezma. I can't deny that Ezma's done plenty of wrong, but Sarah did say that she didn't notice a change in Ezma's personality until after Ezma's parents died. Something about this still isn't adding up.

Sarah turns her head and we both watch a police cruiser pull into the lot. It's difficult to tell, but I can see two people in the front of the vehicle as they park alongside Sarah's car. The driver rolls down the window and beckons for Sarah to come over. In the dim light, I can see that the officer is none other than Officer Harris. The same woman who arrested my mother the other day. Sarah walks over and stands beside the car. I can't make out much of what's being said. Harris makes a subtle gesture toward me. Sarah looks over her shoulder at me, then back at Harris and shakes her head. At first the conversation is quiet and formal. As it progresses, I notice Sarah becoming more anxious and Harris growing frustrated. They both raise their voices just enough for me to hear some of what's being said.

"...not what I asked you," Harris hisses, "You want to play games with me? Fine. I'll drag you right down to the county jail and you can talk with him about it. Is that what you want?"

"I said I would take care of it," Sarah responds, "Why the hell do you guys keep harassing me?"

"You know how this works, Miss Fenton," Harris growls, "I won't warn you again."

"No one gave me any details," Sarah replies, "How do you expect me to do anything if I don't have a clear list of instructions?" Instructions? What is she talking about?

"I told you exactly who to talk to, who to get the info from, and where to take it," Harris growls, "In case you haven't noticed, this task has fallen to you and number four."

"Then why aren't you bothering her?" Sarah demands, "Quit putting this all on me."

"I'm not going to argue with you about this, now do what you're told or I'll be back." Sarah backs off and Harris rolls up the window before backing out of the lot and driving away. Sarah is left standing beside the curb, running her fingers through her hair and gritting her teeth.

"What was that all about?" I ask. She shakes her head and walks over to me.

"Nothing, just forget about it," she answers.

"Why was she pointing at me?" I demand.

"I said forget about it!" she snaps, "Now get out of here. We're done talking, alright? I just...I need a minute to myself."

"If it has something to do with me, I think I have a right to know!" I argue.

"She just asked who you were," Sarah responds, "Forget it. Go home. We're done, alright?"

"She knows damn well who I am, Sarah!" I growl, "She arrested my mother and was around the day I was asked about Michael's murder. What's really going on?" She sits down on the edge of the curb and claps her palm to her face.

"Just go," she murmurs, "We'll talk some other time." With that I shake my head and turn to leave. I glance back at her as I'm leaving. What did Harris want with her?

Chapter 17

Three days have passed since my mother's death. That day, after Sarah walked away at Hunter's Ridge, Ezma and I returned to the van and waited for Sarah to leave. Once the car passed by our hiding spot, Ezma gave me a choice. Stay and help dispose of the bodies, or go back home and wait for her there. I chose the former. I still don't know what compelled me to do it. One by one, we loaded Jack and Stella's bodies into the back of the van. We left my mother's behind, feeling it best to leave her in the shack for the time being. She may have been a pain in my ass in life, but she still deserved better than what we had planned for the others. After that, we drove the bodies to the ravine and tossed them down into it. The entire time I just felt numb.

"What happened to her?" I asked.

"To who?"

"Addison," I answered, "Who do you think? What really happened to her?" Ezma was sitting on her knees near the ravine. We'd just thrown the second body into the ravine and she appeared to have cooled off. That calmness wouldn't last much longer.

"What? Are you deaf?" she snorted, standing up as she spoke, "You heard what I told those two degenerates. I killed her. I stand by what I said. I don't give a rat's ass about it. Addison was evil. I was only doing what I felt was right."

"Were you, really?" I growled, "Come on, Ezma! You murdered three people! I saw you kill two of them! How can you say it's the right thing to do?"

"It is if you kill the right people," she grumbled. She paused for a moment, staring down into the ravine. For a moment, I was worried she might kill me too.

"I wasn't planning to kill her..." she murmurs, "I really wasn't. I was...I was so furious with her! She hurt my cousin in one of the worst ways anyone ever could; and then had the audacity to tell me I should 'get over it.' That I should be happy that he was still alive. Yeah, maybe he is...but now he's cold and bitter. Nothing like the guy I always knew growing up. He was all smiles, intelligent, caring. She took it away and faced no consequences for it. I'm not delusional, Zoey. Addison admitted to lying...right to my face...and I guess I just snapped. If I hadn't killed her already, I might not have killed Jack and Stella. I just figured, what's the point? I'm already going to Hell, aren't I? What's another two stains on my soul gonna hurt?"

"What was really in the boxes?" I demanded.

"The hell do you think?" she snapped, "It was trash, Zoey! I didn't cut her up, I'm not that fucked in the head! I didn't lie about the contents and I didn't lie about the saw, the blood, or anything else. I do little projects around the house, I really did cut my finger on the blade. Addison died weeks ago. If I was going to cut her up, I would have done it right away."

Ezma met me outside our houses the night I got back from the gas station. I felt it was best that she not know what Sarah and I talked about, so I lied and said she never showed. I thought about concocting some story, maybe twisting up what Sarah told me in the process, but the effort didn't seem worth it. Ezma seemed to buy that Sarah never showed up, but after the way I confronted her about the boxes on Saturday, I feel it possible that she doesn't believe me. That when she cursed under her breath and muttered to herself in response to my news, she knew it was a lie. When I got back to my house Saturday evening, I did my best to make it seem like nothing unusual had taken place. I told my dad that we'd gone shooting, that we'd talked and laughed, the usual. That night I dreamed of the events that took place at Hunter's Ridge. The horrid sound of Jack choking on his own blood, the sight of Stella taking a bullet to the forehead, even the torture we put Sarah through. I was left to ask myself the same question over and over again as I struggled to sleep. Am I a monster? Did I do the right thing? The answer seemed obvious.

I sat there and let two people die in front of me. I had a gun, I could have stopped it, so why didn't I? It seemed unreal, all of it, like something out of a movie. If I'd shot Ezma, things only would have gotten worse for me, and somewhere in the back of my mind I knew that. I couldn't betray the only ally I had in that situation. I didn't have a shred of trust for Sarah until I met her at the station, until I witnessed that crooked cop threatening her.

I didn't leave my room at all on Sunday. Ezma didn't try to call me, didn't come to the house. Nothing. Monday morning it was the same. No word from her. I started to get worried, but went about my business as usual. I started becoming increasingly paranoid, just waiting for something to come up in the news. Dad ended up taking a trip over to the Cedar Springs Motel to try and find my mother. When he came up empty handed, he made a few more calls and began contemplating whether or not to file a missing persons report. Considering the way Mom would often disappear in the past, it probably didn't seem all that unusual to him.

When he asked me if I'd heard from her toward the end of the weekend, I lied and said I hadn't. As I spoke to him, the images of my mother's body in that shack flashed through my mind. When I came home from school on Monday, he said that he'd filed a report with the police. All day at school that day, I endured stares and whispers in the hallways. Everyone was still talking about my fight with Lisa Trent. I spotted her in the cafeteria, but she didn't notice me. The entire day I was bracing myself for a fight that never came.

It's now Tuesday morning and just about six-thirty. I've been dressed and ready to go since about five. I haven't been able to sleep all that well since Saturday. Still in somewhat of a daze, I've been lying on my bed, staring up at the ceiling for over an hour now. Dad came in at one point to ask if I wanted breakfast. I refused and he asked me if I was feeling alright. I lied and said I was fine. Truth is I haven't had much of an appetite as of late. I mean, what am I supposed to do? How does this get solved, how do I get out of it? I wish I could go back in time, tell myself not to shoot at the shack...maybe even further than that and just tell Dad that I didn't want Mom to come here. Then that way that whole mess would have been avoided too. If only, if only. I can say that all I want, but it doesn't solve anything. My only hope right now is that Ezma can do something to get us out of this mess.

The bus is going to be here soon and I need to get up and get outside to meet it. Part of me just wants to lie here and take a sick day. I doubt one day would cause any harm. I'm already behind anyway, why not make it a little worse? I'm an accomplice to murder, so who cares if I graduate? I'll probably spend the rest of my life in prison at this rate. I'm stuck with Ezma whether I like it or not. No telling what she might do if I decide I want out. Can I continue to assume the 'rogue killer' is someone else? After everything I've seen? I suppose it's still possible she wasn't involved in those murders, but even so, I need to be wary of Ezma from now on. I sit up and make my way down to the front door. Stepping outside, I see Ezma standing on her front porch, smoking a cigarette and appearing to be lost in thought. She notices me walk out and waves.

"Not planning to take the bus, are you?"

"I was thinking about it," I reply, "Is that your way of offering me a ride?" She chuckles and I smile. Once I start talking to her, I think again about the murders. I can't decide if this is the right thing to do or not. Does it even make sense to go back to her after everything she's done? Does it matter? Part of me feels that what happened was more than justified...and that part of me has the greatest influence here. If someone had killed my dad, would I have stood by and let them get away with it? No, never. No good person would, right?

"Come on over, neighbor," she says, putting out her cigarette, "We need to talk." I walk down the stone pathway and out the front gate, all the while feeling somewhat relieved that she wants to talk. She hops off the porch and takes her keys from her coat pocket.

"Heard anything from Sarah at all?" she asks, climbing into the driver seat. I close the door and she does the same.

"Still nothing" I lie, "Haven't spoken to her since Hunter's Ridge." She starts the van and begins backing it out of the driveway.

"We'll wait a couple more days. Rachel knows how to get in touch with me. If Sarah's having issues finding you or whatever, she can just ask Rachel and go from there," she says, "I don't know what made her decide to skip out, but that really ticks me off." She puts the van in gear and pulls forward.

"Any idea what we're going to do from here?" I ask, "About the other deaths? Michael and Melissa?"

"Not really," she admits, "I had one idea, but it's not what I would call a good one."

"Mind if I ask what it is?"

"I'm thinking of calling Rachel's dumb ass back over to my place again," she says, "If Sarah doesn't want to talk, then maybe we can get something out of Rachel instead."

"Isn't Rachel going to be pissed off about Sarah? I imagine she's already heard about it by now."

"Rachel's a chump," Ezma snorts, "She isn't going to do anything. Actually, you know what, why don't you look for her at school today? Maybe she'll tell you something useful. If I'm around she'll hold back."

"I suppose that makes sense. Can't say I'm looking forward to it."

"Just keep a cool head and it'll be fine," she assures me, "Be persistent too. Depending on what she tells you today, I may or may not ask her to come by." I think back to what Sarah told me at the gas station, and what I heard Officer Harris say to her. From the looks of it, Sarah was being blackmailed. Harris referred to an unknown person as 'number four.' She made it sound like there were at least four key players in whatever she and Sarah are involved in, and said 'it fell to Sarah and number four.' If there are four...and two are out...does that mean Harris was referring to Michael and Melissa? What do they all have in common, besides their relation to one another? Sarah and Michael, even Rachel have warned me about Ezma to some extent. Michael barely spoke to me and Melissa never said a word to me. There has to be more that I'm not seeing.

"Then who else would be responsible?" I inquire. Come on...think... what else is there? Wait...Ezma said something to Michael the day I met him. She mentioned a 'second job' and asked him what he 'hoped to accomplish.' Does Ezma know about the blackmailing? And if she does know about it...then does that make her the killer? Is she picking them off to protect herself from whatever Harris is doing?

"That's what we need to figure out," she replies, "So far the only thing the deaths have in common were threats...against me."

"I don't remember Michael threatening you."

"He did after you left," she says, "Said I was trash and that I deserved to die, all that fun stuff." What about that girl? The one with the ribbon? Come to think of it, she seems to be around shortly before something bad happens. No, that can't be right, can it? What about the missing rope from Ezma's tree? Wouldn't it make more sense that Ezma took it? No, that doesn't make sense either. We cleaned up the crime scene on Saturday. Why would she risk taking something from her own house like that? Unless she wanted to cover her own tracks, avoid any sales records. If she'd bought a rope around the time of Melissa's death, it wouldn't look good for her. On top of that, maybe she wanted me to see that it was missing...to lead me around like an idiot and cast suspicion away from herself. Two birds with one stone. Keep me on her side and fly under the radar. Regardless, I want to know what that girl with the ribbon is doing. It can't just be mere coincidence that she's around at the times she is.

"Do you happen to remember seeing anyone at the library that day you spoke to Micheal? That weird girl with the ribbon?"

"What weird girl?"

"I was walking back to the counter and bumped into her," I explain, "She looked to be about our age, about your height with black hair and green eyes, pale as a ghost. She seemed kind of mild mannered, quiet. She had her hair held in a ponytail with a red ribbon."

"Oh, I know who you're talking about," Ezma replies, "That's my cousin, Bernadette. I keep seeing her around and wondering why the hell she's here in the first place."

"Why do you say that?" I ask.

"She's from out of town," Ezma explains, "I don't see or talk to her much. Suffice it to say we have some things we need to discuss. It's not something I want to do and I imagine she doesn't either. Either way, due to the circumstances, I'm not going to be the one to approach her. She needs to come to me if she wants to talk. The reason I'm wondering why she's around is because I thought she was living out of the state or something, I don't remember. I haven't spoken to her in a couple of years. Why did you mention seeing her?"

"Well now I don't know if I should say it," I reply, "I noticed that she seems to be around shortly before someone dies. At least that's how it was with Michael and Melissa."

"So you were thinking she might be involved somehow?"

"Yeah, pretty much," I say with a shrug.

"I don't think she would be, but it is possible she might know something," Ezma continues, "I'd say chat her up if you get the chance.

We pull up at the school building and I step out of the vehicle. She drives off and I start walking to the front of the building. Along the way, I notice a red ribbon bobbing up and down in the crowd. It takes me a moment to realize it, but it's the same girl I was just telling Ezma about. I quicken my pace and keep my eye on her. She walks into the building and before I can follow, I hear a familiar voice behind me. I turn to see Rachel standing before me.

"Hey, I've been looking for you," Rachel says, cocking her head and crossing her arms, "You got a minute?"

"No, I...fine, whatever," I groan, pinching the bridge of my nose. Doing so brings instant regret and tears to my eyes.

"Sorry, did I interrupt something?"

"It doesn't matter," I reply, letting my arm drop to my side, "I was wanting to talk to you, anyway."

"Really? That's unusual," she says, "Usually you seem eager to get away from me."

"Have you seen a girl with a red ribbon around here?" I ask, "I just saw her a minute ago."

"Were you following her or something? You looked like you were in a hurry."

"I was trying to talk to her," I explain, "Do you know her?"

"Yeah, I do. She's a new student," Rachel explains, "Not as new as you, but she moved here about two-and-a-half months ago. Her name's Bernadette. Why are you suddenly curious about her?"

"You got time to listen?" I ask. She nods.

"Class doesn't start for a while," she says, "I can stick around for a bit."

"I'm gonna start by assuming you know about Sarah and that whole mess?"

"That's part of why I wanted to speak with you, yes," she nods, "Speaking of which, just what the hell do you think you were doing? I told you Ezma was trouble and now here we are."

"Yeah, that's great," I sigh, "but did Sarah tell you what Ezma said about the two recent deaths? Michael and Melissa?"

"She says Ezma didn't claim responsibility for either murder. She told me everything. She's recuperating with a shattered forearm and a hand full of broken fingers, so thanks for that. You're in over your head,

Zoey. I've seen people outside the Westons and Nolans get hurt before and here it is happening again."

"Let's not get too off track. The reason I'm asking about Bernadette is that I've noticed that she seems to be around before people die," I explain, "She was at the library the day Michael was killed and I remember seeing her across the street the day Melissa was threatening Ezma with a bat."

"Wait, are you accusing my friend of murder?" she snorts, "You can't be serious! She's this quiet, bookish gal with a soft spot for animals; she's harmless. Look, don't let Ezma try and fool you on this one. If she said anything terrible about Bernadette, it isn't true. All that aside, I need to discuss something related to all of this with you."

"And what is that?"

"Since you were with Ezma the day she killed Jack and Stella and tortured Sarah, it could potentially make you a target for other members of my family," she explains, "I don't know what they would do, but there are others as bad, if not worse, than Jack and Stella. If I tell them to leave you alone, they'll listen to me. You won't have to worry about retaliation that way. This goes away if anything like torturing my cousin happens again, you got that? Not because I'll tell them to forget it, but because they won't listen to me if it happens a second time." Back at Hunter's Ridge, Ezma and Jack mentioned an attempt on Ezma's life; firing at her through her living room window. All I have is what I've heard, but since Jack admitted to it, I have to assume that it could have happened. Maybe next time I'm at Ezma's, I'll take a closer look at the living room.

"At Hunter's Ridge, I heard Ezma and Jack mention something about an attempt on Ezma's life right after Addison disappeared," I say, "Is that the kind of thing you're talking about?"

"That's exactly what I'm talking about," Rachel nods, "I try to stay out of that nonsense as much as I can. I don't see the point in it, but as far as I know, I'm the only one in my family with that perspective."

"If what you're saying is true, then I guess there's no harm in taking you up on your offer," I reply, "Last thing I want is my dad getting hurt for something I did. I imagine I'm not the only one they'd target, am I?"

"It wouldn't surprise me," she answers, "Anything else you want to ask me?"

"Is there anything else you can tell me about Bernadette?" I ask, "I mean...she looks a lot like Ezma, I'm sure you've noticed by now. Is she related or something?" Rachel shifts her weight and uncrosses her arms.

"Yeah, she is," Rachel replies, "Back when I was friends with Ezma, I met her cousin and that's who Bernadette is. I don't remember from what side of the family or anything like that, though. I remember thinking she was Ezma's twin at first. I still struggle to tell them apart."

"So you quit speaking to Ezma, but not her cousin?" I ask.

"Yeah, it was...awkward...to say the least," she explains, "That's a whole story in itself. I don't have time to go into all the details. Anyway, I don't think she's had anything to do with the murders. She's a loyal friend, she'd never do something like that. Feel free to try talking to her if you'd like, I just don't think you're going to find anything interesting. If Ezma isn't the one who killed my sister, then we'll have to try something else."

"What do you mean?"

"I mean we'll have to look back on everything that's happened so far, see if there's anything we might have missed," she explains, "Of course, that means talking to Ezma and I don't know how much of that I can stomach. Even so, I want to know who killed my sister. This doesn't mean I drop her as a suspect, though. Deal?" She holds out her hand and I heave a sigh.

"Fine, whatever you want," I sigh, "I don't want my dad getting hurt and I'm sure you don't want anymore bloodshed either, right?"

"If I hear anything, I'll let you know," she says, starting to walk away, "Be careful, Zoey." She walks off and disappears through the front doors.

Chapter 18

I don't see Bernadette much throughout the day; only in the hallways a couple of times. Lisa Trent spots me for the first time since the fight and glares at me from across the cafeteria, still sporting a black eye and bruises around her neck. I almost wish she was the murderer, then at least I'd have an excuse to hit her again. When the day comes to an end, I start scanning the halls for Bernadette. Halfway out of the building, I spot the red ribbon bobbing along in the crowd. I try to make my way toward her, but the crowd is so dense it's next to impossible. She moves outside and I follow after her. From there I lose sight of her for a moment. When I see her again, she's even further away, rounding the corner.

I push past a few people and continue after her, quickening my pace as I go. When I reach the corner of the building, I see that she's disappeared again. Great, she probably boarded one of the buses. There's no way I can follow her at this point. I let out a sigh and begin walking to the student parking lot, feeling frustrated at not being able to catch up with Bernadette. Whatever. I guess I'll have to wait until tomorrow. Before I set foot in the parking lot, I can see Ezma's van parked nearby and Ezma herself sitting on the edge of the sidewalk.

"Hey, you're alive," she smiles, standing up, "Did you happen to catch Rachel today?"

"Yeah, I did," I nod, following her to the van, "Went better than expected. Didn't lose my temper like I worried I might."

"Did you happen to talk to Bernadette at all?"

"I tried catching up to her a minute ago, but I lost her near the buses," I continue climbing into the van, "Rachel says she still considers you a suspect in Michael and Melissa's deaths. Other than that she seems willing to cooperate to some extent." Ezma starts the engine and begins backing out of the lot.

"Meaning what?"

"It means she'll tell me if she hears anything new or useful, and also that she would be at least somewhat fine with helping us figure out who's behind the recent murders," I explain, "That's pretty much it. She talked about Bernadette a little, but nothing all that important." Once we pull up in Ezma's driveway, I climb out and she says she needs to get back to the library. I thank her for the ride and she backs into the street and drives away. I walk up to my room and sit down on the end of the bed. I'm not sure what to do with myself. I have a lot on my mind, but there's not much I can do about it right now. Maybe I should walk the library book back and find another one. I haven't pestered Ezma at work yet. I doubt she would care, but I'd rather not get her in trouble. Either way the book needs to go back. I'd rather not wait to take it on its last day. Whatever...I guess it's not like I have much else to do. I swipe the book off my pillow and drop my backpack by the foot of the bed.

Before I leave, I make a quick stop in the kitchen to grab something to eat. My appetite seems to be coming back and my stomach feels like it's full of pins. Dad's left the newspaper sitting on the table again. I glance through it, searching for anything new that might be relevant to me. Sure enough I find an article that mentions my mother is missing. Last seen at the motel where she was kidnapped. I still haven't asked Ezma about that; if she has any plan to deal with my mother's body. I hear what sounds like a bus stop near the house and look up from the paper.

I peer out the kitchen window to see the school bus sitting along the opposite side of the street. What's it doing here? I'm the only one on this street who's in high school. At least that's what I thought. It begins to pull away and I notice someone familiar standing on the sidewalk. It's Bernadette. She's facing the end of the street and staring down at her phone. She pockets it and begins walking down the street. I race out the front door and close it behind me. What do I do now? I can't just chase her down, she doesn't even know me. I walk to the front gate and step out onto the sidewalk, keeping my eye on her the entire time.

I don't know why I'm even bothering. If I want to say something to her I can wait till tomorrow; but what is she doing here? I don't think she lives around here. I've seen her across the street a few times, but she was just talking to people. Every time it looked like something quick and formal. I start after her, making certain to stay out of her line of sight. She stops at the end of the street and turns to face the Becketts' old house. Boarded up and deserted; a constant reminder of the horrors that took place within. Before I can do or say anything, she trots off through the side gate and into the backyard.

For a moment I consider walking away. I mean, yeah I'm curious, but I'd rather not stalk her. I stand there for a moment going over the options in my head. I don't know what compels me to do it, but I decide to follow her. I stop at the gate and glance around to see if anyone is watching. I sneak to the side of the house and stand near the edge of the building. It sounds like she's trying to pry the door open. I hear the cracking of wood and the sound of the back door swinging open. She steps into the house right as I glance around the corner. It's only for a second, but I glimpse a crowbar in one of her hands and a flashlight in the other. Is she just one of those thrill seekers who break in from time to time?

I stoop below the windows and move toward the door. I can hear her walking further and further away, her footsteps fading as she goes. Glancing through the doorway, I find that it's difficult to see. Even if I had a flashlight, it would just give me away. I make my way inside and be sure to stay off to the side and out of her way. I follow her through the dining room and toward the living room, all the while dreading the moment I might step on a loose floorboard. The house looks as if it was abandoned right after the killings. That alone has me dreading what I might find in here. Bernadette pauses in the living room and I crouch behind a sofa, holding my breath. She moves the flashlight around the room and I duck out of sight as the beam swings toward me.

"I should burn this place down..." Bernadette mutters, "Doubt anyone will miss it." She turns and continues down the hallway, looking into the individual rooms as she goes. I step out from behind the couch and follow her once she vanishes into a room at the end of the hall. Halfway down the hallway, I freeze and panic when I realize she's coming back out of the room. My split second decision leads me to dart into the nearest room as quietly as I can. The flashlight beam washes over the walls and I duck behind a bed. I can see Bernadette out in the hallway, glancing at her phone. I take mine out of my pocket and set it to silent. Last thing I need is someone calling me while I'm in here.

Bernadette shakes her head, appearing frustrated. She turns and walks back into the room she was in. While my phone is still out, I use the screen as a makeshift flashlight and shine it around on the carpet and wall behind me. It doesn't take me long to regret it. It's faded from the years, but blood spatters are still visible along the walls and on the carpet. I move away from the bloodstains and toward the closet, revolted by my discovery. I'm standing where two people were butchered. Just the thought gives me the creeps. In the other room, I can hear Bernadette moving things around. Whatever it is, it sounds heavy. I can hear it scraping across the hardwood floor. Next I hear something being dragged out of the room and I move back behind the bed.

Bernadette drags a rug out of the room and pushes it into a bathroom across the hall. She kicks it a few times to get it to stay put before going back into the room. What is she doing in there? Little over a minute passes and I hear something metallic clack on the hardwood. The flashlight beam catches the wall and I duck down until she passes. Her footsteps fade as she heads toward the back door. Maybe now I can see what it was she was doing. I move out in the hallway, again using my phone as a flashlight. It's difficult to see very far, even with the screen's brightness level turned all the way up. Once inside the room, I start looking around.

I can see where the rug she moved used to be. The dust around the edges is wiped away where she dragged it into the hallway, and caked on in layers everywhere else. A dresser appears to have been pushed toward the wall, probably to get it off the rug. What I find most peculiar is the fact that one of the boards in the floor has been removed. Upon closer inspection, I see that it's a secret compartment built into the floor. Bernadette must have removed whatever was inside. I assume it was whatever made the metallic clunking sound earlier. My discovery leaves me with even more questions. If she'd been in here before and used the compartment to store something, then why would it just now be disturbed? And why break open the door if you'd been in here recently? Wouldn't you just go back inside the way you came? She knew what she was looking for and where to find it...which would mean that she may have been here prior to the murders. Come to think of it, I remember Ezma telling me she had a cousin who was here before then. Could Bernadette be who Ezma was referring to?

I need to tell Ezma what I found. The deafening silence in this old house is giving me the creeps. I walk back out into the hallway with my mind racing, and a flurry of questions yet to be answered. I imagine Ezma will be interested to know that her cousin was looking around the Becketts' old house, whatever the reason might be. Once I get to the dining room, I'm taken by surprise. Bernadette rushes up behind me and puts a knife to my throat. My heart is pounding as I struggle to keep calm.

"Is there a reason you're following me?" Bernadette demands. I can feel myself beginning to sweat.

"I wasn't," I lie.

"Bullshit," she snarls, increasing pressure on the blade, "Which one was it, huh? Who paid you?"

"What are you talking about?"

"Don't fucking lie to me!" Bernadette hisses, "I know you were paid off! They always are! They look for someone who can get to me without raising suspicion, then they send them after me! Now tell me who hired you!"

"I don't know what you're talking about, I swear! No one hired me to do anything!"

"I'm gonna give you one last chance to start telling me the truth," she snarls, "You got that? One more shot. You fuck it up and I'll cut you!"

"I'm not lying to you!" I insist, "I live across the street, I just saw you walk in here!"

"Wait a minute...where at?"

"Across the street, you whackjob!" I snarl. She removes the knife from my throat and prods me in the back with it.

"Get moving, outside where I can see you," Bernadette orders, "Keep your hands on the back of your head. No sudden movements." I do as she requests and begin walking toward the door. Once outside, she spins me around and places the blade to my throat again.

"Wait a minute, I know you..." she says, her eyes widening, "You're that girl who was following me today. You're Zoey, right? Ezma's friend? Crap..."

"Yeah," I choke, "Is that bad?"

"It is for me," Bernadette mutters, removing the knife, "How the hell am I supposed to explain this to Ezma?" She places the knife back in a sheath under her coat and goes back into the house.

"Stay here for a minute," she says, "I left something in there." She disappears into the house and I'm left more confused than ever. That little outburst has me doubting that she's as harmless as I was told. Moments later, she comes back out of the house with a tin box under her arm. It looks like it could have fit in that compartment. She closes the door and places her hand against it with her head bowed. She stands there for almost half a minute, before turning to face me. This is the first time I've been able to really look at her. I can see why Rachel once thought Ezma had a twin.

"Come on, let's go..." she murmurs, walking past me, "...and for what it's worth, I'm sorry..."

"How did you know where to find that box?" I ask. She ignores my question and continues to the sidewalk. Moments later, she disappears around the corner. I consider following her, but think better of it. Whatever is going on, it seems best to leave her alone for now.

Chapter 19

I end up walking all the way to the library without paying much attention to my surroundings. So much so that I almost step out in front of traffic at a crosswalk. I'm still a little shaken up. What do I do now? I suppose all I can do is talk to Ezma about it. Who was Bernadette talking about? People following her, paying them to find her? Is she serious or paranoid? I have to find out what's going on with her. Once at the library, I walk inside and toss the book in the return bin. Right as I do so, I hear Ezma calling to me.

"Hey, Zoey!" Ezma calls, waving as she trots toward me, "Come to visit me at work?"

"Something like that. Are you still on the clock?"

"No, I'm heading out," she explains, "Is something wrong? You seem a little shaken up."

"That obvious?"

"What happened? Someone attack you again?" she asks.

"How about we walk and talk?" I suggest, "I'd rather not discuss it here." We walk outside and start walking toward the parking lot.

"I had a run-in with Bernadette," I explain, "I found her outside the old Beckett house. I followed her into the house and heard her muttering about wanting to burn the place down, and how she doubted anyone would miss it."

"That's odd," she replies.

"So, I went into one of the bedrooms, turned out it was the murder scene, judging from the bloodstains all over the place, kind of gave me the creeps, but that's not the point. She goes and drags this rug out of the next room over, then before that I heard her moving a dresser around. When she left the room, there was a little compartment in the floor that was left open. I know she took a tin box out of it, but I haven't a clue what was in it."

"Do you think she was storing something in the house?" Ezma asks. We've just arrived at her van and we both climb in.

"I thought about that too, like maybe she'd explored it before and wanted to hide something, but it didn't look that way. The room looked like it had just been disturbed, like no one had been in there in years. According to what Rachel said, she's only been here for a little while, so that seems unlikely." We pull out of the lot and start driving down the main street.

"So what happened after that? What shook you up?"

"After I looked in the room she'd been moving things around in, I figured she was gone and I didn't need to stick around any longer, you know? I'd heard her leave, or so I thought, so I went back to the door. Halfway there, she jumps out and puts a knife to my throat, starts going on about people being paid to find her, demands to know who paid me off, then she marches me out the back door after I told her I live across the street. She knew who I was, asked me if I was your friend. I asked her if that was a problem, then she said it was for her and muttered something about having to explain herself to you."

"Explain herself to me?"

"I don't know what she meant by that. Before she left I asked her how she knew where to find the tin box. She ignored me and just walked off. I know you told me about a cousin who visited the house prior to the murders once before. Was Bernadette that cousin?"

"I can't remember if it was her or my cousin Renee," Ezma admits, "My memory is a little fuzzy on that one. Bernadette was around enough, so it's possible. She's from my dad's side of the family, so that would give her reason to be there, since she'd be a blood relative of my half-sister too. That's really odd she threatened you like that. She always seemed like the last person who would ever do something like that. Scares me to think of what may have changed. Whatever happened to make her do that must have really taken a toll on her. I'm sorry that happened to you."

"Don't worry about it," I assure her, "She apologized afterward. I'm not planning on holding it against her."

* * *

That night, I'm back in my room, thinking about the incident with Bernadette. Even with what she did today, I find it hard to place her as Melissa and Michael's killer. She just sounded scared and somewhat paranoid. She had a knife and was threatening to slit my throat with it. The murders were all the result of a combination of an unknown drug injected into the neck and subsequent strangulation. If she was going to kill me, she could have done so right there in the house without anyone to witness it. I haven't had any extended interactions with Bernadette, but what happened to the two victims seems to be the work of someone different. Regardless, I need to keep an eye on her, just in case. I'm going to have to suck it up and try talking to Bernadette at least one more time. She knows something, even if it might not be directly linked to the murders. I need to find out what that is.

The next day, I find myself sitting in class, trying to think of what to say. No matter how many times I go over things in my head, it all comes back to strolling up to her and starting a conversation somehow. Yeah...good luck with that. The bell rings and everyone starts making their way to the cafeteria. Like usual, I go a different route, making my way to the back of the building. Somewhere quiet where I can think. So far it seems like no one really cares that I go back there. Just as long as I don't leave campus, I doubt I'll get in much trouble. It's not like it's deserted, though. Students sometimes walk through the pair of double doors where I sit; on their way to the portables outside. None of them pay any attention to me, so it all works out fine.

I don't have an appetite at the moment, otherwise I'm sure I'd be digging through my bag for something to eat. Near the doors is a loading platform with a small staircase on one side. That's where I'm sitting at the moment. Back against the wall, in the corner at the top of the stairs. I should be searching the cafeteria, looking to see if Bernadette's around. She seems to be a loner from what I've seen. Doesn't seem all that surprising, considering she's inclined to pull knives on people. The nearby doors open up and someone walks out. I turn my head to see that it's Bernadette. She looks to her left, then right at me.

"Oh...hey..." she murmurs.

"You wouldn't happen to have a knife on you...would you?" I ask, half-joking.

"Oh...that, um...no." She shakes her head and shifts her weight.

"Did you want to talk to me or something?" I ask.

"Well, first thing was I wanted to apologize for what happened," she says, taking a step forward, "Um...you mind if I join you?"

"Be my guest," I say with a shrug. She walks up the stairs and sits a few feet away from me along the wall.

"Not the most comfortable spot, is it?" she says, adjusting her back on the wall a few times, "Wall's all jagged."

"Better than the noise in the cafeteria," I reply, "So what the hell was that yesterday?"

"My paranoia getting the better of me," she answers, "I don't even know where to start. There's a lot to this and I'm not even sure you're going to believe me."

"Try me."

"I knew Myra Beckett," she explains, "I'm her cousin, Bernadette Blanche. I imagine you're wondering what I took from the house, aren't you?"

"Yeah, kind of."

"It wasn't much," she continues, "Just some old photos and mementos she kept. Things I passed off to her while she was living there. Her parents were disgusting people. How much do you know about that place? About what happened in that house?"

"Quite a bit," I answer, "I've researched it a fair amount."

"Then you're aware of the abuse my cousin endured?"

"I heard there were allegations of rape and prostitution," I reply, "They beat her and kept her locked in that room." The more I look at this girl, the more of Ezma I see in her. She's got the same jet-black hair, green eyes, and prominent cheekbones. The differences seem to be her nose, a little wider than Ezma's, her thinner lips, and bushier eyebrows.

"That they did," she confirms, "Those things in the floor compartment, I gave those to her when her parents weren't paying attention. I tried to convince mine that something was wrong, but they didn't believe me. Even when the Becketts tried to bring me into it."

"Bring you into it?"

"One day while I was visiting, I witnessed an argument between

Myra and her father. She was ten at the time, I was eight. This was the first of six days I was there. My parents were always fighting with one another and when my dad walked out on us around that time, my mom decided to hand me off to the Becketts while she took some time for herself. That first day was bad, but it was just the start of what was to come. I had heard shouting and snarling, that kind of thing, so I went to see what was wrong. I was that kind of kid. Not really afraid of anything, just curious."

"So what happened?" I ask.

"This gets kind of dark, are you sure you don't mind listening?"

"It's fine," I insist, "Go on."

"If you're sure," she sighs, tilting her head back, "Anyway...so I walked in and her step-father, David, he shouts at me, asks me what the hell I think I'm doing, that sort of thing. Smacked me right across the face, knocked me on my rear. I was in shock. I didn't know what to do. That was the first time anyone had ever hit me. He shouts at me to stand up, to get out of the room, then when I continued to sit there, not knowing how to react, he grabbed me by my hair and dragged me out of the room. By that point I was crying and screaming. More out of fear than anything. The next day I realized I had a bruise on my cheek. That got David and his wife all riled up. They told me to tell my mother that I got hit with a ball. That Myra and I were playing catch in the yard. I asked him why and he said he'd hit me again if I said anything different."

"Jeez..."

"Then on the third day I was there," Bernadette continues, "Myra spilled something in the kitchen and they threw her in her room. Locked her up and left her in there. I protested and they tossed me in with her. Things just got even worse from there. That was the day I found out what they were really doing to her."

"You mean selling her?" I inquire. She nods and exhales.

"What kind of sick people do that to a child?" Bernadette mutters, "Anyway...David came back down the hall, unlocked the door and came in with two creeps. Money was exchanged and I'd had enough. I tried to run and David grabbed me, shoved me back in the room and hit me so hard I passed out. When I woke up, Myra was curled up on her bed, bawling her eyes out. The next day or so is just a blur to me.

All I can remember is Myra crying so hard that she fell asleep. I was in and out of consciousness for a while. I had nightmares until I left, and for a while after that too. I didn't dare tell my mother what happened. I was terrified that something would happen to me or Myra. I didn't talk about it until Ezma's mother came by a few years later...right before the murders."

"Why'd she come by?"

"She'd seen Myra trying to escape one night before that," Bernadette explains, "She wanted to know if my mother had seen anything strange over there. At the time, she hadn't spoken to the Becketts in a few years. She didn't buy the story about the ball. She accused them of abusing me and I never saw Myra again after that. I never admitted to being hit until the night Ezma's mother was there. Everything just came pouring out. My mother was furious, but as much as she wanted the Becketts dead, she didn't want to spend the rest of her life in jail, and thus abandon me in the process. Especially after what I'd just told her. Ezma's mother understood, but my own mother swore she wouldn't say anything about what Ezma's mother had proposed. Hell, she encouraged her. I still remember my mother telling her to make their deaths slow and painful. She kept her word. Never said a thing to law enforcement about the meeting."

"So...Rachel said you're her friend," I begin, trying to steer the conversation in another direction, "How come you're...you know..."

"Being friendly with the Nolans?" she finishes.

"Well...yeah," I say with a shrug.

"Have Ezma or Rachel said anything about me?" she asks, "Anything regarding my friendship with Rachel?"

"A little, but not very much," I reply, "It sounded like there was some bad blood between you and Ezma."

"Yeah, there is," she sighs, tilting her head back, "I had hoped that maybe I could talk to her at some point...clear the air. Problem is I never seem to get around to it. Truth be told, I still feel terrible about it, and I'm a little afraid to approach her after not having spoken for so long. Here I was at the center of a falling out between two close friends, not knowing what to do. Ezma acted like she didn't care that I was still Rachel's friend, but I know she did."

"What happened between them?" I ask.

"Something about Ezma changed about two years ago," Bernadette explains, "It was like she just snapped. She had a lot that went wrong in her life. Her parents weren't exactly angels, but at least they weren't anywhere near as bad as Myra's parents. After they died, Ezma was distraught. Losing your parents when you're a kid...it'd be rough on anyone. I think Brian's death is what changed her the most. Yeah, the two of them were at each other's throats more than I care to admit, but they were in that whole mess together. Once he was gone, Ezma started to change. It's like she's just not herself anymore. If you'd known her before two years ago, I'm sure you'd see it too. It's difficult to put it all into words."

"I think I understand," I say, "How does all that tie in with you and Rachel?"

"Did she ever tell you about Rachel's cousin supposedly attacking her and Brian one night?" she asks.

"Yeah she told me the whole story," I nod, "Rachel shared her version of events too. To be honest, I have no idea who's telling the truth about that."

"That makes two of us," Bernadette replies, "Ezma was expecting me to be on her side about it and Rachel was doing the same. Eventually I told them to deal with it themselves since I didn't want to be involved. Around that time was when Ezma and Rachel started becoming frustrated with one another. Things had been rough between them for at least a couple of months by that point. It wasn't long after that when the rest of the Nolans started giving her grief too. I don't know what was going through Rachel's mind, but she walked away, presumably because she didn't want things to get worse than they already were. I tried to explain that to Ezma, but she wasn't having it. She decided that Rachel was a traitor and didn't want anything to do with her after that."

"Wow, that's depressing."

"Right?" she says, "I know I felt bad, but I can't imagine how hard it was on Ezma and Rachel. Personally I think Rachel had it the worst. Ezma was so wrapped up in her anger that it sort of protected her, you know? Rachel's never been that way. She's always been pretty calm, despite getting easily frustrated nowadays. At least that's how it looks so far. I don't think she has a mean bone in her body, but my God...her aunt is terrible. Probably not happy about having to take care of her brother's kids."

"What do you mean?" I ask.

"Rachel's aunt, her father's sister, she's sort of taken over for Rachel's parents since they're in prison for at least a few more years. If you know about the Beckett murders, I imagine you can guess why Rachel's parents are locked up."

"There was something about Nolans and tax evasion or something, I don't remember exactly what I read," I say, "I just know Ezma's dad brought evidence against them." Bernadette nods and takes a moment to sneeze into her elbow. She sniffs a couple of times and clears her throat.

"Yeah, Ezma's dad worked for the Nolans at one of their stores, didn't really get along with Rachel's dad for reasons I'm not familiar with," Bernadette explains, "So that's why and how he had the evidence in the first place. Kind of his way of making sure he could screw over the Nolans if he ever felt like they did it to him first. Kind of petty, but I understand the reasoning. Rachel's dad is kind of a snob and his sister isn't much better. Melissa was pretty terrible too. Almost like a clone of her aunt. Borderline psychopath, if not a full one. Can't say I was sorry to see her go."

"I saw you across the street the day she was threatening Ezma," I recall, "You were sitting on the front step of the old Beckett house."

"Yeah, I saw that whole thing," she replies, "I'm sorry you two had to put up with that. I heard Melissa threatening to do it the day before. I was over at their place with Rachel and Melissa was up in arms over what happened to Rachel's car. Rachel was trying to talk her out of going to Ezma's. Then when Melissa ran off and did it, Rachel was livid. She said it was idiotic and childish, and of course Melissa didn't like that. She felt like she was defending her sister and here Rachel was sounding all "ungrateful" as Melissa put it. Rachel stormed off after that. Went right out the front door and out the front gate. I followed her and she ranted about it for a few minutes or so."

"What'd she say about it?" I ask, "I mean...if you don't mind me asking."

"No, no it's fine," she assures me, "I don't remember every word, but she said something about an accident Melissa was in when she was eleven. Hit by a truck while she was on her bike. Barely survived it.

Rachel said something about wishing Melissa had died. It was kind of sad in a way. I mean, I didn't grow up around any siblings myself, but I can't imagine being so frustrated with one that I wished death upon them."

"Yeah, I'm in the same boat," I say, "Only child."

"Well, there's something we have in common," she smiles, "Although, there is a rumor in my family that I have a sister. Story seems a little crazy, though. I think it's just something someone made up."

"What kind of story?" I inquire.

"Well, what happened was one of my cousins, he went and joined the Navy right out of high school, and before he left, he was telling his older sister that he'd heard from our late great-aunt Edith that Ezma and I are twins and that we were both born to Ezma's parents. Apparently they weren't planning on having two kids and couldn't afford it. So the story goes that they split the two of us up and tried to keep it all under wraps. They didn't want me to feel like I'd been abandoned, so they told me I was Ezma's cousin and that my mother was my biological one. I can't tell you how many times I've looked at old photos of Ezma's mother and the woman who raised me, comparing them over and over again. Ezma doesn't really look all that much like her mother and I don't look much like mine. Similar, yeah, but that's about it. The cousin who supposedly heard that, he's known for telling whoppers and stirring the pot, so that's another reason I don't believe any of it. The only two things that still make me wonder is that our birthdays are only one day apart, December 8th, mine, and Ezma's, December 9th."

"Do you know the exact times?" I ask.

"Ezma sometime around eleven and me close to one," she answers, "Still, we don't look like any twins I've ever seen. I mean, I've seen fraternal twins who look nothing alike, then identical ones and we sure as hell aren't that. Too many subtle differences if you look close enough. Different lips and noses, granted it's not very noticeable. Plus she's an inch taller than me too. Or at least she was the whole time we were growing up. I don't know if I caught up or not."

"Could be half-identical or something," I say.

"I've never heard of that. Half-identical? Is that a thing?"

"Yeah, but I don't know a whole lot about it," I admit, "I have a pair of twins in my family, but they're mirror-image twins. Identical, but also sort of different. Something that's on the right side of one's face is on the left of the other's, that kind of thing."

"Hmm...I'll have to look into that sometime," she says.

"So, on the topic of siblings, and I can't believe I'm asking this, but... how's Rachel holding up?" I ask, "Can't be easy losing her sister the way she did."

"She's not having an easy time," Bernadette answers, "Rachel's been pretty shaken up lately. She felt terrible after Melissa died. She said, 'Well...I guess I got my wish.' Depressing, isn't it?"

"Yeah, no kidding."

"She's still beating herself up over what she said, not cutting herself much slack. It's sad to watch. Why can't you believe you asked me how she's doing?"

"Let's just say she and I don't get along," I answer, "She's got it out for Ezma and it pisses me off."

"I hear you on that one," Bernadette replies, "I know she's upset and feels like she got the short end of the stick, but still, that's my cousin... or possible sister, I don't know. You know what I mean. Anyway, I've been thinking that maybe it's time I stop being a coward and just talk to Ezma. Maybe I'll do that today."

"If you wanna follow me to the parking lot after school, she'll probably be there," I suggest, "She often is."

"Sounds good to me," Bernadette says, "Probably miss my bus, though. I guess I'm walking again. I don't expect a ride from her with the way things are between us."

"Before I forget to ask, there were a few other things I wanted to know," I say, "You know...about yesterday."

"Shoot."

"You said something about being paranoid earlier," I continue, "You didn't really go into detail."

"Oh...that," she sighs, "That's a long story. Well...after David Beckett was killed, there were people who still remained loyal to him. They liked being able to get away with whatever the hell they wanted. They were taking dirty money to keep their mouths shut, abusing their power for shits and giggles...that all stopped once Beckett wasn't around anymore. They started a crackdown on police corruption about five months after his death. Pissed a lot of people off. The crackdown started with the police hunting down and catching the sick fucks who victimized Myra. Lot of people lost their jobs, some went to prison, it messed up a few families. Small price to pay if you ask me."

"And so those people still come after you?"

"Sometimes," she says, "Now with the murders that have happened here recently, I'm more on edge than ever. Don't forget, it was the Nolans who helped bring down the Becketts. My enemies want the Nolans dead just as much as the Westons...and me."

"Ezma and I have been trying to figure out what's going on with that," I explain, "That's actually why I was following you yesterday. Not that I thought you had anything to do with it, it's just...well..."

"Well what?" she asks, raising an eyebrow.

"We both noticed that you were nearby before both of the murders," I say, feeling a little bad for saying it.

"Oh so you do think I had something to do with it," she chuckles, "Seriously though...I still think about that. Some cop came and spoke to me the other day after the library incident. Said someone had mentioned I was at the library at the time. To be honest with you, it wasn't anything to do with that. I was just trying to get up the gumption to say something to Ezma. I don't really know how to start that conversation, so I started overthinking it, you know?"

"Well, maybe after today, you won't have to anymore," I smile.

Chapter 20

At the end of the school day, I meet Bernadette outside in the front of the building. It takes me a minute to find her, but she soon calls out to me with a wave. She's standing near the flagpole, keeping her distance from a few others who are working to lower the flag for the day.

"Hey, you showed up," I say.

"Not gonna lie, I thought about leaving," she admits, "I don't expect this to go all that well." We start making our way to the parking lot while we speak.

"Why do you think that?"

"I just don't think she'll forgive me for it," she explains, "God this is going to be awkward."

"Don't overthink it." Sure enough, Ezma is waiting near her van. Sitting on the edge of the sidewalk, a cigarette in her hand. In her other hand she's holding her phone, engrossed in whatever she's looking at. Some ashes fall from the end of the cigarette as we approach. She looks up, pockets her phone, and gets to her feet, tossing the cigarette on the ground in front of her. She puts it out with the toe of her boot and smiles. The three of us stand around for an uncomfortable amount of time, waiting for someone to say something. Bernadette seems like she's wanting to run away and keeps wringing her fingers while looking in various directions. I clear my throat and take a deep breath.

"So...um...are either of you going to say something?" I ask.

"Well, I guess I'll go first," Bernadette says with a heavy exhale, "Ezma, I'm sorry. I know when we stopped talking, you made it sound like you were fine with me maintaining a friendship with Rachel... but you weren't. I didn't know what to do in that situation, we'd both been friends with Rachel for years, I didn't want to throw it away and leave her alone because of something between the two of you. It's been bothering me ever since it happened. I wish I could go back and fix everything, but I can't. I'm sorry. For everything. I would like nothing more than to put this behind us." A tense moment of silence follows as Bernadette finishes speaking. Ezma takes a moment to think, then holds out her hand. Bernadette shakes it and the two of them step back.

"I'm sorry too," Ezma apologizes, "What I did was unfair to you. I shouldn't have treated you the way I did. You're right, it was between me and Rachel, and instead of leaving it there, I made it your problem."

"Apology accepted," Bernadette replies.

"I have to say, I'm glad to see you in one piece," Ezma says, "I heard someone died like a year or so ago. I was worried it might have been you until I started seeing you around. Was it a rumor or something?"

"Unfortunately it isn't. Someone did die," Bernadette replies, "It was our cousin Matilda Redforde. Shot dead about two years ago."

"Jesus..." Ezma whispers, "How old was she?"

"Just turned seventeen the week before," Bernadette explains, "Disgusting. Cops were convinced it was premeditated."

"I bet the Nolans had something to do with that," Ezma mutters, "I got into a fight with one of them back when Brian was still alive. That would be around the same time Matilda died if it was around two years ago. I know the Nolans are still pissed about what my dad did to them and they're scattered all over this state and parts of the surrounding ones. Wouldn't surprise me one bit if they saw what happened here as a violation of our truce, even though one of theirs started it. Just the excuse they needed to do something heinous to one of ours."

"I thought the same thing at first," Bernadette says, "but I don't think the Nolans were in on it. I mean sure, the truce has been flimsy ever since it was first enacted, but I get the feeling that something else is going on. I mean, look at what's happened around here in a short span of time. Two dead Nolans. I doubt anyone in our family had anything to do with that. If you ask me, it's related to the crackdown the cops started in their own departments after David Beckett died. We get so caught up with what happened between our family and the Nolans that it's easy to forget that both sides still have a common enemy out there. One we can't always see."

"I take it that's why you put a knife to my throat yesterday?"

"I heard about that," Ezma says.

"Did you have to tell her about that?" Bernadette moans, clasping both hands to her face and dragging them downward, "Not exactly smart to bring that up after I just apologized for everything else."

"What prompted you to threaten her like that?" Ezma asks.

"I thought someone hired her to follow me yesterday," Bernadette explains, "Coming back to Pryor Creek has had me on edge. This is where it all started after all."

"I wanted to ask you about that," Ezma says, "Why are you all of a sudden here in Pryor Creek again? And not just that, but why are you attending school here too? I thought you lived in Westview, like fifty miles from here?"

"I did until about a year and a half ago," Bernadette explains, "I'm living in Clover Bay now. You know what place I'm talking about?"

"Yeah, I know which one," Ezma nods, "Something like fifteen miles north?"

"That's the one," Bernadette confirms, "My mother got a job there after she quit her old one in Westview and she didn't want to have to commute so far every day. Long story, but the point is she was being underpaid and some other issues, so she quit. Anyway, we moved to Clover Bay and I was attending school there for a while, until some problems arose there, things I don't want to get into right now. After that I ended up having to switch schools and came here."

"I seem to see you around here on weekends too," Ezma continues, "Why are you hanging around here so much if you live in Clover Bay?"

"Well, I do live there, but not right now," Bernadette explains, "My mother just got re-married and there's a ton of drama going on over at my house. So I asked Aunt Tillie if I could stay with her for a little while, but she doesn't have room. So instead she's paying for me to stay in a hotel on the other side of town till things cool down. I've been there for a couple of weeks now. I'm hoping I can get back home soon, but it's not looking good."

"I see," Ezma says, removing her keys from her coat pocket, "Well, if you'd like to come with us, I'd love to talk more. Do some catching up."

"Sure," Bernadette smiles, "I'd like that."

* * *

During the drive back to Ezma's, I learn that this "Aunt Tillie" is the woman who Ezma mentioned when I first met her. The aunt who's helping to support her. Once back at the house, I plop down on the couch and Bernadette trots upstairs to use the bathroom. Ezma asks me if I want anything and I decline the offer. She tells me she restocked the fridge and cupboards and to ask if I change my mind. She vanishes into the kitchen and I hear her sifting through the fridge. Moments later, her cell starts ringing and she comes back into the room. She picks it up off the coffee table and puts it to her ear.

"Hello?" she says, "This is her. Hang on a second." She covers the phone with her free hand and waves to get my attention.

"What is it?" I ask.

"I'm gonna be out in the back for a second," she explains, starting out of the room, "Just let Bernadette know so she doesn't wonder, alright?" I nod and she leaves the room. Seconds later, I hear the back door open and close. It almost slipped my mind, but there was something I meant to do. Standing up from couch, I turn and face the living room window. After pulling the curtains back, I see that one of the sections of glass seems to be newer than the others. I let the curtain fall back into place and face the wall opposite to the window. A series of picture frames are hanging from it. One by one, I start checking behind them until I find what I'm looking for. A small hole hidden behind one of them. I let the frame swing back into place and take a step back. Ezma wasn't kidding. Someone did fire a round through her window. Bernadette comes back down the stairs and I feel a mild sense of awkwardness when she catches me examining the frames.

"What's with that look?" she chuckles, coming to join me, "You look guilty."

"I just feel like I'm snooping is all," I explain, "Is this you and Ezma?" I point to a frame that shows a picture of three girls who appear to be around twelve years old. Bernadette nods and takes the frame off the wall.

"Yeah, I remember this," she replies, "Couple years before Myra's parents were killed. That's her there with us." She points to a somber, red-haired girl standing beside them.

"She looks sad," I observe.

"She often was," Bernadette says, putting the frame back on the wall, "I still remember the way people thought we were all sisters. Maybe there's a reason for that with me and Ezma, but I guess it was just the luck of the draw with Myra. If she changed her hair and didn't have freckles, we might've passed for triplets. I tried to get her to do it, but she was afraid of how her parents would react. Can't say I blame her. Where's Ezma at?"

"She's out back talking to someone," I explain, sitting down on the couch as I speak, "She got a call right after you went up stairs." She seats herself on the opposite end of the couch and stretches her arms over her head.

"Makes sense," she yawns, "Just thought I'd ask."

Ezma joins us soon after and the two of them start talking again almost right off the bat. I'm not hearing much of anything that's new to me. I take my phone out of my pocket and open the browser. What Bernadette said earlier about the shooting has piqued my interest. I'd rather be able to use an actual computer, but I guess this will suffice. I start looking around online and eventually come across an article concerning the shooting Bernadette mentioned. Before I get even a few lines down, something about their conversation catches my attention.

"Well...I do know a little about Myra," Bernadette says. Ezma has just asked if she knows what happened to her.

"Anything you can tell me, anything at all, I'd very much appreciate it," Ezma replies.

"All I know for certain is that she was still in Pryor Creek for about eight months after the murders," Bernadette explains, "I heard she was placed in foster care for that time. Poor gal...her luck just never seemed to improve. She ended up being abused there too. She lost the sight in her left eye because of it. I don't know specifics, but I heard they stuck a needle in her eye as punishment."

"Once or on more than one occasion?" Ezma asks.

"They made a habit of it," Bernadette explains, "I know because she told me herself."

"So you've spoken to her recently?" Ezma inquires.

"Yeah, several times," Bernadette nods, "Last time was a long time ago, though. So maybe not recently. About two years ago. She's living around here somewhere; or she was at the time. Can't say for sure where she is now. Last we spoke, I found that she ran away from her foster parents' house a few weeks before she turned eighteen. I have no idea where she's living, but she must be getting by somehow. She has a cell, but it could be one of those pre-paid ones for all I know. Could've stolen all she needed for that just about anywhere."

"Do you still have the number?" Ezma asks.

"Yeah, but all I ever get these days is her voicemail," Bernadette explains, "Here, let me see your phone. I'll put the number in there." I look back at my phone and try to open the browser again. It closes out and I let out a sigh. I guess it's not that important.

* * *

Later that night, I'm back in my room, still curious to find out as much as I can about the events Bernadette described earlier that day. How deep does this go? I glance at the clock and exhale my held breath. It's almost nine o' clock. I'm staring at the article that wouldn't stay loaded on my phone. What I've found is as confusing as it is unsettling. The article states that there was a shooting, just as Bernadette described, but it also says that Bernadette was the one who died. One sentence reads: "...17-year-old Bernadette Blanche was gunned down in a grocery store parking lot..."

What the hell is going on? Why does it say Bernadette was the one killed? If the article is right, then who was talking with us today? I open a new browser tab and start looking for information on Matilda Redforde. I have to sift through a few articles, but after about ten minutes, I find one about Matilda. Matilda Redforde, dead at eighteen from an "apparent suicide." Her "body was discovered lying beneath a bridge. Redforde showed symptoms of severe paranoia before her death, claiming that there were people out to kill her." There's a photo of both girls on each of the articles and the one of Bernadette looks just like the Bernadette I said goodbye to only hours before. Did she fake her death? Or is she an impostor?

With everything that's going on between these families, it seems likely that she could have felt the need to fake her death. Regardless of whatever is going on, she lied to us. If she's not really Bernadette, then how did she know about the compartment in the floor? According to her, there were only two people who knew about it. Bernadette and Myra. So does that mean...? No, that's ridiculous...right? I tap my fingers on the desk for almost a minute, thinking about what to do next. I take my phone off the desk and dial Ezma's number. With bated breath, I wait as the phone rings.

"Hello?"

"Hey Ezma, it's Zoey. Listen, I'm sorry to bother you so late, but there's something I need to talk to you about."

"Well, nine isn't what I'd consider to be late, but what is it?" she asks.

"It's about Bernadette," I answer, "I found something strange. There are several articles that say she was killed in a shooting. The same shooting our Bernadette was talking about today. The one she said killed Matilda."

"What? Wait, I need to see this for myself, can you send me the links?"

"I'm sending them right now," I reply, "I don't know what to do from here. She's lying to us, whoever she is." Several minutes later, Ezma opened the links I sent and glanced over the articles. She's just as bewildered as I am, and neither of us are sure of what to do next.

"There's not much we can do at the moment," Ezma sighs, "Just don't mention it to her. We don't want to arouse her suspicion."

"Why keep playing this game with her, though? Shouldn't we try to find out who she really is?"

"We will, but we don't want her to run off before then," Ezma explains. I suppose that makes sense. I think back to the picture on the wall at Ezma's house, the one of Ezma, Bernadette, and Myra, and what Bernadette said about Myra looking similar to them.

"So, while I was at your house today, Bernadette was telling me about one of the photos on your wall. The one with you, her, and Myra in it. This is going to sound kind of far-fetched, but...I noticed how similar she looks to you and Bernadette."

"Are you saying what I think you're saying?" Ezma asks.

"Yes, I'm wondering if our Bernadette might actually be Myra," I explain, "I mean, if Bernadette and Matilda are both dead, then who does that leave?"

"No one," Ezma replies, "It was just us three who looked alike. As far as I know, no one else in our family comes close. Myra had brown eyes, red hair, and freckles. I guess she could just dye her hair, but the other two..."

"Contacts and makeup," I say, "My aunt uses contacts that change her eye color."

"I would assume that someone hiding freckles would be a little more concerned with touching up their makeup," Ezma says, "I didn't see her do anything like that today."

"She did use the restroom right after we got to your house," I point out, "She could have been doing it then."

"True, she could have. Find her again tomorrow and try to think of some way to smudge her makeup. Something that seems like an innocent mistake."

"And what would that be?"

"I haven't the slightest clue," Ezma admits, "Look, I'll try to think of something too. Just give it some thought. If I come up with anything, I'll let you know."

Chapter 21

The next morning, Ezma drops me off as usual and I head into the school building, still uncertain of what sort of stunt I'm going to pull. Bernadette is nowhere in sight. I'm not sure if that's good or bad at this point. Part of me wants her nearby so I can keep an eye on her. Before I fell asleep last night, I started going over everything I could think of. Everything I know about Bernadette so far. While she was in the Beckett house, she mentioned that she'd like to burn the place down. That was before she even knew I was there. Still that doesn't prove anything. From the sound of it, there's more than one person who'd like to see that place burn to the ground. Right before I get to the door, I hear Rachel's voice. I furrow my brow and roll my eyes.

"Hey, can I talk to you for a sec?" Rachel says as I turn to face her.

"What could it possibly be now?" I groan.

"I'm going to assume that means yes," Rachel replies, "It won't take long, I promise."

"What is it?"

"I caught a few Beckett Sympathizers poking around near my place last night," she explains, "I just wanted to warn you that they might be around your neighborhood too."

"Beckett Sympathizers?" I repeat.

"Corrupt cops and other folks who benefited from the kickbacks and privileges David Beckett afforded them before he was killed," Rachel explains, "There's no telling how many are still around, but those that remain are still pretty sore about the whole thing." Bernadette never called them Beckett Sympathizers, but I wonder if these are the same people she was talking about?

"And why should I be concerned?" I ask, "Not to sound naive, I'm just looking for details."

"The police departments in not only this county, but the surrounding ones, are still cleaning up the network of corrupt officers. You never know which ones might be old cronies of Beckett. They hide it well and the decent cops struggle to identify them. I know the two I saw yesterday to be some of the corrupt ones. Cybil Harris and Jerry Benson. Remember those names." Harris and Benson. They were the two officers who spoke to me after Michael's death. Harris was the one threatening Rachel at the gas station. I remember the names on their pins, "C. Harris" and "J. Benson." I describe them both to Rachel and she nods.

"That's them," she confirms, "Those are the only two I know of for sure. Avoid them if you can and don't say anything to them about what's been going on, even if they pressure you."

"And why are you telling me this?" I inquire, "I thought you were still upset about what happened to Sarah?"

"I am, but this is something outside of that," Rachel explains, "The Beckett Sympathizers are a threat to everyone, regardless of whether or not they're involved in this ridiculous feud. Just make sure to keep an eye out for them. Here, you mind if I see your phone for a second?" She removes hers from her coat pocket and holds her free hand out in front of her.

"You're not planning on throwing it or something, are you?" I ask, half-joking. She shakes her head.

"No, of course not," she insists, "I'm not that terrible. I just wanted to put my number in it."

"Why?" I ask, handing my phone to her. She hands me hers and starts typing her number into mine.

"I'm trying to be better than my awful family," she explains, "I've said to Ezma at least a few times before that we should be focused on the Sympathizers, not each other. That's all in the past as far as I'm concerned. Even so, my family, Jack and Stella the worst two offenders among them, decided that revenge was more important. I know it's terrible, but I'm somewhat relieved they aren't around anymore. I feel like only Sarah and I have our heads on straight. Within our own family, of course. Overall, you seem decent, and I'd prefer to limit the causalities, so to speak. I'll call you if I find out anything you need to know. Feel free to do the same for me if you'd like. Give me a call when Ezma decides on a time for us to talk." We exchange phones and I pocket mine. She turns to leave, but I stop her.

"One more thing," I say, "I want to talk to you about Bernadette."

"What about her?" Rachel asks.

"What do you know about her?"

"Why are you asking me this?" she inquires.

"Yesterday she mentioned a shooting that took the life of her cousin Matilda," I explain, "The problem is when I looked it up, the articles I found all said that it was Bernadette who died. Matilda's death was never linked to Bernadette's and assumed to be a suicide."

"You can't be serious. How and why would she do that? I've known her for years, I'm telling you, she's exactly like the Bernadette I've always known. There must be a misunderstanding. I'll need to see these articles you're talking about," Rachel replies, crossing her arms, "I can't just take your word on something this serious."

"That's fine, I'd be skeptical too," I say, shifting my weight, "Have you noticed her obsessing over her makeup or anything?"

"Well, she does check it every so often," Rachel shrugs, "No more than any other girl. Why?"

"I'll explain later, but other than that, have you noticed any odd habits?" She takes a moment to think about it before she responds.

"There is one thing I noticed," Rachel says, "She flinches when people make sudden movements; but I assume that was tied to abuse. She mentioned it the first time it happened."

"Did she say what happened?" I ask.

"No," Rachel replies, shaking her head, "Just something about being hit when she was a kid. Nothing about who did it or why. I felt bad since I can sort of relate, but...whatever, that's not the point. I'll meet you out here after two-o'-clock. We'll swing by the library and you can show me what you found there."

"I'll be here." She nods and walks away, disappearing into the last remaining fragments of the crowd. I take a deep breath and follow her inside.

* * *

At lunch, I make my way to my usual spot in the back of the building.

My plan is to wait here for Bernadette. She saw me and waved in the cafeteria a few minutes ago. I have a feeling she's going to follow me out here. I set my backpack near the wall and remove a bottle of water from one of the side pockets. It took me all morning, but I think I have an idea. When she comes out, I'm going to "accidentally" slip on the stairs and splash some of the water in her face. I'm only hoping I get enough on her and that this half-assed plan actually works. I stand near the top of the stairs and wait with the bottle uncapped. Sure enough, about two minutes later, Bernadette comes out the doors and I clench my teeth. One foot, two, a fake smile and...

"Hey Bernadette," I smile, taking a third step down the stairs. To my surprise, I slip for real and tumble into her. We both land in a heap near the door and half the water spills on her face and neck. I try to make my next move look just as real and "accidentally" smear some of the water across her face with the sleeve of my jacket. She sits up and I repeatedly apologize while she wipes the water off her face.

"I am so sorry about that, I really am," I apologize, "You alright?" I help her up and see that I smudged a good deal of her makeup, but there's nothing to see, except what looks like rosacea on her cheek.

"What? What are you looking at?" she demands, sounding irritated. It's then that I realize I'm staring.

"Oh...um...sorry, I just..."

"Everything's all smeared, isn't it?" she grumbles, rolling her eyes. She examines her reflection in the door window, and after a moment, claps a palm to her face in frustration.

"Well shit..." she mutters.

"I'm really sorry, I didn't mean to..."

"No, no it's fine, I'm just not sure what to do," she explains, "I don't want to waste the rest of lunch fixing everything." She runs her fingers through her hair and curses under her breath.

"That bad?" I ask with caution.

"You see the redness, right?" she asks, "The rosacea? You know what that is?"

"Yes, and I can see it."

"I'm really self-conscious about it," she explains, "You think anyone's in the restrooms down here this time of day?"

"Doubtful," I reply, "Everyone's on the other side of the building around this time."

"Well good, at least I have that," she replies, taking hold of the door, "I'll be back in a minute. I'm gonna go wash everything off the best I can."

"You sure?"

"Yeah, it's fine," she insists, "Back in a few." She disappears into the building and I return to the loading platform where I sit down beside my bag. I take my phone out and dial Ezma's number. She said before that she's usually on her own lunch break around this time. Maybe I can catch her. The phone rings three times and I anticipate getting her voicemail. To my relief, she picks up.

"Hey Zoey. What's going on?"

"It's not Myra," I say, "I screwed up her makeup and didn't see any freckles."

"Wow you figured something out?" Ezma chuckles.

"It's not funny," I groan, "It was embarrassing if anything. I'll tell you about it later. Any idea what I should do next?"

"No, not at the moment." she answers, "Like I said last night, just keep an eye on her. Don't try anything else. We need to make sure we don't scare her off."

"Got it. I'll have to cut this short. I don't know how long she's going to be gone."

"No worries," she assures me, "I'll see you later."

"About that," I begin, "Um...I told Rachel about the articles, about Bernadette."

"Right, and...?"

"She wants me to show her the articles at the library," I explain, "So um...she'll probably be with me."

"And I assume Bernadette might show up too?" Ezma asks, "I don't want to see Rachel right now, but...fine, just this once. I'm not making any promises, though. I still reserve the right to toss her out of the van if she starts getting on my nerves."

"Bernadette will act as a buffer," I reply, "I'm sure it'll be fine."

"I'll keep Bernadette busy while you show Rachel the articles," Ezma says, "You know where they are and how to find them?"

"I just have to fetch the links from my email, the ones I sent you last night. It's no big deal."

"Alright, I hope you know what you're doing."

"Don't worry about it. Just think of what you're gonna do to distract her. I'll see you later." I hang up the phone and place it back in my pocket mere seconds before Bernadette comes back out. She's removed most of of her makeup and in the process made her face even more red than it was. She walks up the steps and sits on the edge of the platform.

"I'm tempted to skip the rest of the day," she groans, lying back on the platform. She places her hands over her face and lets out a muffled moan.

"I would, but I have to meet someone after two," I reply.

"No reason we can't come back then," she says, "I was going to go sit over at the park or something. Maybe read a book or whatever. You know of anything worth doing around here?"

"Not really," I say, shaking my head, "I'm even newer around here than you are."

"Yeah, that's right..." she murmurs, "Forgot about that..."

* * *

Just after two, I find myself standing at the front of the building and leaning with my back against the flagpole. No one I'm supposed to meet is anywhere nearby. Bernadette gave me her cell number before walking off to the park at lunch. If she didn't want to be seen in class, then I doubt she wants to be seen here. I'm about to dial her number when she startles me from behind.

"Sorry about that," she chuckles. She has the hood of her jacket up over her head and her hair hiding some of her face.

"It's fine," I assure her, still glancing around.

"No Rachel yet?" Bernadette asks.

"Not yet...wait, there she is, she's coming." Rachel's making her way toward us. She seems miffed about something. She spots Bernadette and I see a trace of a smile appear on Rachel's face.

"Well...I'm here," Rachel sighs, "Lead the way."

"You sure you'll be okay around Ezma for a bit?" I ask, "She usually comes up here to-"

"Yeah, I've see her drop you here a couple of times, it's fine," Rachel interrupts, "Now let's get moving."

"Jeez, what's eating at you?" Bernadette mutters. We start walking to the parking lot as she speaks.

"Nothing, I got in some petty argument with someone," Rachel answers with a dismissive wave. She doesn't make eye contact and keeps looking ahead.

"What happened?" Bernadette inquires.

"Like I said, something petty," Rachel replies, "Bumped into some girl and she dropped some papers. Went all over the place and her obnoxious friend was shouting at me for it so I walked off. Just...long day and now I'm sure Ezma isn't going to be too happy to see me. She never is. Can't really blame her."

"I'll keep her in line if need be," Bernadette offers, "Don't worry about it."

"I take it you feel bad about what happened between you two?" I ask.

"Of course I do," Rachel insists, "I want to work it out, but...I don't know how do that. Back when we were friends, she was all I had when my family started turning on me. Furious that I was associating with a Weston. The hell did I care? Why was what my parents did my problem? I didn't tell them to go butcher a few people and neither did Ezma. Nothing her parents did had anything to do with her and I felt like I was the only one who could see that...and it all fell apart anyway."

"So why'd you side with your family in the end?" I ask.

"I didn't feel like I had a choice in the matter," Rachel explains, "There was some huge fight between my cousin, Ezma, and her brother, and I just remember being in shock. I didn't know who to believe. Sarah's one of the few people in my family who I knew I could trust, who wouldn't just pick a fight with the Westons out of spite. Ezma had always been a good friend to me, she was kind and civil even when she had every right to be angry with my family. Everything changed after that incident. It was like she'd bottled all her anger up over the years, and now here she was letting it all loose. The rest of my family was through the roof, furious about what happened. They threatened to throw me out on the street if I kept talking to her. At first I thought, "What do I care? I hate my family." Thought maybe if it came down to it, I could stay with Ezma and her brother, but after Brian was found dead, I started to feel uneasy. I thought maybe everyone was right about Ezma. Sometimes the people you think would never do something terrible, do exactly that."

"That explains why you kept warning me about her," I say.

"She's not the person I once knew," Rachel sighs, "Not anymore. If I had it my way, the incident with her, Sarah, and Brian would never have happened and we'd still be friends. Unfortunately that's not how the world works. Things happen, people change, life goes on. That's all there is to it. Even with how frustrated I am with her and everything she's done since, I still wish she knew how sorry I was for walking away in the first place." The three of us walk the rest of the way in silence, arriving at the parking lot about a minute later. Ezma is standing with her back against her van with her hands in her coat pockets and a cigarette in her mouth.

"We ready to go?" I ask Ezma. She glances at me, nods, then blows a puff of smoke in front of her. It's quickly carried off in the breeze and she tosses the remainder of the cigarette on the pavement.

"Get in, I guess," Ezma sighs, walking to the driver side. Rachel, Bernadette, and I all trade glances before climbing in.

Chapter 22

The ride to the library is tense and awkward. Ezma and Rachel remain silent the entire way. Bernadette and I are the only ones who say anything. I swear you could cut the air with a knife. Pulling up at the library brings a sense of relief for me and Bernadette. The four of us walk inside and split up. Ezma seems to relax a little and appears to be pretending that Rachel isn't around. Rachel walks off to the computers, arms crossed and shaking her head. It's the first time I've ever seen her look depressed. She sits down at one of the computers and I drag a chair from one of the others.

"Let's just get this over with so I can leave," Rachel sighs, tilting her head back and staring at the ceiling, "I swear I can feel the hate she has for me. It's suffocating."

"I'm sorry about all that," I say.

"Don't let anything I said earlier influence you too much. I still maintain that she's dangerous," Rachel warns, "Yeah, I do feel sorry for the part I played, but it doesn't change what she's done since."

"Even I have to admit that now," I reply, skimming through my emails as I speak. The links should be here somewhere."

"Just hurry and pull up the articles," Rachel orders, "Ezma keeps giving me the evil eye over there." I glance away from the screen without moving my head and spot Bernadette and Ezma sitting in two chairs near the wall. Sure enough, Ezma is scowling at Rachel. Bernadette appears to be trying to get her attention.

"Here they are," I say, opening the links, "Look them over." Rachel takes a couple of minutes to read the first article, re-reading some of it multiple times.

"This can't be right..." she whispers, "Bernadette...she looks a lot like this girl in the photo."

"What do you mean a lot? She looks exactly like her."

"Not entirely," Rachel points out, using the mouse to point to a spot on Bernadette's photo. The girl in the photo has one key difference, one that I didn't notice before.

"Look at her ears," Rachel says, "This Bernadette's ears don't stick out. Our Bernadette's ears do." I glance past the monitor and look at Bernadette. She has her hood down and her hair tucked behind her ears. I look back at the photo and again at our Bernadette. I open the article with the photo of Matilda and it's the same thing. Matilda's ears don't stick out.

"That's not Bernadette Blanche," I whisper.

"The hell is going on here?" Rachel mumbles. Her voice trails off and she sits back in her chair, lost in thought.

"Does she have any other siblings?" I ask, "Ezma?"

"No, just Myra." Rachel admits that I've convinced her that something is wrong. She leaves a minute or so later, refusing to get back in the van with Ezma again. I'm somewhat relieved to hear it. Before she leaves, she and Ezma exchange glances from afar. Ezma continues to scowl and Bernadette seems irritated by this behavior. Rachel shakes her head and walks out the door. She isn't gone for long. She comes back in the door less than ten seconds later and comes straight toward me.

"Come with me. Now," she orders.

"What's going on?" I ask. She doesn't say anything and leads me down a few rows of shelves and out of earshot of the others. We come near a window and she gestures toward it. "What's the big deal?"

"Benson and Harris," she explains, "They're in that cruiser." I glance out the window and spot the police cruiser, pulled up alongside Ezma's van. Before I can say anything else, Bernadette and Ezma come up behind us. Ezma remains silent and lags behind Bernadette.

"Something wrong?" Bernadette asks, sounding concerned.

"Check outside," Rachel replies. Ezma and Bernadette both walk toward the window and glance out at the cruiser.

"Those two again..." Ezma growls, "I thought they were fired months ago?"

"Apparently not..." Rachel mutters.

"I don't understand," Bernadette says, "What's the big deal?"

"They're crooked cops," Rachel replies, "I was telling Zoey this morning that I've seen these two near my house lately. Clearly they're up to something."

"Why the hell are they following us?" Ezma demands, "Trying to scare us or something?"

"Hell if I know," Rachel grumbles, brushing past Bernadette and Ezma, "I'm going out the back. Zoey, I'll call you if I see anything unusual. I'm gonna head home. Just be careful, all of you." She walks off and disappears behind a bookshelf. I think back to what I saw at the gas station and begin to wonder if Rachel is the fourth person Harris mentioned. Is that why she's trying to avoid those two officers? Several seconds pass and once Rachel is assumed to be out of earshot, Ezma mutters something about incoherent and leads me and Bernadette back toward the front of the building.

"So what are we going to do?" I ask, "Just drive off and act like we don't know what they're doing?"

"That's exactly what we're going to do," Ezma answers, "Get straight in the van and don't look at them." We walk out the front doors and do what Ezma says, climbing in the van and leaving without looking at Benson or Harris. The cruiser catches up to us on the main road minutes later. Ezma grips the steering wheel so hard that her knuckles turn white. I can tell she's grinding her teeth. We stop at a light and she glances in the rear-view mirror.

"Just waiting for me to make a mistake..." Ezma grumbles.

"We're only a few more minutes from your place, just keep a cool head," Bernadette says, "I assume you don't have anything illegal in the car?"

"No, nothing," Ezma replies, "Doesn't mean they won't try to plant something, though." The light turns green and we pull forward. Benson and Harris remain right on our tail to the end of the street and halfway down the next, before finally turning down a side street and vanishing.

"About damn time..." Bernadette mutters. Ezma exhales her held breath and soon pulls into the driveway.

"They might come back around here soon," Ezma says, shutting off the engine, "Wouldn't be surprised if they're feigning a loss of interest." We climb out of the vehicle and close the doors, then head into the house. Ezma unlocks the door and once inside, I plop down on the couch. Bernadette sits on one end of the couch and Ezma goes straight into the kitchen.

"Either of you want anything?" she asks, "Something to eat, drink?"

"I don't have much of an appetite, but thanks," I reply.

"I'm good too," Bernadette says. Ezma comes back with a bottle of water and steps over to the window beside the couch. She unscrews the cap and holds it in her teeth while she pulls the curtain back and looks outside.

"I knew it..." she growls, "Both of them are out there again. They're parked across the street." Bernadette gets up from the couch and looks out the window on the opposite side of the door.

"Did any of us do something to cause this?" Bernadette asks, "Anything at all?"

"It might be about Saturday," I suggest, "That's all I can think of."

"What happened on Saturday?" Bernadette inquires.

"Goddammit, they probably found her..." Ezma mumbles.

"Found who?" Bernadette asks, "What's going on?"

"It's private," Ezma answers, still looking out the window. I turn on the couch and look out the same window as Ezma. Across the street is the cruiser and a mustard yellow car that appears to have been pulled over. The two officers are speaking to the driver about something unknown.

"I don't buy what I'm seeing..." Ezma murmurs, "I bet that guy's someone they know."

"It wouldn't surprise me," Bernadette says, backing away from the window, "Looks like they're almost finished talking. Just wish I could hear what they're saying."

"Same," I say.

"I want to know what you two were talking about a minute ago," Bernadette demands, "Whatever it is, I don't care. I need to know the facts."

"I said it's private..." Ezma mutters.

"I know that, but when I see two corrupt cops following us around, I have to wonder what they think they have on us," Bernadette snarls, "What happened on Saturday?"

"It's not open for discussion," Ezma growls. The two cops get back in the cruiser and depart the scene, leaving the man they were speaking to standing by his car. He climbs back into it and shuts the door, before glancing across the street at us. Can he see us watching him? He starts the car and does a U-turn in the street, before parking just outside the house.

"Why were they following us, Ezma?" Bernadette demands.

"Something that got out of hand!" Ezma answers, "Alright?"

"And what does that mean?" Bernadette inquires. Outside I can see the man in the car glancing repeatedly at the house while fiddling with something between the seats.

"Am I the only one watching that guy out there?" I ask.

"What are you talking about?" Ezma demands, throwing back the curtain. As soon as she does so, her eyes widen and she lets the curtain fall back into place.

"Get down!" she screams, dragging me off the couch. We both hit the floor as a series of gunshots ring out. The window behind me shatters and glass flies everywhere. Bullets riddle the walls and tear through cabinets and other furniture, destroying a mirror, a display case, and multiple pictures. It's difficult to tell how many shots are fired, but there has to be at least thirty. When they finally stop, Ezma jumps to her feet, swipes up the shotgun by the fireplace and points it out the window.

She opens fire on the yellow car, the tires screeching and failing to catch the pavement. The blast impacts the side of the vehicle and it swerves into a streetlamp. The impact rips the streetlamp out of the ground and sends it toppling down onto the car. Ezma throws open the front door and approaches the car with her weapon raised. Bernadette and I get to our feet and watch from the porch, both of us prepared to throw ourselves on the ground for a second time. It's difficult to tell, but it looks like the driver is slumped over the steering wheel. Ezma stops for a moment and glances through the side windows. Once she's satisfied that there aren't any others in the vehicle, she wrenches the driver side door open and pulls the driver from behind the wheel, an Uzi still clutched in one hand. Ezma turns and begins walking back to the house as people start coming out onto their front lawns.

"Zoey, he got your house too!" Ezma shouts from the street, "Bernadette, call the damn cops!" I jump off the porch and race to my house to see that several rounds have gone through the walls, door, and windows. I fling the door open and start racing through the house.

"Dad! Dad are you alright? Dad!" I shout, checking the kitchen, the living room, and finally his study. That's where I find him, collapsed on the floor and unconscious. Blood is seeping through his shirt and staining the carpet.

"No, no, no, no!" I panic, grabbing the phone. I dial 911 and wait as tears begin streaming down my cheeks. I can't lose him, I just can't. I follow the operator's instructions and work to stop the bleeding. It feels like an eternity before I hear sirens approaching. A team of paramedics race into the house and take over. Police cruisers accompany the ambulance. I stand nearby, watching helplessly as my dad is carried out on a stretcher and into the back of the ambulance. Within minutes, the vehicle has pulled away, leaving me to join Ezma and Bernadette in dealing with the police.

Ezma is detained and put in the back of one of the cruisers, much to Bernadette's objection. The cop who cuffs her insists that she's not under arrest, but Bernadette's still not happy about it. She curses up a storm and pulls on her hair, pacing around the yard while two other officers try to calm her down. Bernadette continues shouting while I sit on my front stoop in shock. Why did he shoot at my house too? No way it was an accident. He was so close to Ezma's place that he must have done it deliberately. Why would they involve my dad? He hasn't done anything wrong...has he?

Chapter 23

"How are you holding up?" Roughly thirty minutes have passed and it was Bernadette who spoke. She's given up on shouting at the police and decided to check on me.

"Where's Ezma?" I ask, "I can't see over the fence at this angle."

"Still in the back of the cruiser," she answers, "They're still talking to her. I heard one of the neighbors saying it was self-defense, but I don't know how much that's gonna help."

"Hopefully she doesn't get taken off to jail," I say, standing up and stretching, "I don't feel like we can trust anyone at this point."

"Looks like they're letting her go," Bernadette observes, pointing at the cruiser. I stand up to see that one of the cops is uncuffing Ezma and another is still speaking to her. Once the cuffs are off, she rubs her wrists and shakes her head.

"Looks like she's safe for now," Bernadette says. We continue watching for over a minute. Ezma leaves and comes into my yard, failing to close the gate as she steps through it.

"Both of you, in the house, right now," she orders, a look of intense anger in her eyes, "We need to talk about what just happened." Bernadette and I exchange glances, remaining in place as we do so.

"Did I fucking stutter?" Ezma snarls, brushing past us, "Inside! Now!"

"Jeez, Ezma," Bernadette mutters, "The hell's your problem?" Ezma pushes the door open and doesn't say a word. Once I close the door, Ezma stands with her arms crossed at the base of the stairs.

"What's going on?" I ask her.

"That's what I want to know," she replies, "Look, I'm sorry I snapped at you both, but if you can't already tell, I'm pretty goddamn pissed right now."

"I still want to know what you two did the other day," Bernadette says, "What the hell do they have on us that they would try and slaughter us like that?"

"It's nothing those idiots would care about!" Ezma insists, "There has to be another reason!"

"What happened?" Bernadette demands, clenching her fists.

"I shot a couple of people," Ezma groans, "There, you happy?"

"And what prompted that?" Bernadette asks, "Who did you shoot?"

"Couple of Nolans, and it was because they kidnapped Zoey's mother!" Ezma answers, pointing at me, "It was because of them that Miss Parker is dead!"

"Why, because they killed her?" Bernadette inquires.

"We did..." I murmur, staring at the floor, "Not intentionally, but... they left her tied up in a shack out at Hunter's Ridge. She'd seen and heard some things she wasn't supposed to. We were out shooting up some old furniture, cans, jars, that kind of thing. The shack was there, we shot at it too, and...and we...we hit her too..."

"You're kidding me..." Bernadette gasps,

"The Nolans who did it came back to get her," Ezma explains, "We followed them and I shot two of them dead."

"We tortured the third one," I admit, "Let her go after we made a deal with her."

"You don't think she was apart of this, do you?" Bernadette asks, "The one you let go?"

"It's possible, but unlikely," Ezma shrugs, "Sarah wouldn't make for a good ally to those two pigs. They'd sooner kill her. That Harris woman, she's been following me around now for weeks. I had a feeling she might do something like this eventually." I wonder if that guy in the car was the real 'number four' Harris mentioned the other night? I wish I could say something, but if I do, Ezma will know I lied to her.

"Do either of you think they might be the ones behind the other deaths? Melissa and Michael?" Bernadette inquires.

"I doubt it," Ezma contends, "Whoever killed Melissa and Michael has a different M.O."

"Right, tranquilizers and strangulation," Bernadette says, "Nothing like what just happened. So this means we have those two corrupt cops to deal with along with whoever else is killing people around here. Great..."

"Zoey, I know you spoke to Rachel recently," Ezma says, "I heard her say she'd call you if something happened earlier at the library. I assume she has your number?"

"Yeah, she does," I nod, "Wanted to be able to keep in touch with me in case anything happened."

"So you have hers too?" Ezma asks.

"Yeah, I do," I nod.

"As much as I don't want to talk to her, we need all hands on deck for this," Ezma says, "Should give her a call at some point. I don't know when. You probably want to get to the hospital at some point, right?"

"Yeah, the sooner the better," I reply.

"Do you have your gun on you?" Ezma asks.

"No, of course not, I was at school all day," I reply.

"Then go get it," Ezma orders, "No telling what else might happen. Better to be prepared."

"I hope neither of you are thinking of doing anything rash," Bernadette says, cocking her head and looking at Ezma.

"Relax, it's just a precaution," Ezma replies, "Not like we're gonna go hunting for anyone."

"I hope so. You two be careful out there. I'll be at the Watercrest Hotel if you need me. Room 310," Bernadette says, going to the door, "I imagine I don't need to accompany you?"

"It's up to you," I reply, "Not a big deal either way."

"Alright then. I'll just go back to the hotel for now," Bernadette says, "I'm gonna go let Aunt Tillie know I'm still in one piece. I imagine this will be all over the news later. See you later."

"Don't want a ride or anything?" Ezma asks, raising an eyebrow.

"I'll take the bus," Bernadette answers, "I don't want to slow you two down. Zoey, let me know if your dad is alright, okay?"

"I'll send you a text," I reply. She nods and walks out the door. As soon as she does, Ezma exhales her held breath and shakes her head. She brushes her hair away from her face and sits on stairs, resting her arms on her knees.

"I hope she isn't taking this time to run off on us," I murmur, "She said three-ten, right?" Ezma nods.

"What were you and Rachel talking about at the library?" she asks, "I saw you two looking at us a few times."

"She pointed out something odd," I answer, "I didn't see it before, but the photo of Bernadette in the news article showed her with ears that don't stick out. Ours has the opposite."

"So it's not the real Bernadette we're talking to," Ezma deduces, "I guess we already knew that, though."

"It's not Matilda either," I continue, "Same thing. Her ears didn't stick out either. I know Myra is your sister, but are there any others?"

"It's possible," Ezma answers, "Myra's mother wasn't the only woman my dad cheated with. I heard Mom arguing with him one night, claimed there were nine total. Might be more, might be less. All around the same time. I still have no idea how they stayed together."

"So it's possible that Bernadette might be another half-sister?" I ask, "What would she even be doing here?"

"She said she knows my Aunt Tillie," Ezma replies, taking her phone out of her pocket, "We'll see about that..." She dials a number and puts the phone on speaker. After three rings, I hear a woman's voice on the other end.

"Hello? Ezma?" the woman says, "I'm in the middle of something, so make it quick."

"Sorry Aunt Tillie, I can call back later if that helps," Ezma replies.

"No, no, it's fine, I just can't talk for long," Tillie insists, "Usually when you call, I'm on the phone with you for close to an hour. Now, what is it?" In the background I can hear kids of various ages shouting, laughing, and talking.

"Have you spoken to Bernadette lately?" Ezma asks.

"Bernadette? No, the only Bernadette I know is your cousin," Tillie answers, "Why do you ask?"

"I met a girl here in town recently," Ezma explains, "She says she's Bernadette Blanche, but from what I understand, she's dead. Died some time ago, how did I not know about that?"

"Well you don't often speak to most of our family," Tillie says, "Doesn't surprise me that something like that went unnoticed. Anyway...this girl, Bernadette? She says she knows me?"

"That's what she told me," Ezma confirms, "Said you paid to put her up in a hotel here for a little while."

"That's definitely odd," Tillie responds, "Well, I haven't put anyone up in a hotel. I don't know anything else."

"I'll let you get back to whatever you're doing," Ezma says, "Talk to you later, Aunt Tillie."

"Bye, Ezma. It was nice to hear from you."

"You too," Ezma says. She hangs up and pockets her phone. She then buries her face in her hands and lets out a muffled groan. Without a word, I trot upstairs and push open my bedroom door. I open the bottom drawer of my nightstand. Tucked inside is my pistol. Loaded along with two of the three magazines beside it. I tuck the magazines in my coat pocket and attach the holster to my hip before walking back downstairs. Ezma has stood up and begun to pace back and forth at the foot of the stairs, lost in thought. Ezma and I go back outside to see that a few vehicles still remain, along with a handful of cops. They're removing the body of the gunman from the street and searching his vehicle. Ezma mutters something under her breath and goes back inside. I do the same and close the door behind us. They're blocking the street and neither of us can leave at the moment.

Ezma tells me she'll be back in a few minutes, then goes out the back door. I stand in the doorway, watching her as she goes. She hops the wooden fence and lands in her backyard. From there, she sneaks into the back of her house and disappears. I sit down on the back stoop and wait for her. A car door slams on the opposite side of the house and I about jump out of my skin. Everything that's happened in the past week has started to take its toll on me. Ezma walks back out of her house, tucking what I assume is her revolver under her coat. She peeks around the side of the house and makes her way to the fence. After a couple of failed attempts, she manages to climb over and falls to the ground on the other side. She hits the ground with a thud and I start toward her.

"You alright?" I ask, helping her to her feet. She nods.

"Yeah, I'm fine," she grunts, "Damn that hurt. I've never been good at hopping fences."

"So, what do we do now?" I ask, "The street is still blocked. We can't take my dad's car or yours until they leave."

"You can try calling the hospital for the time being," she suggests, accompanying me into the house, "That's what I would do. We're just gonna have to wait unless you feel like walking a few miles there and back." Yeah...I'm not about to do that. I'm already exhausted as it is. I doubt I'd make it even halfway there with how I feel at the moment. Once we're back inside, I sit down at the kitchen table and call the hospital. Ezma sits on the couch in the living room, watching the news. It soon comes to my attention that a news crew has been outside the house for a little while now.

The woman I speak to at the hospital tells me that my dad is still in surgery and that she doesn't know his status at the moment. I thank her for her time and ask if she can call me back once he's out. She says she will and I hang up the phone and fold my arms on the table in front of me. I can hear Ezma muttering to herself in the other room, something about the media and "invasion of privacy." I'm guessing she doesn't like having a camera crew filming her house. I can't say I like it either, but there's not much I can do about it. They'll wrap things up and leave at some point. Until then, I'd rather stay inside where they can't see me.

I doze off at the table for about thirty minutes, coming to when Ezma walks into the kitchen and starts looking through the fridge. She tells me that the news crews are gone and the cops look to be getting ready to leave. I grunt without lifting my head up and fall back asleep. This time when I come to, I feel dizzy. I lift my head up and see Ezma sitting in front of me at the table. She's looking at her phone which sits on the table in front of her. She has her head propped up with her fist mashed into her cheek and looks to be on the verge of falling asleep.

"I think they're just about done," Ezma murmurs, "Took them long enough. I was starting to wonder if they'd be here all night."

"Good. Now I just need the hospital to call me back."

"What'd they tell you the first time you called them?" she asks.

"Just that he was in surgery. No idea how he's doing." Moments later the phone rings and I snatch it up.

"Hello?"

"Yes, I'm looking for Miss Parker," says the woman on the other end.

"That's me," I confirm, "I just called a little while ago."

"Right, well it looks like your father is out of surgery and stable," she replies, "You're welcome to come down and visit him any time. Visiting hours are until eight o' clock, but we'll make exceptions for family members; especially under the current circumstances."

"Thank you so much, I'll be there soon."

"No problem, ma'am." I hang up and breathe a sigh of relief. It's as though a weight has been lifted off my shoulders.

"I assume he's alive?" Ezma asks, now appearing more awake.

"Yeah, he's stable," I reply, getting up from my seat. Come on, let's get to the hospital."

Chapter 24

Ezma and I arrive at the hospital about fifteen minutes later. I waste no time in trotting up to the counter. I'm directed to room 517, and Ezma and I hurry to the nearest elevator. Twice I catch people staring at us. With this whole mess being televised only a short time ago, I feel even more like an outcast than usual. Ezma seems none too happy about the looks.

"I don't see what's so interesting about us," she mutters, following me into the elevator, "It's not like we're the ones who shot up a couple of houses..."

"Maybe they think you're a badass," I tease, hitting the button for the fifth floor. The doors close and the elevator begins to ascend.

"Badass?" she snorts, "Why because I killed the guy?"

"I assume they mentioned that part on the news?"

"Oh you bet they did," she groans, "Had my picture up and everything. I still want to march down to the news station and tear them a new one." The doors open and we step into a crowded hallway.

"I hope you're kidding about that," I say, scanning the room numbers for 517.

"Not really," she admits, "They concocted some grade-A bullshit about me back when I got into that fight with Sarah. Those beanbags hurt like hell. Totally unnecessary. I wasn't even facing them when they fired the first one, I was shouting at Sarah. Those so-called reporters made it sound like I ran at the officer."

"Here it is, five-seventeen." Before I get too far into the room, a couple of doctors stop me.

"Hey, whoa, who are you two?" one of them asks.

"I'm Zoey Parker," I answer, "I'm his daughter. This is Walter Parker's room, right?"

"Yes it is," he nods, "Is this your sister?" Before I can respond, Ezma does it for me.

"Yeah, I'm her sister," she nods, "Why do you ask?"

"It's family only right now," he replies, "Just checking. We'll leave you three alone. He's still asleep, just so you know. He might not wake up for quite a while." He and his companion exit the room, leaving me and Ezma alone with my father.

"I was hoping he might be awake," I sigh, sitting in one of the chairs along the wall, "I knew it was unlikely, but...I just thought maybe I could apologize."

"What for?" Ezma asks, glancing around the room.

"For getting him involved in this," I reply.

"It's not like you're responsible for what happened," Ezma says. A few moments of silence follows and I glance over at my father, still fast asleep.

"Maybe I should come back later," I sigh, leaning back in my chair, "Looks like he's out cold. By the way, did you happen to recognize the gunman?" Ezma shakes her head and crosses her arms.

"Nope. No one I've ever seen. If he's a Beckett Sympathizer, I wouldn't know. It was too soon for them to I.D. the body, so I didn't hear anything on the news either. Anyway...what do you want to do? Wait here a little longer or leave now?"

"I'd prefer to wait," I answer, "How long do you think we should stick around?"

"That's up to you," she grunts, getting to her feet, "I'll be back in a bit. I'm gonna go look for the cafeteria. You want anything?"

"No, not right now," I say, shaking my head, "Don't have much of an appetite."

"Alright, no problem," she smiles, "See you in a little while." I nod and she leaves the room. I sit in silence, my head still spinning from all that's happened. I wish now more than ever that I could turn back time. Dad was always there for me when I needed him. He doesn't deserve this. I just want all of this to stop. I never thought for one moment that when I came to Pryor Creek, I would end up in the middle of something like this. Now I'm missing home more than ever. My friends, the rest of my family. Life wasn't perfect, but at least I wasn't getting shot at.

Next time my dad could end up dead...or me...or Ezma. What would I even do if my dad were to die on me? Where would I go? I imagine I'd fall to pieces for at least a little while. That would do wonders for graduating on time. One more slip up and I'll have to stay behind for another year. I can't help but wonder what the rest of my family is going to think of this when they find out. I'll get an earful, I'm sure. Just as I begin to consider going to find Ezma, my dad begins to stir. He blinks a few times and squints as he turns his head toward me.

"Zoey?" he asks, "That you?"

"Yeah...yeah I'm here," I smile, "How are you feeling?"

"Tired," he yawns, "Everything's still kind of hazy."

"Do you remember what happened?"

"Yeah, kind of," he nods, "I remember hearing gunshots, then the next thing I know I had this searing pain in my ribs and...everything went black after that. How are you holding up? You didn't get hit, did you?"

"No, I'm fine. So is Ezma. She's here with me. She went to go get some food."

"Any idea what happened?" he asks.

"It was a drive-by shooting."

"Was it random or...?" he asks.

"We don't know yet," I answer, "I imagine we won't for a few more days, maybe longer."

"What happened to the shooter?"

"He's dead," I reply, "Ezma shot him."

"Well at least there's that," he sighs, "Don't need to worry about him coming back."

"Yeah, pretty much." There's a brief pause before he speaks again.

"You gonna be alright on your own for a while?" he asks.

"I'm fine," I assure him, "I'm more worried about you. Do you want me to stay?"

"You don't have to," he says, shaking his head, "I'm starting to think I made a mistake when I brought us here. Helen's missing, I'm laid up in a hospital bed, you're getting into fights at school. How's your nose been?"

"Fine," I reply, "Still sensitive as ever, but fine as long as I don't touch it."

"Good to hear," he yawns. I hear footsteps behind me and glance over my shoulder to see Ezma walking into the room.

"Is he awake?" she asks, stopping a few feet from the door.

"You can come in, it's fine," I reply.

"Oh, okay I just, you know...didn't want to interrupt anything."

"Hi Mr. Parker," she smiles, giving a small wave.

"How are you doing, Ezma?" Dad asks.

"Fine," she says, "A little shaken up still."

"I can imagine," he replies, "I heard you shot the guy who did this."

"Yeah, I did," she nods, "Still processing that too."

"Did you find the cafeteria?" I ask, "Noticed you don't have anything with you."

"I found it, but I didn't see anything that looked good," she answers, "So I left." I'm not sure if this is a good idea or not, but now that this mess I'm in has gotten my dad involved, I feel like I should tell Ezma what I saw at the gas station.

"Something wrong?" she asks, reading my expression. I shake my head.

"Come on, let's go out in the hallway for a second," I reply, getting up from my chair, "I need to talk to you about something. We'll be back in a few minutes, Dad."

"I'll be here," he smiles. Ezma and I make our way out into the hallway. We walk all the way to the end and stand near a window, the only place without any people nearby. I clear my throat and take a deep breath.

"You're gonna hate me for this, but..." I begin. The words get caught in my throat. Part of me still thinks this is a bad idea, but I suppose I don't have much choice. If Sarah can tell us something, then Ezma needs to know what I saw.

"What is it?" she asks, looking concerned.

"Sarah showed up at the gas station the other night," I say, "I lied." She stares down at the floor with her hand over her face, shaking her head. She looks up again and slaps me across the face, before grabbing me by the front of my jacket.

"I knew it! I knew you were lying to me!" she growls, "Just what the hell is wrong with you? You think this is a game? You can just try again if you make a mistake?" I notice a few people staring and she reads my expression. She lets go of me and runs her fingers through her hair in frustration.

"It wasn't anything personal, so quit taking it like it is!" I hiss, "I barely know you! I wasn't here when all this crap started! I didn't want to say something I shouldn't."

"If you want to get through this, you're going to need my help. I imagine you realize that now, but still, Zoey...never fucking lie to me again! You got that? Not about this!"

"I won't."

"What did Sarah tell you?" she demands, crossing her arms.

"It wasn't about what she said," I reply, "Trust me on this, it was just more of the same thing Rachel always says. Stay away from Ezma, Ezma's crazy, that sort of thing."

"Really?" she snorts, "You say that right after you admit to lying to me? Trust you?"

"Will you quit rubbing it in, I had my reasons and I said I wouldn't do it again," I growl, "Now look...when I was at the gas station, our conversation was cut short. One of those cops, the ones who were outside the library today. Harris, Cybil Harris. She was threatening Sarah."

"You're kidding. Why would she bother hassling Sarah?"

"I have no idea," I answer, shaking my head, "It sounded like Sarah was being blackmailed. She said that there were four people, two were out, and whatever Harris wanted Sarah to do fell to Sarah and someone Harris referred to as 'number four.' Any idea what she might have been talking about?"

"Not a clue," Ezma replies.

"What about the day at the library?" I ask, "You really didn't know anything about blackmailing? What about what you said to Michael?"

"What?"

"The thing about his second job or something," I reply, "I thought maybe you were referring to him doing something, I don't know."

"That was something else entirely," she explains, "He took a second job and was making a hash of it. He was a bumbling employee and I was just giving him crap for it." Somehow I don't buy that. Was I over-thinking it? Maybe, but I have to assume that she might be lying to me.

"My thought was that maybe you...maybe you were..."

"You thought I was the one killing people off," she finishes.

"No, I just thought maybe you knew something about the blackmailing, that maybe Michael was part of it since he ended up dead," I say, "Like I said, Harris mentioned others, and she was threatening Sarah over not having done whatever she was being forced to do. I felt it safe to assume that Harris and her partner might be killing the people they blackmailed as retaliation for not doing what they were told to do." Ezma looks over her shoulder, then back at me. She exhales her held breath and shifts her weight.

"I think we need to pay Sarah a visit, and soon," Ezma replies, "What you just told me stays between us. I don't know where Sarah lives, so I'm going to need you to call Rachel and ask. Come on, we need to hurry. Let's go tell your dad we're leaving." I follow her back into the room and Dad turns his head as we step inside.

"You two have plans or something?" Dad asks.

"Yeah, I guess you could say that," Ezma says, "We um...we forgot we were going to go visit someone and it's starting to get late, so..."

"Right," I nod, "Are you feeling alright?" I ask my dad.

"I'm fine," he assures me, "Plenty of staff around if I need anything. You got your phone with you?"

"Yeah, I do," I nod.

"Alright, just keep it charged," he says, "Might need to call you at some point. I'm gonna try getting in touch with family at some point. I don't know when that'll be. I'm barely awake as it is. Maybe tomorrow. Anyway...I won't object to another visit tomorrow." We both smile and I give him a hug. Ezma stands up from her chair and Dad and I say goodbye to one another. Ezma follows me out of the room and we head back to the elevator. Once there, I see that a few other people are waiting for it to arrive.

"Glad to see he's awake and talking," Ezma says as we stop behind the others, "He's in it for the long haul, I imagine."

"He's tough," I reply, "I'm sure he'll be fine." One of the women waiting for the elevator glances over her shoulder at us and quickly turns away. One of the men clears his throat and gives us a dirty look.

"See something interesting?" Ezma growls. The man snorts and looks back at the elevator as the doors open. Several people step out of it and brush past us. We both board and the doors close behind us.

I hit the button for the ground floor and see that the lights for the fourth and second floors are lit up as well. I roll my eyes and wait as the elevator descends to the fourth floor. The doors open and the man who sneered at us exits. He brushes past Ezma and mutters something under his breath.

"I heard you..." she hisses. He makes an obscene gesture without looking back and disappears into the crowd.

"Should I ask?" I sigh.

"It's not important," she mutters. The doors close and we wait for the elevator to reach the second floor. One of the women glances at Ezma and rolls her eyes.

"I saw that..." Ezma grumbles.

"Ezma, chill out..." I urge.

"Anyone got the guts to say what they're thinking? Huh?" Ezma growls.

"You're being paranoid," I mutter, glaring at her, "Just chill out." The woman leaves once the doors open, followed by two others. The doors close again, leaving only us.

"I'm not being paranoid, you saw them. I know you did."

"Yeah? Screw 'em. Let's just get out of here." The doors open again and we walk out into the hallway. I take my phone out of my pocket and dial Rachel's number.

"Once you've lived with people acting like that around you for a few years, then you can tell me how to feel about it," Ezma mutters.

"I'm not trying to start a fight, alright? Jeez. I just didn't want to cause a shouting match in the elevator. I'm not happy about it either." I listen as the phone rings a few times and goes to voicemail. Frustrated, I hang up and try again. Walking through the lobby, I see a few more people give us dirty looks. One person sitting on a bench whispers something to their companion. I grit my teeth and resist the temptation to say something. Once back at the van, the two of us climb in and I hang up the phone a second time.

"I take it she's not answering?" Ezma asks as I dial a third time.

"Nope, I just keep getting her voicemail," I answer. For the third time in a row, the call goes to voicemail and hang up. I put the phone back in my pocket and shrug.

"Alright, I guess we're stopping by her place," Ezma murmurs, starting the van.

We pull out of the parking lot and turn onto the main road. The entire way to Rachel's place, Ezma and I discuss what to do. She tells me that I should stay in the van and try to remain hidden. If anything happens I can help her. Her reasoning is that she doesn't trust the rest of Rachel's family and doesn't want to take any chances. Apparently she's not exactly a welcome guest. It's starting to get dark. Ezma switches the headlights on and we drive the rest of the way in silence. Eventually, we come to a private road with a gate that sits ajar. Ezma pulls through and I climb out of my seat and crouch down behind it. Coming up on the house, I see that it's at least twice the size of my own, maybe even more.

"Alright," Ezma says, parking the van, "I'll keep one of the windows cracked. Should be close enough to the door to hear. If anything happens, you come running. Got that?" I nod and she exits the vehicle. The silence is broken up only by the sound of Ezma's fading footsteps. From behind the seat, I watch her approach the door and pound on it with her fist. She does it a second time, and shortly thereafter, Rachel opens the door. It's difficult to hear, but I can just make out what's being said.

"What are you doing here?" Rachel demands, "You know you're not supposed to be here. You're lucky I'm the one who answered the door."

"Yeah, yeah, I know, never mind that. I need to talk to you about something," Ezma replies, "Don't worry, I don't plan to be here long."

"What is it?"

"I need to know where Sarah lives."

"Why would I tell you that?" Rachel ask, "After what you did, I'd rather you stay away from her."

"I don't know if you've been paying attention to the news or not, but my house was just shot up by some lunatic. Zoey's too, and her dad's in the hospital because of it."

"What? What happened?"

"Drive-by shooting," Ezma answers, "Some scumbag emptied an Uzi. I need to talk to Sarah, something happened to her the other night and I need to ask her about it."

"What are you talking about?"

"She met Zoey at the gas station the other night," Ezma explains, "Zoey said that Sarah was being threatened by that Harris officer. You know, one of the ones from the library today?"

"I know who you're talking about," Rachel says, "I don't know anything about Sarah meeting anyone at a gas station. If that's the case, then why isn't Zoey here with you?"

"She's at the hospital with her dad," Ezma lies.

"What happened after I left the library? Did those two cops follow you?"

"They did," Ezma confirms, "We saw them talking to the gunman across the street, right before he opened fire on us."

"I doubt Sarah had anything to do with it," Rachel replies, "She isn't like that."

"I wasn't suggesting that Sarah was involved in the shooting," Ezma argues, "I just want to find out if she she can tell us anything about Harris, about why this happened in the first place. I want to know why Harris was threatening her and if there's anything else Harris might have planned. You know as well as I do that the sympathizers are bad news, Rachel. We need to do whatever we can to protect ourselves." Rachel stares down at her feet for a moment, then looks back up at Ezma.

"Fine. If there are sympathizers threatening my cousin, I want to know why," she says, "If anything else happens to her, there will be consequences."

"I won't lay a hand on her, you have my word," Ezma assures her, "Any bad blood between us can wait. Right now, this is about all of us." Rachel brushes her hair away from her eyes and takes a deep breath.

"She's across town, about a block from the Watercrest Hotel," Rachel says, "She's got a rundown little house on Yew Street. Black with a red roof. Address is 1474. It's right at the end of the street. If she's not there, call me and we'll figure out what to do next. I'd go with you, but I have some things here that need my attention. I'll call Sarah and let her know you're coming."

"Thank you, Rachel," Ezma replies, "I'll let you know if anything comes up." Ezma takes out her phone and the two of them exchange numbers. Ezma comes back to the van and climbs in. Rachel turns and walks back into the house, closing the door behind her.

"Did you catch any of that?" Ezma asks, starting the vehicle.

"Yeah, I heard the whole thing," I grunt, climbing back into my seat. Ezma turns the van around and begins driving toward the gate.

"No matter what she does, we don't harm her. Not unless she pulls something. Just be ready for anything."

Chapter 25

Twenty minutes pass and we arrive on Yew Street. Ezma slows the vehicle and we start looking for somewhere to park. We pull over to the side of the road, in front of one of the many cars parked along the street. We climb out of the van and walk up to the door. The porch light is on, along with a few lights inside. I can hear the TV blaring on the other side of the door. Ezma knocks a few times, but no one answers. I press my ear to the door and for a moment I'm certain I can hear movement. The sound of footsteps can be heard, but it's very faint.

"Could you hear anything?" Ezma asks.

"Yeah it sounded like footsteps," I answer, "It was hard to hear, but I'm certain I heard them."

"She's probably ignoring us," Ezma replies, "Hang on a sec, I'll call Rachel, see if she can figure out what's going on. She was suppose to give Sarah a heads-up." She removes her phone and walks to the curb, where she sits down and dials her phone. I take one last look in the window and join Ezma on the curb. She places the phone on speaker so we can both hear.

"What is it, Ezma?" Rachel asks.

"I'm at Sarah's place and she's not answering the door," Ezma explains, "Any idea why?"

"Well you did break her arm," Rachel retorts, "I'd love to tell you why she's not coming to the door, but she's not answering her phone."

"So she doesn't even know we're supposed to be here?" Ezma snorts, "Great, that's comforting. I can hear her walking around in there doing only God knows what."

"So she's home?" Rachel asks.

"It sure seems that way," Ezma replies, "The TV is blaring and I can hear footsteps."

"Stay where you are and don't touch anything," Rachel says, "I'll be there soon." She hangs up and Ezma puts her phone back in her pocket.

"Great, now I get to deal with two Nolans," Ezma grumbles, searching her coat for her lighter.

"Now what?"

"Wait for her, I guess," Ezma shrugs, lighting a cigarette. She places her lighter back in her pocket and blows a puff of smoke into the air.

"Yeah, cuz it's not gonna raise any questions when she finds me sitting here."

"I was gonna have you sit back in the van," Ezma replies, "She won't be here for a while, relax."

"Whatever, I'm getting back in the van before Sarah sees me," I grunt, getting to my feet. I brush myself off and as I do so, a sliver of light spills out onto the front lawn. I hear the door open, but the second Ezma and I turn to look, the door quickly shuts.

"What's the matter, Sarah?" Ezma taunts, "Feeling shy?"

"Here's an idea, how about we don't make her angry?" I hiss, walking over to the van. I place my hand on the door handle and curse under my breath.

"What's wrong?" Ezma asks.

"Sarah just saw us both, so now there's no use getting in the van," I explain, "She'll just say something to Rachel." Ezma gets to her feet as I speak and flicks the ashes from the end of her cigarette.

"Brace yourself then," Ezma says, walking back over to the door, "Rachel's probably gonna have something to say about it. I'm gonna try one more time to get Sarah to talk to us." She walks back up to the door and knocks a few more times. After the third knock she tilts her head back in frustration. She throws her hands up in the air and turns on her heel.

"Whatever, I don't care anymore," she mutters, joining me by the van. Several minutes later, Rachel pulls up in what I assume is a borrowed car. She climbs out and just as Ezma predicted, she immediately asks why I'm here.

"She was with me at your place," Ezma explains, "You didn't see her in the front of the van?"

"No I guess I didn't," Rachel sighs, rolling her eyes, "How am I supposed to trust you when you lie to me?"

"I had my reasons," Ezma replies, "Quit worrying about it and do what you came here to do. We'll wait here."

"I don't need you ordering me around, Ezma," Rachel mutters, making her way to the front door. She knocks and waits a few moments before knocking a second time.

"Sarah!" she calls, "I've been trying to call you! Answer the damn door!" She knocks a couple more times and backs away from the door.

"Weird, we just saw her open the door before you got here," Ezma says.

"Well neither of us actually saw her," I admit, "We just saw the door open. Both of us had our backs turned. She opened the door, saw us, then shut it; all in about two seconds."

"I have a spare key in the car," Rachel says, "I'll be right back. You two stay put." She opens the passenger-side door and starts looking through the glove compartment. She comes back and motions for us to follow her up to the door. She opens the door and pokes her head inside.

"Hey! Sarah!" Rachel shouts, "The hell's going on? Why aren't you answering your phone?" She beckons us inside and closes the door behind us. Rachel picks the remote up off the couch and mutes the TV.

"Goddamn that was loud," she says, "Sarah! Where are you? You two stay by the door, something's not right." She walks off and starts looking through the other rooms. She walks down the hallway and into a dark room at the end of it. Seconds tick by and she flips the light on.

"Christ!" she shouts. She stumbles back toward the door with her hands over her mouth. She trips, her back hits the wall, and she slides down it into a seated position, her hands still over her mouth.

"What? What's wrong?" Ezma demands, rushing down the hallway with me in tow. Entering the room, we see that Sarah's body is lying on the floor with a cord wrapped around her neck.

"Oh my God..." I gasp, standing near Rachel. Ezma steps over the body and kneels down beside it. She examines the neck, much to Rachel's dislike.

"Don't touch her!" Rachel snaps, "It's a crime scene, quit messing with it!" Ezma ignores her and keeps looking.

"Ezma, I hate to admit it, but she's right on this one."

"There's an injection site on the neck," Ezma says, standing up,

"Looks like someone drugged her before they strangled her. Probably sodium thiopental or something like it."

"So it's the same person?" I ask, "The same one who killed Michael and Melissa?"

"You sure seem knowledgeable about the killer's methods," Rachel growls, getting to her feet.

"Are you implying that I had something to do with this?" Ezma snorts, "I don't have time to steal this crap, much less use it."

"Where would you even steal something like that from?" I ask.

"Hospital might have some, but good luck figuring out where they stash it, or if they even have any for that matter."

"Again, you seem to know a lot about this sort of thing," Rachel growls, "You're really gonna sit there and act all innocent?"

"How would I even pull this off, Rachel? Come on! Explain it to me!"

"You probably broke in here and killed her before you called!" Rachel rages.

"Why would I kill her, then call you and say she's not answering her door? Use your head!" Ezma snarls, "If I was going to kill someone, I wouldn't call their kin five minutes later while I have a smoke at the crime scene!"

"I still think it's weird that everyone who dies is in my family, and always had some kind of confrontation with you beforehand!" Rachel hisses, "It could never be anymore obvious to me! I already know you killed Addison!"

"Prove it!" Ezma sneers.

"Sarah told me you admitted to it!" Rachel growls, "That's proof enough for me!"

"Yeah, cuz that'll hold up in court," Ezma retorts.

"Any chance the two of you could quit arguing and help me come up with a plan?" I interrupt, "What do we do about this?"

"That's a good question," Rachel says, "What do we do about this? You got any ideas, Ezma? You're the expert on making bodies disappear!"

"I've got nothing, Rachel," Ezma grumbles, brushing past her, "I don't know what you expect me to do." She exits the room and walks out into the hallway. Rachel follows her.

"That's your answer?" Rachel snorts, "Just gonna ignore me? A little help would be nice! We can't involve the cops, not with those sympathizers among them. Not to mention you two are already involved in a murder investigation."

"If you wanna roll her up in a tarp and take her out to Hunter's Ridge or something, be my guest," Ezma grumbles.

"Is that where you dumped Addison's body?" Rachel demands.

"No, and I wouldn't tell you where it was, anyway!" Ezma rages, "I don't care whose side you're on in this, what happened to Eric was sick! Addison being let off the hook was just plain wrong!"

"Again, can we focus on the situation at hand?" I demand, "Come on! Quit arguing and help me figure something out! This isn't just about you two!"

"I tried to warn you about this a million times!" Rachel snarls at me, "Why you didn't listen is beyond me! Are you happy now? Is this what you wanted?"

"I just assumed you had some kind of bias toward Ezma!"

"What bias?" Rachel asks.

"The fact that her family cost yours millions in legal payouts!" I snap. Clearly taken aback, it shows on her face. A flash of anger flickers in her eyes and she turns toward Ezma.

"What else have you told her about me?" Rachel demands.

"She didn't tell me about it, I found out myself," I explain, "I was researching the Beckett murders and it came up in one of the articles. I know about the deal between your families too, the reason for the murders, all of it. So when I read that, what was I supposed to think? You just seemed like some petty moron with a few good reasons to hate Ezma and her family."

"You really think I give a damn about the money we lost because of that?" Rachel shouts.

"Which is why you were driving a convertible until I smashed it up, right?" Ezma replies.

"It was old, you moron! That was bought long before my family had their fortune sunk!" Rachel replies, "Speaking of which, it's still not fixed. Do you ever plan on paying for it?"

"Oh now you care?" Ezma snorts, "Where was the anger the day after it happened?"

"Oh I'm plenty angry!" Rachel snarls, "I'm angry about a lot of things, Ezma! I'm angry about the way your family betrayed us after the murders were carried out! Yeah, my family was doing some things they shouldn't have been, but you Westons only brought that to the attention of the court so they could save your own asses!"

"Like hell we did!" Ezma thunders, "My dad brought it up because you were trying to bargain for a plea deal that would reduce your sentences by fingering us at the masterminds!"

"You were the masterminds!" Rachel bellows, "We only went along with it because of what an unbelievable bastard David Beckett was! There wasn't a soul for miles around who didn't want to see him and his wife dead!"

"Yeah, no one except the prosecution," Ezma retorts, "Everyone who supported him kept calling bullshit, saying he was set up and that he never committed any of the crimes he was guilty of, as if the mountains of evidence someone just pulled out of their ass!"

"What does that have to do with anything?" Rachel demands.

"What the hell do we do with the body?" I shout.

"I don't know!" Rachel snaps, "I already said I didn't know! I don't want to be involved in this! They'll consider me a suspect along with you two!"

"Just can't have a stain like that on your record, now can you?" Ezma retorts, "Imagine, Rachel being lumped in with crazy ol' Ezma, the neighborhood psychopath. So now that you might be placed in my situation, you've decided you care?"

"Just leave...both of you..." Rachel mutters, plopping down on the couch, "Right now. I need some time to think."

"Fine, do whatever you want," Ezma grumbles, opening the door, "Whoever is behind this knows what they're doing. It isn't me, and it will never be me, no matter how much you want it to be true. Maybe once you've had some time to think, you can give me a call. We'll decide what to do from there." I follow her out the door and close it behind us.

"So that's it? We're just gonna leave?" I ask, getting in the van.

"Hey, you heard her," Ezma replies, "She said she wants to be alone." Ezma pulls the van away from the curb and I let out a sigh. Things are just getting worse and worse. Neither of us speak until we reach the hotel. Once there, we spend several minutes trying to find a parking place.

During much of this time, Ezma grumbles under her breath, cursing about the way people keep backing out without looking or taking the spot she was looking to grab for herself. At one point she honks the horn at two people having a casual conversation in the middle of the parking lot, right in our way. Both of them jump in alarm and Ezma giggles as they shout at her and walk away. I'm somewhat amazed that she hasn't blown up and started shouting at anyone yet. She does utter a few choice words about the people she startled, but not much else. Once she parks the van, we start toward the front of the building.

"Room three-ten, right?" Ezma asks, walking in through the front doors.

"Yeah, that's what I remember her saying." We make our way to the nearest elevator and to my relief, no one is standing around waiting. Ezma seems to struggle with keeping her mouth shut at the right time. I don't trust that she won't say something stupid if there's a repeat of what happened at the hospital. The doors open and we step inside. Ezma hits the third floor button and I lean against the wall.

"I can't stop thinking about what happened to Sarah," Ezma sighs, "Someone's running loose around here and I don't want Bernadette to get caught up in it."

"So far it's been Nolans that were targeted, right?"

"Yeah...so far..." she replies, glancing at me, then at the opening doors, "I guess that provides some degree of comfort, but if another Nolan falls victim to this person, there's no telling how Rachel and the other Nolans will react." I follow her out into the hall and brush my hair away from my face.

"So what's the solution?" I ask.

"I don't know. Leave town?" Ezma answers. We come to room 310 and Ezma knocks on the door. We stand there waiting for a few seconds and she knocks again. Still nothing. Growing impatient, Ezma pounds her fist on the door.

"Bernadette, it's Ezma!" she calls. Footsteps can be heard on the other side of the door, followed by the sound of the locks being undone. The door creaks open and Bernadette pokes her head out.

"Hey, you made it," Bernadette smiles, "How was the hospital visit?"

"Fine," I reply, following Ezma into the room, "He's awake and talking."

"That's a relief," Bernadette says, closing the door behind us. On the bed is the tin I witnessed Bernadette take from the abandoned house. Inside is a pair of gold rings, each adorned with rubies and diamonds, and a small picture frame with a photo of a senior woman with white hair inside. Sitting beside the tin are a few other items, including an antique hair clip, a silver locket, and a paring knife with an aged wooden handle and well worn blade. Bernadette catches me looking at them and sits down on the bed beside them.

"They were my grandma Hilda's," Bernadette explains, answering my question before I can ask, "I gave them to Myra in the hopes that it would bring her some comfort. I guess she forgot about them." Ezma, who's been glancing around the room, turns her attention to Bernadette.

"I see," I reply, not sure of what to say next.

"Looks like she meant a lot to the two of you," Ezma observes.

"She was the only one who ever seemed to give a damn about me and Myra," Bernadette replies, "Once she was gone, that's when everything started. Myra's parents were scared of Hilda. As long as she was around, Myra was untouchable. She used to take Myra and me for the weekends, holidays, that sort of thing. It was the only time I ever saw her smile."

"What's with the paring knife?" Ezma asks.

"Grandma Hilda used to peel apples with it," Bernadette explains, "She'd do it all in one go with the skin in one long strip. After she died, I took it from her kitchen and gave it to Myra. Partly as a memento and partly as a means of defense. Anyway...you hear anything else about the shooting?"

"No, nothing," Ezma sighs, "Made a stop by Sarah Fenton's place a little bit ago."

"Rachel's cousin?" Bernadette asks, "Why'd you decide to go see her?"

"We hoped maybe she could tell us something about the shooting," Ezma answers, "Found her dead in her bedroom."

"You can't be serious," Bernadette gasps, "What happened to her?"

"I'm guessing it was someone she knew," Ezma replies, "There wasn't any sign of forced entry. The only signs of a struggle were in the bedroom. Whoever killed her, Sarah must have felt comfortable letting them follow her in there. She was killed the same way Michael and the others were."

"I suppose that narrows things down," Bernadette says, "Who could she have known that wanted her dead?"

"That's what I was hoping to discuss while we're here," Ezma says, plopping down in an armchair, "I don't know where to go from here. I was hoping maybe you might have a few suggestions."

"Don't look at me," Bernadette says with a shrug, "I'm not an expert on this sort of thing."

"Maybe if we start back at the beginning," Ezma suggests, "They have to have something in common. Other than their relation to one another, of course." My phone rings and I excuse myself to the bathroom and sit on the edge of the tub. It's my Aunt Lizzy calling. I imagine she heard what happened by this point.

"Hello?"

"Oh good, you answered," Aunt Lizzy says, sounding relieved, "Christ, I thought maybe you got shot too."

"So you heard about that, huh?" I reply.

"Damn right I did! Was it random or did someone order it? Do you know?"

"We don't know yet," I answer, "It's still early."

"No one shoots at my niece...no one," Aunt Lizzy growls, "What on earth is going on up in that town?"

"What do you mean?"

"First that library incident, then that girl was strung up in a tree, my sister is missing, and now you and your father are getting shot at," she rants, "I heard your friend killed the son of a bitch. The gunman. Good for her. Glad to see you've got some good friends up there."

"I have a feeling you'd like her. Her name's Ezma."

"Ezma?"

"Short for Ezmarelda," I explain. While I'm talking, I start pacing around the bathroom. My hand bumps a vial on the counter. It falls toward the trash can and bounces off the rim before rolling across the floor.

"I see. Well, perhaps I'll meet her someday. For now I'm just glad to hear you're safe. How's your father doing? Is he alright?"

"Yeah, I was just at the hospital," I answer, picking up the vial, "He um...he's awake...was awake. Resting comfortably." I glance at the label on the vial and see that it says 'sodium thiopental.' My heart skips a beat.

"Good, I'm glad," she replies, "I'm stuck here in Fort Walton for a couple of days. Your Aunt Becky's house burned down and she's staying with me for now."

"Burned down? Is she alright?"

"She's just fine," Aunt Lizzy assures me, "I'll have to fill you in when I come visit. Stay out of trouble, okay kiddo? No more getting shot at."

"I'll try."

"Alright, keep your chin up," she smiles, "I'll call and check in on you later. If you don't hear from me tonight, I'll call in the morning."

"Thanks Aunt Lizzy. Talk to you later."

"Talk to you later, Zoey." I hang up the phone and look down at the vial in my hand. Ezma mentioned this stuff at Sarah's house. Why does Bernadette have it? I pocket the vial and start looking around the bathroom. I glance down in the trash can beside the sink. Nothing. I check the drawers, being certain to keep silent. A brush, a hair dryer, hair clips, still nothing. I look in the cabinet above the sink, and just as I'm almost finished searching it, a box of what I assume is toothpaste falls into the sink. I pick it up and realize it feels funny, like whatever is inside is smaller than it should be.

I open one end of the box and give it a few light shakes over the counter. A syringe slides out. It's difficult to see, but there's blood around the end of it and on the needle. I set it on the counter for a moment, then put my ear to the door. I can hear Ezma and Bernadette talking. I put the syringe back in the box and place it in the cabinet. I open up the door, my heart pounding in my chest, and return to my seat. If Bernadette has this vial, that needle...she must be the one we're looking for. The one who killed Sarah, Michael, and Melissa.

"...it just seems kind of weird is all," Ezma says as I leave the bathroom, "I mean, with all that's happened since Brian died."

"It can be pretty awkward around her sometimes," Bernadette admits, "Rachel almost never brings it up and I try not to mention it myself."

"Awkward seems like an understatement," Ezma snorts, "I mean hell, she's gotta be thinking about how much she hates me every time she looks at you."

"She doesn't hate you," Bernadette contends, "She hates herself more than anything. She feels like she abandoned you. Not to say she isn't upset with you for a long list of reasons."

"Well she did abandon me!" Ezma replies, "Hell I'm glad she feels bad about it! She deserves to!" I glance at my phone for a moment, trying to think of what to do next. My chair is sitting at an angle where Bernadette isn't looking directly at me, but all it would take is a quick turn of her head to change that. Maybe it doesn't matter. Our killer is right in front of us and it's going to get messy regardless of how I do this.

"I think she's still holding onto the idea that you'll forgive her," Bernadette says, "It's like I told her before, I think that era's over, you know? The damage is done."

"I still haven't decided if I can forgive her," Ezma replies, "Do I think about it every once in a while? Yeah. I'll admit that much. Like you said, though...I think that time is over. Even if I did forgive her, it wouldn't change what happened." Right after she finishes her sentence, I remove the vial from my pocket and grip it in my hand. How am I going to do this?

"I still think you two should sit down and talk about it sometime," Bernadette suggests, "Maybe it would help bring you both some closure at the very least." Bernadette shrugs and lies back on the bed, staring up at the ceiling.

"I suppose it couldn't hurt," Ezma replies, shifting in her chair, "I'll give it some thought." I place the vial on the end table between our seats and Ezma glances at me in confusion. She picks it up and examines it.

"I could come with you if it would help," Bernadette offers, sitting up. Ezma hides the vial in her coat as Bernadette gets up off the bed and starts toward the bathroom.

"I don't know, I think it should just be a one-on-one sort of thing," Ezma continues.

"Well my offer stands, in case you change your mind," Bernadette smiles, "Hang on, I'll be back out in a sec." She closes the bathroom door behind her and I exhale my held breath. Ezma takes the vial out of her coat and looks it over.

"Did you happen to find a syringe too?" she asks.

"Yeah, it's in the medicine cabinet," I murmur.

"I knew it...that sneaky little shit," Ezma mumbles, "Can't say I'm all that upset about the Nolans, but still..."

"What do we do now?" I ask.

"Just play it cool for now," Ezma answers, "We don't want her to run off on us." The toilet flushes and Ezma hides the vial again. Moments later, the bathroom door opens and Bernadette comes out. She has a wet rag in one hand and her cell in the other. She stops for a moment, looking down at the screen.

"Media's going crazy over that shooting still," she sighs, pocketing her phone.

"Not surprising," Ezma says, "They'll talk it to death for weeks, I'm sure." Bernadette strides past us and starts using the rag on the television screen.

"Yeah, I know," she replies, "That's why I'm annoyed. We're involved, so now we get to be the topic of discussion, you know? There... better. I don't understand how people get smudges all over the screen like that. I mean, why are you touching the screen? You're supposed to watch it." She walks back toward the bathroom, shaking her head. Without warning, she grabs Ezma around the neck and pulls her out of the chair. I stand up in a panic and watch the two of them struggle on the floor.

"What the hell are you doing?" I demand, drawing my pistol. Ezma gets loose and I see that Bernadette has stolen her revolver. Ezma retreats several feet away and glares at Bernadette. Something is wrong. Ezma's eyes are now two colors, one brown, one green, and on one of her cheeks are over a dozen freckles.

"Hello, Myra..." Bernadette grunts, getting to her feet, "I suppose I can drop the act now. Looks like you lost a lens." Ezma glances at the mirror on the wall and glares at Bernadette. Bernadette tosses the rag to the side and cocks her weapon. The vial is lying on the floor between the two of them.

"What's going on?" I demand, "Who are you?" I point my weapon at Bernadette, who moves so she can keep an eye on us both. She keeps her weapon trained on Myra, only making fleeting glances toward me.

"I'm Ezma Weston," Bernadette replies, "The real one."

"Real one?" I repeat.

"Myra kidnapped me two years ago, isn't that right?" Ezma continues, "You remember that, don't you?"

"Clear as day," Myra smirks.

"Why were you picking off the Nolans?" I ask Ezma.

"They were partnered with Beckett Sympathizers," Ezma explains, "They were stalking you and Myra, bringing information back to the sympathizers."

"They were being blackmailed!" I shout, "I saw them threatening Sarah at the gas station, they had something on her!"

"Oh I know all about that," Ezma replies, "I tried talking them over to my side, but they refused."

"So you killed them?" I snarl.

"Loose ends, they knew who I really was and I couldn't risk them going to the sympathizers with that information!" Ezma explains, "I gave them an out and they refused! Besides, Melissa and Michael were trash! They're better off dead!"

"What about Sarah?" I demand, "She wasn't like them!"

"And you believed her?" Ezma snorts, "She got my brother addicted to opiates! Did she tell you about that? About how she used to be a user too? I have to admit, I was shocked to see that she was sober. I imagine Brian's death shocked her into rehab!"

"If you gave a damn about Brian, you wouldn't have shoved him out the door when he had a drinking problem," Myra scolds, "Quit acting like you cared, it's pathetic."

"It was you, wasn't it?" Ezma snarls, "You killed him because he found you out, right? You used his drug addiction to make it look like a suicide." Myra gives a few slow, sarcastic claps.

"You're a regular detective, aren't you?" Myra smirks, "Tell me, what else did you figure out?"

"You killed Addison for the same reason, didn't you?" Ezma accuses, "You did something wrong, she got suspicious."

"Like you care," Myra snorts, "We both know what she was like. It's like I've said before, some people are better off dead. I'm sure we can agree on that."

"Addison may have deserved it, but that doesn't excuse what you did to get to her in the first place," Ezma hisses, "You took my name, my house, my life! I have a plate in my head because of you! I knew it was a mistake to take you in. You must have been stalking me for months. How else could you pull this off? How else could you fool everyone for so long?"

"Seems I didn't hit you hard enough," Myra sneers, "You're right, I did stalk you."

"You need to face what happened to you," Ezma snarls, "You can't just keep pretending to be me. It's over, Myra. I'm taking you somewhere to get help."

"Like hell you are!" Myra shouts, charging at Ezma. Myra's on Ezma so fast that she has little time to react. The revolver falls from Ezma's hand and tumbles across the floor. Ezma slugs Myra in the jaw and tries to pin her arms down. Myra rolls with enough force to fling her sister off. Myra reaches for the pistol and Ezma pulls a knife, the same one she held to my throat at the Beckett house. She slams it point down on the floor, narrowly missing Myra's hand. The knife serves its purpose and prevents Myra from reaching the pistol. Ezma picks up the revolver and points it at Myra.

"Get up and back away..." Ezma orders, "I don't want to shoot you, but I will..." Myra scowls at Ezma for a moment, then complies with her order. Ezma gets to her feet and backs away, never taking her eyes off Myra for even a second.

"It all started when you called me one day," Ezma continues, "You said you'd ran away from home. You told me you were scared, that you didn't know what to do. I told you I'd help you and I tried...but the second I mentioned taking you to an inpatient facility, you disappeared. Ran off in the night and left me scared to death and wondering where you went. Then one night, two weeks later, you barged into my house and abducted me!"

"Funny how I remember it differently..." Myra growls.

"I lost my memory because of you, that's why it took so long for me to come back," Ezma explains, "I didn't know who I was, where I was, nothing. I started becoming paranoid of the staff and escaped the hospital one night. I was certain something would happen to me if I stayed. My memory started coming back over the next year, piece by shattered piece, until I finally put it all together. The flashbacks, the nightmares...I was remembering what you did to me that night. It was the perfect crime. Everything fell in your favor. Your sicko foster parents didn't give a damn that you went missing and since you took over my life, no one had any reason to suspect that something had happened to me." By this point, Myra has become incredibly agitated. Clenching and unclenching her fists, gritting her teeth, and visibly sweating. She backs away, slowly at first, then bolts for the door.

"Grab her!" Ezma shouts, running toward her. Before we can get to her, Myra slips out the door and darts down the hall, leaving Ezma and I standing in the doorway. Two people in the hallway are now staring at us.

"Back inside, back inside," Ezma orders, pushing me into the room. She closes the door behind us and takes out her cell.

"I can't believe what just happened..." I murmur. I holster my pistol and hold my hands against the sides of head, then let them drop to my sides. I think back to what Sarah told me at the gas station, that she saw Ezma cutting the brake lines, how Ezma's personality seemed to change sometime after that.

"She's going to head for my house first," Ezma says, putting the phone to her ear, "Now that I have my revolver back, my bet is she's going to get my shotgun."

"There's no way we're going to catch up to her in time," I argue, "Is it even worth going back there?"

"Hold on a second," she says putting a finger to her lips, "Hey, Rachel...hold on I'm gonna put you on speaker."

"What is it?" Rachel asks, her voice crackling over the speaker.

"I need you to meet me at the Watercrest Hotel, right now," Ezma urges, "I need you to come get me and Zoey, something has come up."
"What kind of something?"

"Ezma's not who you think she is, she's an impostor, she ran off to find a weapon," Ezma says, "Look, I'll explain when you get here, just meet me out front as soon as you can. Please, just hurry."

"Whoa, whoa, whoa, I'm not going anywhere until you explain what you just said," Rachel declares, "What's this about Ezma?"

"I can't afford to waste time with you on the phone, just get here now!" Ezma orders. She hangs up the phone and starts packing things up around the room. She pulls her knife from the floor and places it back in its sheath.

"Come on, help me with this stuff, we need to be quick about it," Ezma orders. She places the contents of the tin box back inside and closes the lid before tossing her clothes in a suitcase she pulls from under the bed.

"How did you know about the tin if that was between Myra and Bernadette?" I ask, retrieving the drug vial and pocketing it.

"When Myra first contacted me, she told me about it," Ezma explains, "She said she'd come back by the house once before but couldn't bring herself to go in and get the tin. I can't blame her after everything that happened. The Becketts screwed her up good. I wish I could kill them a second time for what they did. Even then it wouldn't be enough."

I take the unused syringes out of the bathroom and she takes the trash bag out of the can, stuffing it in her suitcase.

"We're going to have to destroy the evidence somehow," Ezma says, answering my question before I can ask it, "No sense leaving it here." Once we're done, we head to the door and out into the hallway.

"Why would she do something like this?" I ask, "Why take over your life?"

"Myra's been through hell," Ezma answers, "Even that's an understatement. I don't know what's wrong with her, I'm not a psychologist or anything. My only guess is that she wants to forget what happened to her. When she and I first met up a couple of years back, she was having vivid nightmares, flashbacks, panic attacks, the works. She was drinking herself stupid and talking about killing herself. She said she wanted the memories to go away. I was terrified for her, but I didn't know what to do. After the Becketts were murdered, the rest of my family cut ties with me, my parents, and brother." We reach an elevator and she hits the button.

"If your Aunt Tillie knows about Bernadette's death, then how are you staying here?" I ask. The elevator begins to descend.

"I made that up, I haven't been in contact with her at all," she admits, "I've been working odd jobs and stealing anything I need to get by. I was living in a tent for a few weeks while I saved up some money. Getting an apartment around here was out of the question. It was cheaper to pay for a room here at this dump. That and a million other reasons I won't bore you with. It's tough pretending to be a dead girl. Hopefully Rachel left after I hung up. She should be here if she did." The doors open and we depart the elevator.

We make our way through the lobby and out the front doors. Sure enough, Rachel is waiting for us. She spots us coming out of the building and steps out of her car, looking at us over the roof of the vehicle.

"Do either of you want to tell me what the hell is going on?" Rachel demands.

"Get in the car," Ezma orders, "Now! Both of you! We're going to my house."

"What? Why?" Rachel asks. Ezma puts her suitcase in the back of the car and gets in. I climb into the passenger seat and close the door.

"Hurry up, get going, I'll explain on the way," Ezma urges. Rachel closes her door, starts the engine, and pulls away from the curb.

"Where is your house, anyway?" Rachel asks, glancing at Ezma in the rear-view mirror.

"The house next to Zoey's," Ezma answers.

"That's Ezma's house," Rachel says, turning down an adjacent street.

"No, I'm Ezma," Ezma declares, "That girl you thought was me, that was Myra. She kidnapped me two years ago. She's been pretending to be me since then."

"You can't be serious..." Rachel murmurs, "Are you telling me the truth?"

"The other Ezma, Myra...she lost a contact lens, her eyes are actually brown. She's been hiding her freckles with makeup," I say.

"That's what it was...that's what seemed off this entire time," Rachel continues, "God I feel so stupid! There were these little things that didn't make sense and I never put them together. Where is she? What happened?"

"I stole her weapon from her," Ezma replies, holding up the revolver, "She ran off and I have reason to believe that she's going back to my house to get my shotgun. After that, I imagine she'll try to leave town. That's why we need to hurry." Rachel speeds up the car and we dart through an empty intersection.

"That's not good," Rachel says, shaking her head, "What do you think she's planning?"

"To kill me and probably you and Zoey too," Ezma answers, "After that, I have no idea. She doesn't want her fantasy world to come crashing down around her. She'll make anyone who threatens that disappear...just like she did to me."

"I'm still not completely sold on this," Rachel declares, glancing at Ezma in the mirror again, "Zoey and I were already sure your name wasn't Bernadette, but I'm going to need more than that."

"Once we catch up to her, you'll see everything you need," Ezma says, "Just know that we're walking into a dangerous situation."

"Is she the one who was killing off the others?" Rachel demands.

"No," Ezma answers, shaking her head, "but that's not important right now, just keep driving."

"I don't know, Ezma, it feels pretty important to me!" Rachel snaps, "Are they still on the loose or what?"

"It's taken care of, now stop asking questions!" Ezma barks, "We have bigger problems right now!" Rachel curses under her breath and clenches her teeth.

"My gut's telling me to pull over," Rachel growls, "I wonder if I should listen?"

"Myra's going to be running loose with a loaded weapon if she isn't already! Stop being stubborn and get your head in the game!"

"Can you really blame me for being skeptical?" Rachel shouts, turning down another street, "The girl I thought was Bernadette is now telling me that she's Ezma! When was the last time that happened to you?"

"Look, I know it's a shock, and I'm sorry we don't have time to go into detail!" Ezma replies, "We'll discuss it later. Assuming we're alive to do so." We pull onto my street and park the car behind Ezma's van, now sitting in the driveway. Ezma readies her revolver and steps out of the vehicle.

"She's probably watching for us," Ezma warns, "Stay low and keep near the van until I give you the signal to follow." The three of us stand behind the van and Ezma pokes her head out. She crouches and trots up to the deck, remaining as quiet as possible. Rachel turns to me with a look of uncertainty on her face. I shrug and she shakes her head. I lean out from behind the van with my weapon ready. Ezma has the door open and is beckoning for us to follow. I motion for Rachel to follow me and we make our way to the deck. Ezma leads us inside with her revolver raised. I glance around the fireplace and see that the shotgun is missing.

"Shit..." Ezma whispers, noticing it too. A light flicks on at the top of

the stairs and the three of us look up to see Myra peering down at us..
A cardboard box is sitting in front of her and her foot is resting atop
it. She has the shotgun in one hand and her other hand hidden behind
her back.

"Myra, put the gun down, we can talk about this," Ezma urges, still
keeping her weapon ready, "Please, think about what you're doing."

"We're beyond that point..." Myra growls. She pushes the box down
the stairs and the three of us back away to avoid it. It crashes into the
wardrobe near the kitchen door and out spills a partially decayed hu-
man head. The smell is overwhelming and I have to cover my nose.

"Christ!" Rachel gasps, clapping her hands over her mouth. She
backs away a few paces and drops to her knees.

"I guess I missed a box. Isn't that right, Zoey?" Myra laughs, "I kept
that one for my own reasons. Couldn't decide whether or not I wanted
to keep the skull or just toss the whole damn thing into her mother's
yard."

"Addison..." Rachel gasps, still staring at the head.

"But of course, life happens and you become rather busy," Myra continues, smiling ear to ear, "Seems my forgetfulness caused it to go bad.
Pity."

"You're sick!" Rachel roars, "I'll kill you for this!"

"No one's killing anyone!" Ezma bellows. Myra removes her hand
from behind her back and holds her palm out before her. Dangling from
one of her fingers is a pearl necklace.

"Plucked this off her corpse," Myra says, "Thought maybe you'd like
a memento, Rachel. I'm sure as hell not about to pawn some dead woman's jewelry." She tosses it to Rachel, who catches it with both hands.
She looks down at it in her hands, then glares up at Myra, too furious
to speak.

"Myra, please, I don't want to see you get hurt!" Ezma pleads, "Just
come down and talk to me."

"Are you serious?" Myra snorts, descending the stairs as she speaks,
"You don't want to see me get hurt? You and everyone else forgot about
me. Abandoned me once the trial began!" She stops at the base of the
stairs and racks the slide of her shotgun in a threatening manner. She
keeps the weapon pointed at the floor and cocks her head.

"That's not true, Myra, we tried to help you!" Ezma insists.

"The main show was over, the stage silent, the fireworks now only a memory. I still wonder if your idiot mother realized what the consequences would be for me? I don't think it crossed her mind even once, did it? No, of course not, she just wanted the glory of taking down my scumbag step-father! Don't get me wrong, I very much appreciated the favor, but it was too little, too late!"

"We can get you help, Myra," Ezma argues, "It doesn't have to be like this!"

"Fuck you, Ezmarelda! Fuck you and your idealistic bullshit!" Myra roars, "I'm a lost cause, Ezma! Don't act like I'll ever get better just because you sit me down with some shrink! You cannot fix what has been done to me, so stop acting like you can! I'm too far gone and I'm smart enough to realize it!"

"You're wrong!" Ezma insists.

"That monster sold me like a piece of cheap art!" Myra shrieks, stepping forward. Ezma holds her ground, but Rachel and I back away. "I was a fucking child! I was raped, Ezma! More times than I can remember! I was beaten, half-drowned in the tub, thrown against walls, starved, and locked up like some kind of animal!"

"He can't hurt you anymore," Ezma replies, "You survived. He's dead and you're not."

"You just don't get it, do you?" Myra growls, pulling her hair, "I can never get away from what happened. I have no words to describe the pain, the violation I suffered! That will stay with me until my last gasping breath! And you know what? It didn't end there...no, of course not. I've never had luck on my side, not in this life! From there I got tossed into a situation that was only marginally better! I can't see out of my left eye because of those fuckoffs!"

"Myra, if I could snap my fingers and make it all go away, I would," Ezma says, "I don't want to lose you! I know we failed you, it haunts me even now."

"I wonder if your parents thought about that as they plummeted off that cliff?" Myra taunts.

"Wait a minute..." Rachel murmurs, looking at Ezma, then at Myra, "You! It was you at the gas station that night! That's why Sarah kept saying she saw Ezma there!"

"You're a regular sleuth, aren't you?" Myra snorts.

"You didn't..." Ezma whispers, "Tell me you didn't..."

"Oh but I did," Myra cackles, "Serves them both right! For leaving me in that hellhole! You still think I'm worth saving?" Myra asks. She and Ezma glare at one another for several tense moments. Before either of them can do anything, Rachel slugs the distracted Myra in the cheek.

"Hell no!" Rachel cries, answering Myra's question. Rachel tries to attack Myra a second time, but Ezma grabs her arm and begins struggling with her.

"The hell do you think you're doing?" Ezma shouts, trying to control a thrashing Rachel.

"Addison was innocent!" Rachel shrieks, "She didn't deserve this! I could give less of a crap about the others, but Addison would never hurt a fly!" Myra points the shotgun at Rachel and Ezma, and before she can fire, I lunge toward the shotgun, pushing it just far enough aside as it goes off. The blast takes the leg off the coffee table and shreds the rug while leaving my ears ringing. Everything sounds as if it's taking place underwater. Rachel and Ezma back off and I attempt to wrestle the weapon from Myra. Ezma snaps out of her shock, but doesn't help me in time to make any difference. Myra punches me in my still broken nose, blinding me with intense pain and sending me stumbling. Myra bashes Ezma in the cheek with the butt of the weapon and sticks the muzzle in Rachel's face.

"I think we all need to take some deep breaths, and calm the fuck down!" Myra shouts, "Give me your keys, Rachel."

"What? Screw you!" Rachel snarls.

"I said hand them over!" Myra hisses. "Why do you even want them?" Rachel asks.

"What, you think I'm stupid?" Myra snorts, "You idiots parked your car behind the van!" Rachel hesitates and glances over at Ezma, then removes her keys from her coat pocket. She glares at Myra with intense hatred as she hands them over.

"Now was that so hard?" Myra sneers, "I'll be leaving now. Don't follow me. I will kill anyone who tries, you got that?" Each of us nods as Myra backs toward the front door. She opens it without taking her eyes off of us, then backs out onto the deck before trotting to Rachel's car. Rachel clenches her fists and starts toward the door, but Ezma grabs her shoulder and stops her. Rachel throws Ezma's arm off and spins around to face her.

"So that's it, then?" Rachel snarls, "You're just gonna let her get away? We don't even know where she's going, we need to stop her right now!"

"The hell do you want me to do, Rachel?" Ezma demands, "If we go after her, she'll start shooting! I'd rather not see either of you dead! I'm sorry for thinking ahead, it was so insensitive of me!"

"There's got to be something we can do," I cut in, "We can't just let her run off like this." Rachel's car starts up and the tires squeal as it pulls away from the curb and takes off down the street.

"The car can be tracked through GPS, but the device can't be tracked with my phone," Rachel explains, "It's my aunt's car and it's her phone that's set up to track it."

"Get on the phone with her," Ezma instructs, "We need to figure out where Myra's heading. Come on." She leads us out the door and I resist the urge to look back at Addison's head. The smell is starting to make me feel nauseated. We step out onto the deck and Ezma closes the door while Rachel dials a number on her phone. The three of us start toward the van and begin climbing in.

"I only just came back and now I'm leaving again," Ezma grumbles, slamming her door shut.

"What do we do about the remains in there?" I ask.

"Nothing," she replies, "Cops'll figure something out. I'm sure they'll show up soon enough since the gun went off." I have a strange feeling in the pit of my stomach. Something that feels almost like homesickness. I stare at my house as the van pulls away, watching until I can't see it anymore. What happens now? What about my dad? My mother and Addison's remains? What happens to me? I'm left asking myself the same question over and over again. Am I doing the right thing?

Epilogue

My eyes flutter open and I feel the sting of sunlight. Ezma's still at the wheel, Rachel's sleeping in the back of the van. We're now about three hours from the wooded area where I kept watch all night. It's been six months since we left Pryor Creek. Rachel ended up stealing her aunt's phone to track the vehicle, but it didn't help much. We found the car about sixty miles away, ditched in a field near an abandoned farm. Her trail went cold from there, but even so we pressed on. I don't think any of us were expecting that she'd ditch the vehicle quite that soon. The gas tank was still about a quarter full and there was nothing to suggest that anything had gone wrong with the rest of it. We searched the area for hours, but nothing came up. No sign of her anywhere.

I heard through Pryor Creek's local paper, and their website, that my father made a full recovery and went back home. Addison's remains were discovered and buried days later. The entire community was in an uproar. Because the remains were discovered in Ezma's house, the police are now searching for her. Since Ezma and I were still suspects in a murder case, the death of Michael, leaving town made us appear guilty. No one but us three understands what's happening. No one knows that it was Myra who killed Addison, that she murdered Jack and Stella, none of it. Ezma keeps going back and forth about what she wants to do. She wants to save Myra, but at the same time she worries she might not be able to. At her lowest, she talks of giving up the search. Rachel and I insist we continue, though for different reasons.

My mother's remains were discovered, identified, and buried back home in Echo Point, alongside her mother and father. I don't have a clue how Dad's taking it, but I can see him having a mixed reaction to all of this. Mom drove him crazy, brought a lot of pain to their relationship, but I think in a way he still cared about her. Still wanted to see her get better. Now she won't ever have that chance. I can't decide if it's tragic or fitting. Mom might have just drank herself to death, anyway...but we'll never know for sure. I still feel guilty about what happened, like I can never truly make up for it. Ezma and Rachel both agree that it wasn't my fault and Ezma reminds me now and again that it was both Myra and me who shot at the shack. Much like a firing squad, neither of us know who hit her. That's a question I'll never have an answer to. I know Ezma's heart is in the right place, but I still feel like I'll carry that guilt for the rest of my life.

Rachel seems to be numb after discovering that Ezma was the one who killed her sister and cousins. She reacted the same way she did to the news of the deaths; with an eerie calm that seemed to mask a storm brewing within her. Rachel confirmed that she, her sister, and her two cousins had been repeatedly threatened with prison time, blackmailed into doing what the Beckett Sympathizers told them to do. Rachel said herself that she can't decide if she's angry at them, at her family, or at Ezma.

I miss my home, my family, even my own bed. Even now I still haven't adjusted to sleeping outside or in the van. I suppose the question is, can I even go back home? The Beckett Sympathizers would track me down and kill me, or worse, someone I care about. No...I can't go home...not until we've sorted this out. Now, even months into this, I fear this may be just another chapter in a story that isn't yet

CPSIA information can be obtained
at www.ICGtesting.com
Printed in the USA
FSOW04n0700131217
42372FS

9 781942 661702